THE
AFTER
GIRLS

THE
AFTER
GIRLS

LEAH KONEN

F+W Media, Inc.

Published by Merit Press
an imprint of F+W Media, Inc.
10151 Carver Road, Suite 200
Blue Ash, Ohio 45242
www.meritpressbooks.com

ISBN 10: 1-4405-6108-7
ISBN 13: 978-1-4405-6108-5
eISBN 10: 1-4405-6109-5
eISBN 13: 978-1-4405-6109-2

Printed in the United States of America.

10 9 8 7 6 5 4 3 2 1

This book is available at quantity discounts for bulk purchases.
For information, please call 1-800-289-0963.

For Kim
and Chrissy

CHAPTER ONE

The rain came down in sheets. That was the thing about North Carolina. It'd be cool and clear one minute, the moon full and bright and just begging you to enjoy the night, and then it would just pour, pour its heart out, and you were fresh out of luck if you happened to be caught in it.

Which they were.

"Come on," Ella said, dragging Sydney by the arm. Even the canopy of trees couldn't protect them. Their clothes were getting soaked, the rain dripping from Ella's hair down her back. It had come on fast, just a few minutes ago, once they were already too far into the woods to turn back.

"Let's leave," Sydney said. "This is ridiculous. We can come back tomorrow."

The wind whipped at them, slapping Ella's hair against her face, but she just gripped Sydney's arm tighter.

Her flashlight found a clearing.

She let go of Sydney and pushed the brush away, stepping forward, and she had no cover. The rain pelted at her, and she turned to see if Sydney had followed.

She had.

And there it was.

The cabin was small, hardly more than a few feet wide. It was nestled snugly in the woods; she and Astrid had found it when they were twelve. It had been theirs ever since.

Now she stared at it, surrounded by streams of rain, soggy red clay. Around it, yellow caution tape warded them off, warning them to stay away.

Ella hadn't been here since Astrid died.

"What are you waiting for?" Sydney yelled above the rain, grabbing her. The two of them ducked under the tape and ran onto the porch. It creaked beneath them, but they had a shelter now, at least.

Sydney shook off. The rain had turned her hair into short little spikes, dyed bright, fire-truck red. "Why did we have to come at night?" she asked.

Ella pointed her flashlight at the tape. "I didn't think we should be prowling around a *crime scene* in broad daylight."

Even in the dim moonlight, Ella could feel her friend rolling her eyes. "It's not a crime scene," Sydney said. Her voice got quieter for a moment. "There was nothing in her system but the pills."

"Then why is the tape still here?" Ella asked. "Maybe they're still looking into it."

"It's the Falling Rock police," Sydney said. "Last time I checked the FRPD wasn't exactly the beacon of thoroughness. Plus, it's only been three days."

Ella felt heavy all of a sudden. She knew what Syd said was true. She'd known it every moment since Astrid died: During the night, when she dreamed about Astrid, seeing her just one more time. In the little things, when she brushed her teeth in the morning. In the quiet spaces of this town, when she stood on her porch and watched the sun go to sleep behind the mountains. She just didn't want to know it. She didn't want it to be true.

Sydney put her hands on Ella's shoulders. "She left us, El. She wanted to."

Ella nodded, and she felt herself shiver under Sydney's touch.

"I know," she said. "But I need to know why."

Inside, the cabin was just as it had been before Astrid died. Abandoned and forgotten, it was nothing more than a room; it was probably built when an outhouse and a well were the way people went about things. It definitely wasn't nice enough to preserve, but it wasn't worth the effort to tear down. There were a lot of places like it here. Maybe one day, some historical society would come and declare it a Civil War relic—some placard-worthy testament to the rural poverty in the post-Antebellum south. But for the past five years, it had been reserved for the three of them—Ella, Sydney, and Astrid.

Ella heard a crack outside, like a branch breaking, and then the creak of the swaying door. She turned her head, shone her flashlight out into the night. Raindrops trickled in through the door, dancing through the beam of light. There was no one there.

"It's just the wind," Sydney said, turning around and shutting the door tight. There was a clap of thunder, and the cabin quaked.

"Wind," Ella repeated. This place was giving her the creeps. Maybe Sydney was right. Maybe they shouldn't have come here at night.

Ella shone her light around the room. This had been their stomping ground. It was where she'd first tasted wine, many hiccups and giggles and a headache to follow, and where Sydney had shown them how to practice French kisses on their hands.

The walls were virtually covered with photos of the three of them—ones that they had put up together. School dances, football games, days spent splashing through the rock quarry. Incriminatingly dorky ones from middle school, their backpacks riding too high up on their shoulders, Ella's jeans flared and stitched with hot pink. The photos were imposing, reminding her of what seemed like another world altogether. Even now, the knowledge of what had passed jolted her, shocked her. It was ruined now. Ella didn't want it to be, but it was.

Thunder growled around them.

"We don't have to stay if you don't want," Sydney said.

"No," Ella said. "We're here now. Let's get the candles."

She walked over to an old armoire from who knows when, its wood decayed, molding from moisture and bugs, covered with dust and cobwebs—it was the only piece of furniture in the place. Ella opened the doors and pulled out a tray of candles and a box of long matches.

She lit them, setting the tray down next to her.

"Let's start here," she said. And she did. Ella pulled out a stack of books. She grabbed the first one—it was one about séances that they'd found in Sydney's aunt's attic. Sydney had dared them to have one, but they'd burst into laughter every single time they'd tried—they'd never gotten that far. Ella flipped her thumb over the pages, then turned it upside-down and shook. Nothing.

"Come on," Ella said. "Help." She shoved a book into Sydney's hands.

Sydney took it, following her lead, while she moved on to the next one. Ella shook it hard, but nothing came out. They worked like that, slowly, meticulously, while the storm ravaged the woods outside and the night got darker and deeper. Wetter. They pulled out every book, every magazine. They shuffled through the blankets they'd tucked around the place to keep them warm while they sat together and downed bottles of wine.

Ella was in the corner, flipping through an old yearbook. It was Sydney's from freshman year. They kept it around to make fun of people's awkward pictures, to look at how young they'd looked just a few years ago. She heard Sydney sigh.

"I know you want to do this," she said. "But what exactly do you think we're going to find?"

Ella kept her eyes glued to the book in her hand.

"Ella?"

"I don't know," she snapped. "There has to be something."

"The police searched the place. There wasn't a note."

"I *know*," Ella said. "But like you said, it's the town police. Maybe they missed something."

"I don't think she left anything," Sydney said. Another clap of thunder sent chills down Ella's spine, and her friend's words left a weight in her stomach.

"She had to, Syd. This was Astrid. She was always scribbling in that journal. She loved to write. The Astrid I know would have left a note."

Sydney's voice was loud, louder than the rain and the wind and creaking of the cabin all put together: "The Astrid you know wouldn't have *killed* herself."

The yearbook dropped to the ground with a thud. Ella looked down, realizing she'd let it go.

"I'm sorry," Sydney said.

Ella looked back up at her friend. The candlelight cast shadows on Sydney's face that made her look eerie. Gaunt.

"Why do you think she decided to do it here?" Ella asked.

Sydney shrugged, and she looked sad. Defeated. "I don't know," she said. "But I don't think anything in here is going to answer that."

Ella nodded, and she didn't object as Sydney's hand touched her shoulder, turning her towards the door. Away. "Let's go," Sydney said. "We've had enough for one night."

But Ella couldn't help it. She looked back, and her heart beat fast as she glanced at the spot on the ground. Astrid's spot.

And for a second, a chilling, nauseating second, it was like she could see Astrid. Lying there. Just like she had been.

Dead.

It was morning when she found her; Ella had led Astrid's mother to the cabin. Sydney wasn't there. Sydney wouldn't know 'til later. Ella didn't know why, but she'd gone in first.

The sight of her friend had frozen her in place. She was stretched out on a blanket, her gorgeous red hair splayed out around her, her blue dress—the same one she'd worn to graduation—crumpled and wrinkled. The key, the one that was always tied around her neck, the one that she never *ever* took off, lay flat on her chest. The cabin smelled like dew and morning. Not death.

It had been like a bad dream. A movie you watched too late at night that stuck with you as your eyes got heavy.

Ella had run, squatting down, her knee knocking over a bottle. A clear orange bottle that didn't rattle because it was empty. Astrid's eyes were staring straight into nothing, wide, like they'd just seen something awful. Something that they wouldn't forget. Her mouth was loose, agape. Her skin was white, way too white. Gray, almost.

Ella didn't scream 'til she touched her, and her cheek was cold. Cold and stiff. And that's when Grace came in. And that's when she heard Grace scream, too.

And that's when they'd both known that Astrid was gone.

"El," she felt a hand on her shoulder. "El," Sydney said again. "What is it?"

Ella shut her eyes tight, praying that all the horrible thoughts would go away. "Nothing," she said. She opened her eyes and the thoughts were still there, but they were lighter, like they'd been covered with vellum. "Nothing. Let's get out of here."

"Good idea," Sydney said, and she opened the door, quickly walking through. The rain had calmed now. They'd still get wet, but they wouldn't get soaked.

Ella took a deep breath, grabbed her purse from the corner, and followed Sydney out the door.

And she shut it tight behind her without looking back.

The wake was the next day.

Ella's room looked like a war zone. Objects in each corner seemed to creep towards her, ready to attack, to finally take over when they'd built up enough troops. She'd been up half the night looking through everything. Every note. Every photo. Everything at all connected to Astrid.

She wanted an answer, even though she knew it wouldn't bring Astrid back—or make all the bad thoughts go away. She still wanted to know why. She wanted to know how she could have missed something so huge. How could she have spent week after week with her friend, her best friend, and not known that she wanted to leave? The guilt ripped at her, enveloped her, drowned her. If only she could find what it was that she'd missed. If only she could see how she'd failed her friend.

There was a knock at the door, and her mom poked her head in. Her cheek was smeared with the drippings of wet clay. Her mom was the official town potter. Ella didn't know her dad—didn't even know who he was. Her mom had been a bit of a . . . *free spirit* . . . in her twenties, and whoever it was had been far out of the picture by the time Ella had come along.

"You awake?" her mom asked softly. She wasn't so much of a free spirit now. She did her pottery and wore dangly earrings, but she was your typical mom, attending PTA meetings and requesting extra stop signs for their street, always asking how your day was and to call "when you get there."

Ella pushed the covers back and sat up, nodding. Her mom gave a quick glance around the room. Under any other circumstances, she would have opened the door without knocking, given the room a once-over, and declared the place fit for pigs. Ella would then point out that it was no worse than the pottery studio upstairs, her mom would counter that it was her one place to be free and messy—plus, Ella used it, too—Ella would note that this was hers, and so on and so forth until Ella dragged herself off the bed and began to hang the clothes to quiet her mother.

But her mom didn't say anything about it now. And that was almost worse.

"Ben's here," she said. Her mom grabbed a sweatshirt, tossing it to her. Ella pulled it on over her pajamas. "You want me to tell him you're up?"

Ella nodded, and her mom walked out of the room, leaving the door open behind her.

She heard Ben's friendly voice, then his heavy footsteps climbing the stairs.

"Hey sleepy," he said, walking inside. Even just into summer his skin was tan, glowing against his dirty blond hair, his brown eyes warm with concern. He normally wore a smile straight out of a Wonder Bread commercial, but it had grown softer these last few days.

"Can I come in?"

Ella heard her mom downstairs, banging pots around in the kitchen. She nodded. For some reason the sight of him standing before her and trying to make things better made her almost want to cry.

"Come lie down with me."

He smiled wider that time. Then he lay by her side and wrapped his arms around her. Ben was big and strong and just a touch heavy like a Southern football player should be. His arms were hefty, and it felt good to be contained. She turned towards him, and their faces were just inches apart. She felt tears rising up in her throat, but she swallowed hard and kept them down.

"Are you okay?" he asked, and his voice felt deeper than usual. As if it were booming right through her. He clasped his hand around hers.

"Not really." Ben's lips were shut tight, like he was afraid to speak and say the wrong thing. She knew the feeling. He was waiting for her to explain. But even though he'd done nothing but be there for her over the last few days, Ella hadn't been able to find the right words. The right way to explain anything to him. But she couldn't help but try.

"I want to know why," she said. "I feel like if I could just find something, some note, some memory, some anything that would give me a clue," she stopped to catch her breath. "I need to know how it got to this. I still can't—I just can't believe it." The last words came out as a choke, and as the tears finally came, she felt her body shake against Ben's strong and solid arms.

"Shhh," he said, rocking her. "Shhhh." But she wondered why he said it, how it was supposed to console her. If she stopped talking about it, the pain wouldn't go away.

"You can never know that," Ben said, stroking her hair. "And it doesn't matter. All that matters now is that she loved you. That she cared about you. She's in a better place."

Ella looked at him then, her eyes wide and soggy, and she wondered where he'd learned to speak in platitudes. She knew she shouldn't care; she knew he was just trying to help, but he wasn't. It was like some kind of sick, twisted fantasy was playing out. The kind inspired by baby-faced young actors who'd rush to the heroine's side when tragedy strikes, unafraid to show emotion, fearlessly kissing away their shiny-haired lady's tears—the same tears that manage never to smear her makeup. Heart-wrenching moments when the whole audience thinks, *I want to be loved like that.*

She'd had those fantasies like everyone else. Particularly when she and Ben started dating. She imagined a tragedy befalling them—nothing real, nothing this bad—and running to her big, strong quarterback of a boyfriend for solace.

Now she knew that it was far less sexy in real life.

It was quiet between them, but their eyes stayed locked.

"Can I kiss you?" Ben asked finally, tracing a finger along her cheek. His voice was almost sheepish. He hadn't asked her that since the day he'd driven her home from French club, sitting in his Jeep. Her fingers were tingling and she'd felt warm and nervous and surprised that someone who seemed so cool, so in control, had to ask before he made a move.

Now it was like they were back at the beginning, starting over. Just not so happy this time.

But Ella nodded anyway, and their lips touched lightly, and just like everything else in her life now, something was different.

She and her mom got to the funeral home right at four. Ben had offered to drive her but she'd said no. The only person she really wanted to be with was Sydney, anyway. The place was already almost full. She guessed that's what happened when someone died so young. She looked around at all the faces, people from school, people from the café, Astrid's neighbors. How many of them had really known her?

Had Ella even really known her?

She felt a hand on her shoulder, and she turned to see Sydney. She was decked out in black lace, tights, combat boots and lipstick that matched her hair. Only she could find a way to look hot for a funeral.

Sydney wrapped her in a hug and held her tight. "I'm so glad you're here," she said. "I've been waiting for you."

"Not too long, I hope," Ella said.

Sydney just shook her head.

Their moms banded together and gave them some space.

"Should we go in?" Sydney asked, nodding to the main room just to their right. Where Astrid would inevitably be.

"I guess," Ella said. "I guess we have to."

The place smelled toxic, like too many lilies, and the first thing she noticed was how ugly the carpeting was—mauve and brown and gaudy florals. Astrid would have hated it. They walked up to a line that led to the casket, which made her feel like she was at some kind of hellish amusement park.

"This is so fucked up," Sydney said, her voice a whisper. "This is like, so. Fucked. Up."

Ella didn't do anything but nod. She didn't know what to say. This was like the official confirmation that made the nightmare of the last few days real. The line moved surprisingly fast, and with each step forward, fear sparked in her stomach, kindling, dancing, growing like fire.

Finally, they were just one away. Ella's breathing grew quick, and Sydney must have noticed. She squeezed her hand tight and didn't let go, even though Ella could feel her palms sweating.

And then they were up, and there was no turning back. Ella walked slowly, her feet like weights, and then there they were. Standing over Astrid's casket. Saying goodbye to their friend.

The first thing she thought was that it wasn't her. Not the Astrid she'd known, not the one she'd been seeing in her dreams. The hair was there, ginger red and carefully set around her, but her clothes were different, her chest was bare. Her face was coated in thick makeup, blush, and orangey foundation that mimicked the color of her dress. You couldn't see the tiny freckles that spattered the bridge of her nose or the crinkly lines at the edges of her eyes.

After a moment, she felt Sydney tug her, and she let herself be led. Grace stood waiting for them in the receiving line, next to three more faces that she didn't know.

Ella didn't have words. The last time she'd spoken to this woman—this woman whom she'd known since she was eleven, who'd been her favorite adult, who was so beautiful, so wild, so fun—the last time she'd spoken to her had been in screams.

So Ella just looked in her eyes, her puffy, messy eyes, and hugged her as quick as she could, walking away without saying anything to the people standing next to her. She didn't want to meet anyone new today.

In moments, Sydney was by her side again. They walked to the middle of the room and grabbed two chairs that were far away enough from anyone else in their school. Ella didn't want to talk to people, and she had a feeling that Sydney didn't either.

So they sat there, Ella staring straight ahead as people moved through the line, Sydney taking sips from a bottle of Diet Coke that was most definitely splashed with rum.

Ella didn't know how long it had been when she saw the man. She noticed him because his cheeks were wet, really wet.

"Who's that?" she asked, nudging Sydney.

"Beats me," Sydney said. "I've never seen him before. Probably an old family friend or something."

The man had blondish-gray hair and tanned leathery skin. He wore a crisp suit like someone who wasn't from around here, and even though he was older, probably in his forties, Ella could tell that he was attractive. That he'd probably been quite the thing in his youth.

He walked up to the casket alone and when he did his body shook. Great gasping sobs that seemed to take over him.

When he stopped shaking he walked over to Grace and held out his hands to hug her, but she stepped back. He leaned forward as if to whisper something in her ear, but she shook her head, and with her two tiny hands she pushed him away.

"Did you see that?" Ella whispered, but Sydney was hunched over her purse, trying to pour the rest of the airplane bottle into her Coke.

"What?" she asked, looking up.

"Grace just pushed that man away."

Sydney sat up straight then, following the man with her eyes as he walked down the aisle and out the door.

She shrugged. "She's distraught."

"You don't think it's weird?"

"Maybe they have a bad history or something. Who knows?" Sydney took another sip of her Coke.

Ella nodded, but she couldn't help looking from the casket to Grace and wondering what it all meant. She couldn't help wondering how well she'd really known her friend.

It was almost a week before Ella dreamed of Astrid again. Blurry, blended days spent mostly in bed. On the phone with Sydney. Occasionally chatting with Ben. Watching TV, one bad reality show bleeding into the next.

They were in the coffee shop, and they were making lattes.

They stood together, side by side, at the giant red machine. Hips almost touching. Astrid pulled the espresso—ground it, tamped it down, hooked the portafilter in, started the machine.

Ella heated the milk. *Simmer simmer. Splash splash.*

"Something is wrong," Astrid said, without looking at Ella.

"What?"

Astrid didn't respond.

"What?"

"Something I can't tell you."

Simmer simmer. Splash splash.

The espresso machine was red. Red like blood.

Ella knew! She would tell Astrid to stop, to wait, to explain. She would tell her it would all be okay. They would hug and dance and drink and cry and be like they were supposed to be, and Astrid wouldn't ever leave.

Simmer simmer. Splash splash. The milk was warming. The pot was hot in her hands.

Ella turned to tell her friend—to stop her—but Astrid was gone, and the black espresso was dripping, dripping into nothing, and the pot of milk was too hot now, falling out of her hands, and it would spill and it would splash and it would hurt and it would burn, and there was nothing that Ella could do.

She awoke with a start. Her friend's name was on her lips, ready to burst out like a scream.

Astrid.

Ella pulled the covers up around her. It was dark out, and the wind surrounded the house, cooing. The dream, so clear just a minute ago, was already disappearing from her; only flashes remained. Images. Red. Astrid's words: "Something is wrong."

And yet, it had felt so real. It had felt like Astrid had really been there, had really, truly been there. Had spoken to her. It had felt that for an instant, maybe things could have changed.

The thought both comforted and terrified her at the very same time.

There was a scratching sound at the window, and Ella jumped. The trees were close to her window, their branches and the awful moonlight casting wraithlike shadows through the curtains and about the room. Another scratch, and the wind cooed again.

It's just a branch it's just a branch it's just a branch . . .

She took a deep breath, and she whipped her sheets back. She ran to the window, and she used all her courage and curiosity to open the curtains. There was nothing, and it was really just a branch. As she turned, the shadows looked so dark and yet soft, like a girl, or a bird, running and flying. Falling.

Ella ran to the door and flipped on the light as fast as she could, and the bulb cast a glow that filled the room, hiding the shadows.

Ella lay back in bed, and she closed her eyes tight, and she took deep breaths, *in and out and in and out*, but she still didn't feel alone.

Sometime in the night, she'd managed to fall back asleep, but she was tired when she woke up. She couldn't remember any more dreams, but she still felt rattled. Unsettled.

She could hear her mother downstairs, making coffee, but she didn't want to see anyone right now. So she walked up to the studio, where she knew she'd be by herself.

Ella squinted as her eyes adjusted to the light cascading through the arched windows, spilling onto a cracked wood floor littered with crumpled newspapers, damp rags, and remnants of clay. She sat down at the wheel. She didn't know what else to do.

The clay felt raw, good between her fingers. Malleable.

She forced it into a mound on the wheel in front of her. It was fresh and new—unformed—it could become anything, anything in the world that she wanted it to.

She pressed her foot down and the wheel began to spin, the clay whirling, taking shape. She dipped her hand in the water and placed her fingers along one edge, turning the lump into a mini mountain, rising up—becoming—right before her eyes.

She dipped her hands in the water again; then pushed her fingers into the middle, turning the mountain into a volcano—tall, strong—rising, growing—she could still do this.

Ella spun the wheel faster, and the volcano rose, grew taller—ready to burst, to explode any moment. Faster and faster.

Ella pressed her fingers along the edge, and it turned, became something again. Hourglass.

Rising.

Existing.

It felt good to have something real in front of her. Not sounds or scratches or visions of her friend or shadows dancing along the wall.

And the hourglass rose, just as it should, and it spun faster. It was a vase. A beautiful fabulous vase that she would sell at the fair—she and her mom always made a bunch of pieces to sell at the fair.

Even now, she could still make.

Real. Fired. Solid.

Existing.

But she blinked and Astrid was before her again. *"Something is wrong."*

And she heard her name being called. Echoing. *"Ella. Ella."*

And then she spun too fast and the perfect pretty twirling hourglass crumpled before her. Ruined.

The failure startled her, and then she heard her name called clearer. Her mother.

Ella pushed the clay down so it crumpled even further. And she found herself scooting away from the wheel, dipping her hands in the water, her fingers dripping all the way down the stairs, and then her mother was there, and she was staring at Ella, asking if anything was wrong, and it wasn't, and okay, then, the phone's for you.

And Ella held it to her ear and she muttered hello, and for a moment it sounded so much like Astrid that she wanted to cry.

But only for a moment.

Because it wasn't Astrid.

It was Grace.

"How are you?" Ella asked, trying to sound calm.

"I'm okay." Her voice sounded hoarse.

Grace had always insisted upon being called by her first name, unlike most other moms in the South. It was one of the many characteristics that made her awesome. That had made Ella love her, like more than an adult, like a friend. Ella hadn't seen her since the funeral.

"I didn't wake you, did I?" Her voice was just like Astrid's. It was uncanny—*terrifying*, even—how much it sounded like her.

Ella shook her head. "No."

The line was quiet a moment, as if Grace were waiting for her to say something else.

Then she spoke. "I need you to come in tomorrow," Grace stammered, her voice cracking, as if she were about to cry.

"Come in?" Ella asked, and for a second she really didn't know what Grace could mean.

"The *café*," she said, and she almost sounded annoyed. Angry. "We need you here. Please."

"Oh," Ella said. Maybe it was the dream, but Trail Mix seemed far away now. Fake, almost, like a coffee shop on TV.

She and Astrid had practically grown up there. They'd been hanging out behind the counter since they were twelve, long before they knew the difference between steel cut and regular oatmeal, agave nectar and sugar, like all of the regulars did. The old owner had died, and Grace inherited the place when they were fifteen—ever since then she and Astrid had been working there. It was perfect. It drew enough backpackers from off the Appalachian Trail to give them plenty of eye candy. And there were lots of kids from school who came by, too. A dream job.

"So will you do it?" Grace asked, and Ella almost expected tears to seep right through the phone. "I don't know what else to do."

Ella imagined Grace, so beautiful and lithe, just like Astrid, wasting away in the house. Astrid's dad had died years ago in a car wreck, long before Ella and Astrid became friends, and now Astrid was gone, too. Grace was all alone now. It must be unbearable.

"What time?" Ella asked, stalling. She heard Grace's heavy breathing on the other end.

"Seven o'clock." Ella felt her heartbeat quicken because she knew that she didn't have a choice. Maybe because she needed the money or maybe because she felt bad for Grace, or maybe, just maybe, because being there could help her learn something—anything—that would help her understand.

"Seven," Ella repeated. "Okay," she said. "I'll be there."

"Thank you," Grace said, relief flooding her voice. "I knew you would help me, Ella."

"Of course," Ella said. "See you tomorrow."

"Tomorrow," Grace echoed back.

And Ella could still hear her heavy breathing as she hung up the phone.

CHAPTER TWO

Sydney decided to go to the party alone.

It was the first big party in over a month, and she'd begged Ella to go. They needed something to take their minds off of Astrid, off of the funeral, off of these last few miserable days. But Ella had said she was tired, that she had to be up early for work the next day. She hadn't even tried to conceal the disdain in her voice when Sydney had asked her to at least consider having some fun.

Ella was going back to the coffee shop, back to a job that would constantly remind her of Astrid. Sydney was going to get drunk. And somehow *she* was the weird one.

Max's parents were gone until Sunday. They were often gone like that: checking B&B's off some Best-of-the-Appalachians list. They'd altogether given up taking their children with them once they were old enough to take care of themselves—Max and his older brother had always seemed sort of like an afterthought to them.

He was who-knows-how-many-beers in when she got there. So was everyone else: scattered across the couch, dotting the staircase, bodies pulsing, protruding from the kitchen. Some of them had been at the funeral, and some of them hadn't, but she knew that there was no one in the entire house who felt anything like her. That's why she needed to drink.

A few weeks ago, she and Ella and Astrid would have pre-gamed beforehand, passed wine around the cabin, and stumbled in together. But tonight, Sydney walked calmly, steadily towards the first sight of liquor. By herself.

"Syd!" Carter yelled as she passed the couch. He jumped up to hug her, and she let him. Carter was nice and dependable, and just a little too touchy.

Carter let go and looked down into her eyes. "I wasn't sure if you'd come."

Sydney shrugged. "I need a distraction." From the couch, Max gave her the obligatory head nod but nothing more. He wasn't one to talk about feelings. He was one to pretend that they didn't exist.

"I'm getting a drink," she said, turning back to Carter. "Do you need one?"

Carter shook his head, and he didn't quite let her go, so she ducked out of his arms and headed straight for the kitchen, pushing through the packed bodies, the summer skin that emanated heat. She didn't really care who was in her way. People expected her to be a little abrasive anyway. It was part of her hair-dyed, eyebrow-pierced, fiddle-punk charm. She picked up the darkest bottle and poured it into a plastic cup, watching it fill. It was deep, muddy—a good place to get lost.

She topped it off with Diet Coke and took a fiery sip and knew in a few minutes that she wouldn't have to think about any of it, that feeling in the cabin and the sadness on Ella's face when she discovered there was nothing to help them, the way Ella had stared at the center of the room as if she'd seen a ghost, the shiny wood of Astrid's casket that looked just like the wood of her fiddle, the thought that picked at her every minute, that wouldn't go away—that she should have known, that she should have done something, that she should have saved her friend—she knew that if she kept on sipping they would leave for a bit, at least until later when they'd come back even worse and with a headache, to boot. But that was later. Now was now.

So she took another sip and waited for the liquor to hit.

Sydney felt strangely famous. Different, definitely different from being up on stage, even during the couple shows that had been big enough to have fancy lights. In that, there was anonymity. She was up high with Max and Carter, and the crowd was apart, in another world. Not aware of her so much as they were the music, the feeling in the air.

This wasn't the same. She'd had two full drinks, and people were touching her. Like she was Jesus or something. They were actually grabbing her clothes. Everyone wanted to know if she was okay. Everyone wanted to know if Astrid's death was a surprise. Everyone wanted to know how the suicide was affecting her, and was she really ready to go to parties? How was Astrid's mom? Was Sydney going to see a shrink about it? Was she sure she hadn't seen it coming?

All the questions that they knew weren't appropriate to ask sober.

Becky was there. *Bubbly Becky.* A chatty girl in their class whose hair was about as blond as could be and whose eyes always looked like they'd just beheld the Holy Grail. She'd worked at Trail Mix with Astrid and Ella, and Sydney had always aimed her visits for when Becky was off the schedule.

"Sssydney," she said, grabbing her shoulder. "Are you okay?"

Syd smiled her widest smile. With the whiskey inside her, it almost felt real. *Okay?* Of course she wasn't okay. She was the opposite. Somewhere inside were all the bad feelings, ready to escape. But not yet, not now. She had the warmth instead, flowing through her body, pulsing through her blood to the beat of the bass that pumped through the house. Sydney couldn't make out any of the words to the song. Someone bumped into her from behind.

"Sure I'm okay," she yelled with way too much enthusiasm. Like she was in some kind of weird drama class exercise.

Becky shook her head like there was no way in hell she believed her. Like Sydney should do a few more character studies before getting any role in the school play.

"I know it must just be *so hard* for you," she said. "Having to go through something so . . . so . . . well, just, you know, so *horrible*, right at the end of the year. Right after graduation!"

Sydney put a hand on her hip and some of the Jack and Diet sloshed out of her cup. It was long past the point when spilling mattered.

"But you don't know, now, do you Beckster?" Syd tapped Becky's nose with the tip of her finger. "Because Astrid wasn't your friend. It didn't happen to you."

Becky's mouth turned to a pout. "No, we weren't like you guys," she stammered. "But I really really liked Astrid, you know? We worked together with her mom. Plus Biology. We dissected a pig," she said, taking a sip of beer.

Sydney scrunched her eyebrows together and threw her free arm around Becky. "Now that's something," she said, squeezing a little too tight. "That'll bring you together."

Becky just nodded, but the thought of formaldehyde and death made Sydney feel ill. She felt something rise to her throat, but she held it down, swallowing hard. "I need some air," she managed, separating herself from Becky, and she made her way through the crowd.

Max was out on the deck, sucking on a cigarette.

The air was what she needed: Appalachian cool. The smoke made the night smell sweet and dark and lovely.

Sydney ambled up to Max and took great deep breaths: in comes the oxygen, out goes Astrid.

"Can I steal a puff?" she asked.

"It's bad for you," he said, in a high-pitched falsetto. It was what she was always telling him.

"Just one won't kill me."

He handed her the cigarette, his fingers just barely brushing hers.

But it didn't work like she wanted it to—maybe it was the smell or the spark of the burning paper or the whiskey, swimming its way through her veins, but she thought of another time and another cigarette, and the way the light on the end of it had just matched Astrid's hair as she took a puff.

It was three, maybe four months ago—just the two of them. The first time Astrid had ever smoked. One of the few times Sydney had ever seen her friend properly drunk.

They were on a porch, and Astrid was drinking strawberry-flavored wine. Her hair was pulled back into a tight ponytail that bounced down her back. Unwashed. She was in a loose tank top, and her only jewelry was the skeleton key that she always wore around her neck. Sydney carefully lifted the key off of Astrid's chest.

"Why do you always wear this?"

Astrid shrugged, her lips a thin, unwavering line. Finally: "Why do you always dye your hair?"

"Because I like it," Sydney said. "Because it makes me feel like me."

"That's why I wear this."

"There's no *deep meaning* behind it?" Sydney asked, almost laughing, because if Ella had been here, that's exactly how she would have said it—except even more serious. "You never take it off."

Astrid narrowed her eyes at Sydney and grabbed the cigarette from her fingers. "Let me try this." It wasn't a question.

She took a drag and then quickly pushed the cigarette back as her body shook with coughs.

At first, Sydney couldn't help but laugh, but then Astrid coughed so hard that her eyes got wet. Syd snubbed the cig on the deck and put her hand on her friend's shoulder. "You okay?"

Astrid lifted herself up and stared around them. Her hand went back to her necklace. She squeezed it. Let it go. Ran her finger along the ribbon that fastened it around her neck.

"Don't tell Ella," Astrid said. "I don't want her to know."

"Know what?" Sydney asked with a laugh. "That you're drunk?"

"I'm not dru-unk," Astrid stammered, but her words were split with another cough. She looked at Sydney, and her eyes looked sad. "I'm here," she said. "I'm me. I'm not anyone else. I haven't gone anywhere."

"I know," Sydney said. "There's nothing wrong with being a little tipsy. It doesn't mean you're not you."

Astrid just shook her head. "I don't like it when people become someone else." She took a deep breath and steadied herself against the railing. Either her head felt like it was spinning or she was ready to cry. "Just don't tell Ella," she said.

Sydney nodded. "And don't tell her about before."

When Sydney had picked Astrid up for the party, she'd watched from the driveway as Grace followed Astrid out the door, screaming at her, running down to the car, forbidding her from leaving, not stopping until they were out of the driveway, heading down the street.

"Why won't you talk to me about it?"

Astrid dropped the necklace and it bounced against her chest. She stared at her, almost instantly sober. "Because I won't," she said. "And I don't want you to, either. Promise me you won't tell Ella."

She hesitated, but she knew there was no winning with Astrid. No pushing. Not about that stuff. She was quiet about her family. She always had been.

"Alright," Sydney said, brushing a loose strand off of Astrid's face. "I won't."

Astrid stared at her then, as Sydney carefully placed a hand on her shoulder. Astrid took a breath and for a second her lips parted, almost as if she were ready to speak, as if telling everything might not really be so bad.

And that was when Brent Avery, the bad-boy dropout Sydney had been gaga for then, walked right up to her, shoved a beer in her hand, and asked her to dance. And she really should have said no, not now, but she didn't. Because he was right there and he was so cute, and even if she stuck around and pressed it's not like Astrid was actually going to tell her anything anyway.

Was she?

"Are you going to smoke or what?" Max asked, and Sydney realized that she was just standing there, holding the cigarette a few inches from her face.

She could still see herself walking away, and her stomach ached with guilt or Jack Daniels or both—and so she took a drag, good and long, and in an instant she could feel it, her head, detaching from her body, spinning, swimming, rising above the pain. Forgetting about every last thing that she should have done but didn't. She tried to exhale slowly like they did in the movies, but instead, she punctuated her breath with coughs—just like Astrid.

She took another one, and then she handed the cigarette back to Max, and now the air outside was swirling around her, and the awful thoughts in her head were getting fuzzier. Tamer. The stars were big and bright and beautiful.

She looked at Max and he looked so cool. So detached from everything. She wanted to be where he was. She felt her body sway and leaned on him for support, her hand catching his shoulder, trailing down his arm; her fingers graced the inside of his palm.

He seemed to get her meaning. And he clasped his hand through hers.

It's not like they'd never hooked up before. They used to date a long time ago, when they'd just started the band and things made more sense. Love and music. Everything pretty. Things were perfect then.

Now, somehow, the two of them had made it up to his bedroom. He hadn't let go of her hand once. He was taking control. She liked that.

Sydney knew it was probably a bad idea, but when his mouth pressed on hers, she couldn't resist. Just like before, when he'd decided that he wanted space, she couldn't do anything but acquiesce. She hadn't wanted to break up the band. To ruin their friendship. She didn't want to make Carter have to choose between the two of them. She thought he'd probably have chosen Max anyway. Max was the leader. Max called the shots.

His lips were warm and familiar. He tasted sweet. His fingers swept her hair away from her face just like they used to. They fell down together, his arms encircling her. She weaved her fingers through his hair, pulling him closer, and as she did she tried to forget about everything else but the feel of his body against hers.

When Sydney woke up, it was just after five. Max was snoring loudly next to her on the bed. The blades of the fan whirred above her, and the air felt cold against her skin. She looked around the room. Posters of their favorite bands, their inspirations, stared back at her, while piles of dirty t-shirts and worn boxers littered the floor. She spotted her bra and dress in the corner and pulled them on quickly. Then she looked at herself in the mirror; her hair was a mess, her mascara was smudged underneath her eyes like she'd been prepped for a *Maxim* photo shoot.

When she stood up her head started screaming at her, as if her brain was peeling away from her skull. She stared down at Max, wondering why she'd been so stupid, so pathetic. Knowing that he didn't want anything more. That he didn't want the real thing. Just the other things.

Wondering if it would happen again.

She walked away slowly, getting her balance, and headed down the stairs. The living room was strewn with plastic cups and a few people still passed out, using a castaway jacket or each other for cushion from the floor.

Sydney found her purse tipped over on the kitchen counter. She scooped the contents back into it and headed out the door, stepping over Carter's sleeping body as she left.

Outside, dew kissed the grass, wetting her sandaled feet. There was a calm breeze, and Sydney gulped in breaths of fresh, real air. She walked along the side of the road; it was a straight-shot from here to her house. Her mother would likely be up with Darcy in two hours. As long as she was in bed by then, she wouldn't ask any questions. She was sure that her mom knew that she went out sometimes, but if she said goodnight and was there in the morning, they seemed to have an unspoken agreement. Especially now during her "time of grief," as her mother liked to call it.

It was quiet out, as if Sydney were the only person in the whole world. If her head weren't pounding, it would have almost been peaceful.

She walked around her house until she reached the backyard. She'd always been the best one at climbing trees, better, always, than the boys in the playground. Better, for sure, than Astrid or Ella, though, with practice, they'd mastered the technique, as well.

The oak tree was a good friend. It was covered in knobs and indents that made climbing an easy task. She slipped off her sandals and hooked them around her wrist. Her bare foot grasped the bark, and she felt, for a second, in control. She grabbed onto branches, shimmying herself up. The tree was old and strong; it had only failed her once, and that was when it was younger and so was she. Her arm had taken six weeks to heal.

When she was high enough, she scooted onto the branch that nearly touched her window. It gave a little beneath her—that was normal—but her stomach seemed to twist, to knot, to rise up to her throat: Jack and Coke and bad decisions and an image of Astrid, a cigarette to her lips, swishing around inside.

She'd left the window open; she only needed to push up the screen. With one leg still wrapped around the branch, she leaned forward and pulled herself inside, ducking her head so she wouldn't hurt it anymore. But once she was in, her stomach contracted, and Sydney whipped around, leaning back out the window.

Her body lurched. One time. Two times. Three times. Her throat burned bitter and acidic as her stomach emptied itself. She lurched forward one more time, hard; the motion brought tears to her eyes.

She shook her head and wiped her hand across her eyes, spitting out all that was left in her mouth. Then she drew the curtains closed, collapsed on her bed, and shut her eyes tight, curling her body in on itself, praying at least for a little more sleep, a little more escape, before the brightness and the realness of the day inevitably took her over.

CHAPTER THREE

Trail Mix smelled the same.

Hazelnut coffee and floury pastries. The chairs were stacked on the tables, and the cash register sat on the counter. Just as if they were opening for any other day. Ella almost wished it was destroyed like her room. That it could show how messed up things were. But it looked like any normal coffee shop.

The sun was already up, streaming through the windows. The world was moving again. A world without Astrid.

There was a boy behind the counter. It was usually just her or Astrid, sometimes Becky. Rarely a boy. And definitely not a cute one. He had curly brown hair and a weak shadow of stubble on his chin. He wore thick-rimmed glasses and a Beatles shirt that he was just a tad too skinny for. He wasn't out-and-out attractive, not like Ben, with his blond hair and tan skin and perfect muscles, but he was good-looking in that *I-listen-to-Indie-music* sort of way.

He stuffed bills in the register without looking up.

"Uh, is Grace here?" Ella asked as the door jingled shut behind her.

He looked up, and in a strange way he looked familiar.

"Sorry, I was counting," he said. He smiled, looking at her intently. Then he moved the till over, lifted up the counter, and walked to the other side.

"I'm Jake," he said, sticking out his hand. He was silent a moment while they shook.

"Astrid and I were cousins," he added. "I saw you at the wake."

"Oh," she said. That must be why he'd looked familiar. But there was more to it than that. It was something in his face.

Jake cleared his throat, and she realized they were still shaking hands. She let go too fast. "Ella," she said. "I'm . . . her best friend."

He nodded, and their hands weren't touching anymore, and in an instant she realized it was his eyes. They were big and wide. They looked so much like Astrid's.

"Are you alright?" he asked, and his eyes narrowed. Concerned. And she saw her, just for a second. Astrid, asking her if she was alright after she and Ben had had a fight. And she missed her so much then, so much that she wanted to crumple up on the floor and just cry. Cry for as long as she could until it all came out.

But she shook her head, trying to get the image of her friend out of her mind. "Sorry," Ella said. "I just—"

But she didn't have time to finish. "Grace," she said, because she was there, standing in the doorway to the back room. An older, sadder version of her daughter. And those same damn eyes. Her red hair was pulled back into a tight bun, errant strands framing either side of her face. She wasn't wearing makeup, like she usually did, like she had at the wake, and now Ella could see her face. Naked before her.

Her eyes—though wide—had deep circles beneath them, as if she hadn't slept in weeks; her cheeks were thin, skeletal, as if she hadn't eaten either. She was still beautiful—how could she not be?—but it was in a different way, a broken way. She looked like one of those messed up Hollywood stars who ends up having to go to rehab or something.

It was hard to imagine this woman blasting a Pink Floyd album or entertaining them with stories of sneaking out of the house when she was younger. Ella had always thought Grace was so cool. So young and hip. She'd ask them about school gossip and rant about the bitchy girls she'd hated when she was their age. Ella had always wanted her own mother to be more like her. Now she barely recognized her.

"Hi, Ella," Grace said finally. "Thanks for coming." She spoke the words slowly, as if each one took energy.

"Hi," Ella said, and on impulse, she rushed behind the counter and wrapped her in a hug. Grace barely hugged her back, her arms hanging limp at her sides, and she didn't utter a single word. Instead she slowly moved out of the way as another woman walked out from the back, pushing her hand out at Ella.

"I'm Claire," she said. "Astrid was my niece."

She had dark auburn hair, not as fiery as Grace's or Astrid's. Not as wild either. It was cut into a short bob and obviously straightened. She, too, was pretty, but in that conservative First Lady sort of way.

"Ella," she said, forcing a smile, giving Ella a firm shake. Then she turned to Grace. "There's still lots you need to show me," she said, and she grabbed her shoulder and directed her back into the office, almost as if she were a child. Grace followed her sister just like she was one.

"My mom's not exactly a chatterer," Jake said, once the two of them were safe in the back.

"Oh, she's your—"

"Yeah," he said. "My dad went back to West Virginia yesterday. We're hanging around for awhile. Helping Aunt Grace get things in order."

Ella just shrugged. She didn't know what to say to that because order didn't seem possible at this point. And she usually liked order.

Jake tossed her a bag of large filters. "You want to start brewing those pots?" he asked, pointing to the row of them on the counter. "We open in less than an hour."

Ella nodded, but she didn't move. Not yet.

"It's weird that I didn't know about you," she said. And it was. Astrid never talked about her family. Ella had never noticed it before, but now it was clear as day. Astrid had never even mentioned them. No stories of grandpas walking 10 miles in the snow, of uncles getting too drunk at Thanksgiving, of cousins making fun of her because she couldn't whistle correctly. No tales, even, of her dad's death. Of what it was like to lose him so young. Of how much she missed him.

Every summer, Christmas, and Thanksgiving, Ella and her mom went up to New Jersey, and she always came back with pictures and inside jokes and scabs on her knees from their annual flag football game. She knew that Grace and Astrid went up to West Virginia sometimes. She knew that there'd been family there. But Astrid had never said all that much about them. And Ella had always been so busy regaling her with fun-family-time memories that she'd never really thought to ask.

Jake was just looking at her, his eyebrows raised.

"I just mean, I've known Astrid forever," she said finally.

"Knew," he said under his breath.

"What?"

"Never mind," he said, and his face sunk, like he almost felt bad about what he'd said. Like maybe he hadn't wanted her to hear.

"It's just that it's weird to hear you talk like that."

"Like what?" she asked. Even though she knew.

"All in the present," he said. "About her."

"It's one phrase," Ella said.

"You said it before, too. That you're her best friend."

"I am."

"You *were*."

Ella shook her head in disbelief. Indie-boy was taking this *way* too far.

"Why are we even fighting about this? It's so stupid."

"Sorry," he said.

She grabbed a large bag of coffee from underneath the counter. She walked around the other side and began setting up the pot. She scooped out each cup with force, some of the grounds escaping onto the floor.

"Maybe," she said, without looking up at him, the one who'd barely known Astrid, the one who she hadn't even heard about until today. "It's easier for you to talk completely accurately because you weren't used to seeing her every single day."

Jake whipped his head up. "Just because we didn't have slumber parties all the time doesn't mean I didn't know her."

Ella threw another scoop of coffee into the machine. She glared at Jake. How dare he?

"Well clearly none of us really knew her," she snapped. "Or we all wouldn't be here, would we?"

"I know you guys were close," Jake said, taking a deep breath. "But it's different. I'm the one who's known her since she was born.

I'm the one that was there for her when she lost her dad. I'm the one who understands Grace."

She shook her head as she flicked on the brew button. She knew Astrid and Grace just as well as he did. She'd probably spent more time with them than he had. Sure, he shared their blood, but had he known which TV shows were Astrid's favorite? Had he known just the way her lips pursed together when she was trying to figure out a math problem? Did he know the way Grace shook her hips around the kitchen when she was making dinner?

Jake didn't say anything else. He just bowed his head and started shuffling bills in the register again.

She knew that he didn't get it. That he couldn't get it.

Because the only one who could have really explained it to him wasn't here to speak.

The shop was surprisingly busy. It almost felt like Astrid's funeral, round two. Everyone was looking at her with understanding eyes, like they wanted to somehow show their support. But, "I'm sorry your best friend killed herself," didn't really jibe with, "Can I have an iced latte?" So they just left her really big tips.

A part of her kept expecting Astrid to pop out of the back office, to hop on the register and take care of a few customers, to show her exactly how she got the foam on her lattes so perfect.

The big pot of house blend was out in a few hours. Jake was on the register and there was a slight lull in customers, so Ella headed to the back room where they stocked extra beans.

As soon as she stepped inside, the sight of Grace and Claire made her tense up. Grace faced the wall, slumped over her desk in a corner of the stock room, papers spread out in front of her, hands on top of them as if they were holding her up. Ella felt like an intruder. She hadn't meant to interrupt—she hadn't known there was anything *to* interrupt. She just wanted to stock the coffee, damn it, but she was already inside. She couldn't turn around now.

Claire leaned over Grace. "Come on," she said quietly, tugging on Grace's arm. "It will be good to go out there. Just for a minute."

Ella moved quietly, grabbing a big bag of the house blend off the first shelf. Their backs were to her, and they still hadn't seemed to notice.

They were quiet for a moment as Ella tip-toed out, but then there was a flash of movement, a yell. "Get away from me," Grace said, jerking her arm from her sister's grasp. "It won't be good," she said, her voice rising. "It can't help me. You can't help me. He can't help me. No one can." And she began to sob.

Ella heard a rattle on the floor. The two women whipped around. Grace stared right at her. Angry.

It took her a second to realize that she'd dropped the bag of coffee. "I'm sorry," she said, kneeling down, the coffee beans pressing into her bare kneecaps. She started to scoop them up with her hands. "I'm really sorry."

"Just get out," Grace said. And then she looked to her sister. "Both of you, just leave me alone," she said. "Please."

And Claire walked towards Ella quickly, the coffee beans crunching beneath her feet. She grabbed Ella by the shoulder, pulling her upright. Beans were still stuck to her shin. Claire pushed her back to the front. Grace's eyes stayed pinned on her until she couldn't see them anymore. Claire closed the door behind her with a thud.

"I'm sorry," Ella said, brushing the coffee beans off her legs. "I was just getting coffee. We ran out. I didn't mean to—"

"Shh," Claire said, putting her finger to her lips in a move that was super patronizing but just the slightest bit comforting. "Don't worry," she said. "I'll get the coffee. I think I saw some more in the cabinet."

Without a pause, she grabbed a rag from the counter and pushed it into Ella's hands. "Here," she said. "Why don't you wipe down the counters?" she asked. "They look dirty."

Ella took the rag obediently. Jake looked at her and gave her a shrug. He must have heard everything, but he didn't look all that surprised. She followed Claire's suggestion on autopilot, sliding the rag across the counter in big even arcs. Claire had swooped in after the storm and she was in charge now. Which was weird because it used to be her and Grace and Astrid who were in charge. She and Astrid used to decide what pots needed brewing. Which counters needed to be cleaned.

She stared back at Jake, standing at the register, ringing up an old woman and handing her a paper cup. She had gray-blue hair you couldn't forget, and she and Astrid had probably helped her a hundred times.

The door continued to jingle and more people walked inside, and Ella walked back towards the espresso machine because Jake was going to need a lot of help.

Even though the place was packed, she'd never felt more alone.

Ben and Sydney picked her up at six. They were headed to Johnny's. It was really called Jumping Johnny's, but the only people who ever called it that were the ones who didn't live in Falling Rock or who were very, very new. Astrid had corrected her when they were younger.

A line of cars sputtered in front of them. Sydney was sprawled across the backseat, leaning against the window, her hair pulled into short pigtails. Ben leaned one arm on the window, cute as ever. Ella sat in the front, hands folded in her lap, waiting for their turn. There was a hole in the back where Astrid would have sat. Right behind her. Ella tried not to look in the side view mirror, but she couldn't help it. She glanced over and emptiness met her, and she knew that this wasn't a dream. This was real.

"What do you girls want?" Ben turned in his seat, looking from her to Sydney. A twangy country act crooned on the radio and Ella turned it down. It was making her nervous.

"The usual," Sydney said. Large fries. Diet Coke.

Ben looked at her, like, *your turn*, but she couldn't seem to think. She couldn't get that damn empty seat out of her mind. She looked away from Ben and back to the side mirror, and for a second, for an infinitesimal second, she wanted to so bad that it was like she could see Astrid right there, and she couldn't help it, she drew her breath in, and the vision was gone.

"Hello, love," Ben said, waving his hand in front of her. "You okay?"

Ella closed her eyes. Opened them again. Stole a quick glance in the side view. Nothing.

"Ellllla," Ben said.

"Sorry," she said. "I got distracted. I'm not hungry."

He looked at her all sad and parent-like. "Come on, Ella," he said. "Just get a little something."

The cars pulled forward, and Ella scanned her eyes across the menu without really reading it. "Just get me a vanilla shake," she said.

"That's my girl." And he rolled down the window, rattling off their orders, getting the super extra value special for himself.

Ben paid for their food, shoved a few greasy bags onto her lap, and they pulled away. They never went inside—anyone who really knew the place knew that if you headed out of the parking lot and just to the left, you'd hit a winding dirt road and a half-mile drive that led to one of the most beautiful lookout points in town. On summer nights with greasy fries and thick milkshakes, it never got old. At least it hadn't until now.

There were a few cars parked when they got there, and Ben backed up to the ledge. It always made Ella nervous when he did this, like they could just roll right over and everything would turn into crushed metal and smushed bodies. She couldn't believe that Astrid was actually dead.

Ben turned off the car, and they got out, opened the hatch in the back, and crawled inside. They fit easier now that it was just the three of them, side by side, Ella in the middle. She passed out the items. She wished that there was a strawberry shake and a thing of chicken tenders with honey mustard in there, too, but there wasn't.

Sydney immediately started chomping and Ben ravaged his cheese-burger but Ella just sipped slowly. The sky was nice. Not gray. And the sun was just going down and splashing everything with pink and purple hues. Ella could see the valley below and the mountains behind, covered in mist, even though the sky was clear. There was a crescent moon, a really pretty one. Damn, it was beautiful out. The world could be so good sometimes. How could Astrid leave it?

Ben and Sydney still had yet to breach the subject of her first day back at work. It was like they were trying to protect her or something. But she wanted to talk about it. God, she wanted to talk about it. More than that, she wanted them to ask. Astrid would have asked.

"So I guess you're not going to ask about work?" she said, looking straight at Sydney. The shake was turning her hand icy, but she didn't sip it. Not yet.

Ben took another bite so he wouldn't have to say anything. He wanted to stay out of this. Clearly.

"Well you obviously want to talk about it," Sydney said. "If you want to talk, talk."

"I want you to want to hear about it." She was looking at both of them now.

"El," Sydney said, brushing her off. "Can we just have a moment—one freaking moment—that's not about Astrid?"

"Well I just spent a day that was all about her, so maybe you could show me a little understanding."

"What do you want me to do?" Sydney asked. "You chose to do that." She looked to Ben for confirmation. "She's the one who wanted to do it."

Ben held his hands up. "You two leave me out of it."

An anger started then, deep in her stomach. Ben was always such a diplomat. It wasn't fair. "You know," she said, staring right at him. "You really should take my side on this."

"Oh, lovely," Sydney said, sarcasm oozing out of every word. "There are *sides* now."

"Yeah," Ella snapped. "There are."

"I told you last night you should go to the party instead," Sydney said. "I knew that going there would make things worse."

"Well I went," Ella said. "And I'm going to go back. And you have to be there for me and listen to me, no matter what. That's your job, Syd. You're the only best friend I have left."

And she jumped out of the car and walked up to the trash can and threw her shake in as hard as she could, but it didn't work like she wanted it to. The lid popped off, and little drops of the cool white goop sprayed her across the face. She whipped around, avoiding Ben and Sydney's eyes, and she opened the passenger door and climbed in, slamming it shut behind her. She opened the glove box and began to ruffle through. There had to be some napkins in there somewhere.

"Ella," Sydney said, but she didn't turn. "Ella."

She just kept looking, but it was already hard to see. The tears made her vision wavy. They came on strong and fast. In a moment, she was full-on crying. Not because of Sydney. Not because of Ben. Not even because of the look Grace gave her or the way every moment in the café had made Astrid's absence feel even more real. She cried for all of it. She cried because things weren't supposed to be this way. She cried because she had vanilla milkshake all over her face.

She felt the car lift up and in a minute, Ben and Sydney had surrounded her.

"Here," Sydney said, pushing a wad of paper napkins in front of her. But Ella couldn't stop. Her body shook now, and she felt Sydney's arms tighten around her and Ben's warm hand on her shoulder. And she shook and she shook until she couldn't shake anymore and then her breath came in gasps, and she looked up and they were still there, still right there for her, and it felt so good to have them. Ella tried to calm her breathing as Sydney took her chin in her hand. Her eyes were intent on her face, and she patted the napkin underneath her eyes and then down her cheeks.

"I'm sorry," Sydney said. "I'm really sorry."

"It's okay," Ella said, her voice coming out so shaky it barely sounded like her.

Sydney let her go, and Ben wrapped his arm around her shoulder. "I'm sorry too, babe," he whispered in her ear. "Let me see," he said, turning her face towards his. "Geez you're a wreck."

"She always was a messy eater," Sydney piped in from behind.

"You still got a little, right there," he said, and he leaned in and kissed the bottom of her lip. He felt warm and safe.

Ben pulled back and made a face, scrunching up his nose. "Next time you get, uhh, *rightfully* pissed at us," he said, "could you please make your point with a chocolate shake?"

She heard Sydney laugh, and she couldn't help it. She did, too.

And for a moment—a small one—the world felt okay again.

Ella couldn't sleep that night. She kept waking, wide-eyed, dreams too fuzzy to remember, but with dark colors, tones that meant they'd been bad. On the third or fourth time, she sat up and pulled her computer onto her lap. She couldn't imagine going back to sleep but reading felt impossible, like the words would blur together if she even tried to look at a page, so she opened the screen, and on impulse, logged onto Facebook. She hadn't been on since Astrid died—seeing a public reaction to everything had felt like way too much. But now she didn't care—she knew that Astrid would be there, words and pictures on a screen. In a pixel world, in the cloud and the data centers far away, it was almost like she was still alive.

Nothing much was new. Her music-obsessed friends were posting links to YouTube videos and reviews, a lonely girl from her English class had put up a sad quote about finding romance at the right time, and it looked like it was the official day for posting your doppelganger. Ella might have done it herself a few weeks ago—everyone said she looked just like the brown-haired girl from that TV show that she didn't really watch—but it all felt so pointless now. How could she really have spent hours on this site before? It was meaningless. It wasn't even real. Just a bunch of people trying to make other people think that they were a certain way. If she'd learned anything lately it was that you couldn't really know people from the outside—and especially not from the Internet.

Ella went to her own profile. Her wall was filled with messages, but her eyes froze on the side of her screen. There she was, like an apparition. The first face in the list of all of her friends. Smiling back at her like nothing in the world was wrong. Like she still *existed*.

Astrid.

Ella couldn't help it—she clicked. She was instantly taken to her profile. Her friends, her activities, her high school, her hometown, listed out as if she were still around. As if she might respond if you sent her a message or invited her to your birthday party.

Ella took a deep breath as she took in the pseudo-memorial— posted photos, goodbye notes, declarations that she was in a happier place. All of a sudden it didn't seem right. Astrid wasn't around anymore. You couldn't touch her. You couldn't hug her. You couldn't make her any better. It wasn't fair.

"Write something . . ." it said at the top of her screen. Calling her. Asking her to join in, too. Even if she wanted to, what would she say?

How could you?

Where did you go?

Was it my fault?

Should I have seen it coming?

Why the hell did you do it right now? Couldn't you have waited until we'd grown up and grown apart and gotten married and then maybe I wouldn't miss you as much as I do?

Ella clicked on the box, and the cursor blinked at her, begging for her to say something to her best friend in the world. Her best friend who wasn't in the world anymore.

She laid her fingers on the keys, and she started to type—slowly, but surely.

All I want to know is why.

She held her finger above the button, waiting to click post. This was what she really felt, what she wanted to say to Astrid, not that she missed her, not that she loved her, even though those things were true, truer now maybe than ever before.

But she couldn't do it. Slowly, she deleted the letters, one by one, and the box was empty again. Waiting.

I miss you.

And she hit enter and flipped the computer shut, flopping back onto the bed and rolling over before she could say anything more.

When Ella got to the café the next morning, Becky was already there, leaning against the counter and looking confused.

"Ella," she said, standing up straight as soon as she saw her, her blue eyes opening wide. "I didn't expect *you* to be here." Her voice was sugary and sympathetic and fake. Like, *Oh, you poor baby. How hard it must be.* There was polite, sure, but Ella hated fake.

"I still work here," Ella said, crossing her arms in front of her.

"Well, yeah," Becky said. "I know. I just can't even *imagine* how hard this must be for you," she said, wrapping Ella in a bony hug. She pulled back, looked her straight in the eyes. "We just all loved Astrid so much. I just never would have expected this from her."

Jake stepped out from the back in time to save her, and Becky immediately forgot her sympathy speech. Her concerned face softened, turned to the beginnings of a smile.

"Hi," he said. "You're Becky?"

Full smile this time: "Yeah."

Then she shot a look at Ella, like, *You didn't tell me a hot guy started here.* Apparently her sadness about Astrid hadn't lasted all that long.

Ella ignored her and headed to the back to get an apron. Becky throwing herself at yet another cute guy was just too much of a train wreck to watch. She pushed the door open slowly, breathing a sigh of relief when she realized no one else was there. No Claire. No Grace. Today would be at least a little less heart-wrenching than the one before. She grabbed her apron and knotted it tight at her waist.

"We still have to brew all these pots," Jake said as soon as she was back up front. "The tables need to be prepped, the counters cleaned, the pastries are in the back, and I'm getting the register together."

"Of course," Becky said. "Where should I start?" She looked at Jake like she'd looked at pretty much every guy on the football team at one point or another. A look that said, *I'm interested. I'm available.*

"Why don't you brew?" Jake asked, without returning her look. So far he seemed immune to Becky's charms. One thing, at least, to count in his favor.

Ella set to work scrubbing as Jake counted out the bills. Soon, the place was bustling, the three of them taking turns at the register and at the espresso machine. They didn't talk about the day before—it was too busy to talk about much.

Around one o'clock there was a lull. Ella was wiping down the espresso machine—she wanted to get it nice and clean before the next rush. Jake was quiet, changing out the tip jar. Becky was dramatically wiping down a few tables.

Ella thought about the day before—she hated what Jake had said, but at the same time, she knew that he never would have said it unless he really loved Astrid. And it was nice to be around someone who cared about her, not someone who felt compelled to say sorry, like Becky. Or someone who would promise to be there, like Ben. Someone who really, truly missed her—maybe not as much as she and Sydney did—but some.

Before she could change her mind, she cleared her throat. She was no good at olive branches but she might as well try. "You like music?" she asked, and immediately she regretted it. What kind of question was that?

"Me?" Jake asked, even though it was so completely obvious that it had been directed at him.

"I mean, do you like going to see music?"

Jake nodded all big and dramatic. "Uh, yeah."

Ella smiled, recovering. "My friend, Sydney," she said. "Well, she's—she was—" Jake winced, but she kept going, "Astrid's friend, too. Anyway, she's in this folksy kind of band and they're playing tonight, and—"

"I'd love to go," he said.

"Oh, I mean," Ella felt the blood rush to her face. She hoped that he didn't think she was hitting on him. She was no Becky. Plus, she had Ben.

"You're asking me, right?" he asked.

"Uh, yeah," she said hesitantly. Inviting him and letting him know about it were two different things. "I mean, and Becky, too," she said. "If you guys want to."

Becky turned around, a pout on her face. "I have dance practice," she said. Of *course* she did.

But Jake just smiled. "Sounds good. I'll be there."

Ella smiled, too, maybe too long, and finally he broke their gaze, looking down at the register. "You mind getting me a roll of quarters?" he asked. "They're right in the back."

"Sure," she said, smiling as she walked to the back room, her phone buzzing from inside her apron. She didn't want him to get the wrong idea. She hoped to hell that he hadn't. Still, a part of her couldn't help being glad that he'd said yes.

But Ella pulled out her phone, and in seconds, the good feeling went away.

Her heart pounded as she stared at the screen—it echoed in her ears, felt like it was going to pump itself right out of her chest. A notification on her phone, from Facebook:

Astrid Allen commented on your post.

Ella's breathing got heavy and all she could think was, *What the hell, what the hell, what the hell?* She held the phone in her hands, willing herself to keep going. It was hard to even do it because her hands were shaking so much, but she clicked to the page she'd been on just last night. Astrid's page.

And there they were, four little words, four little horrible, terrifying, comforting, wonderful words. Right underneath her post. From Astrid. *From Astrid Allen.*

I miss you, too.

She didn't know how long she stood there, but she heard Jake's voice in the distance, and soon her body was moving of its own accord. Autopilot, like she'd rehearsed this. Door open. Apron off. Around the counter. Towards the door.

"I have to go," she said to Jake, without even looking over.

"What?"

"I'm not well," she said. "I have to go."

She didn't wait for an answer, just pushed through the door and walked.

Away from the shop. The people. She had to get away.

But she had nowhere to go but home, and in minutes, she was there, at her old familiar door, pushing it open, her mom asking why she was home so early, mumbling an excuse. She climbed the stairs two at a time, and then she was in her room, and she went straight to her computer and flipped it open.

The page was still there, and before she could lose her nerve, she hit refresh.

Ella felt herself gasp—out of fear or relief she couldn't tell—and she kept hitting it, over and over and over. *Refresh, refresh, refresh!*

But it was no use—there was nothing she could do.

Those four little words.

I miss you, too.

Those four little words were gone.

CHAPTER FOUR

Sydney's fiddle had a broken string.

She'd been putting it off—real, productive tasks seemed difficult lately (hair-brushing, making a sandwich, watching Darcy)—but now she had no choice. She had a show tonight and practice in two hours.

The drive to her aunt and uncle's was a little less than twenty minutes. The road was windy, curving around hills, the lanes just big enough to let two cars pass. Led Zeppelin was playing on the radio. Crooning, metal poetry.

Syd hated speed limits. They assumed that every driver had the same limitations, the same abilities. Her car was old and tiny. It made a lot of noise, never shut up, really, but it handled the turns well, even when she did go quite a bit faster than she should.

It was misting today. Not actual rain, but enough to make the sky sad and gloomy, the mountains blurry, moody, in the distance—they didn't call it the Blue Ridge for nothing. Sydney followed the highway around the side of a hill, and her aunt and uncle's house came into view. The music had changed, and now Paul and John and George and Ringo were telling her it was all getting better, a little better, all the time.

But she didn't believe them.

She parked the car in the back. She opened the door and stepped out, the red clay on the ground made darker by the wetness of the weather, squishing beneath her feet.

A wooden sign reading "Sid's Music Repairs" swayed back and forth in front of the shop. She'd been named after her uncle, a simple one-letter swap making her version more girl-appropriate, or at least distinguished from his. She pulled back the screen door, the squeaking announcing her presence.

The shop was an all-purpose kind of place. In the front was quite the sampling of used instruments, brass saxophones in need of a good polish, acoustic guitars grown scratchy with heavy use. There was a counter and a workroom behind it where Uncle Sid did his repairs. Tune-ups for those who hadn't learned how, new strings, and pretty much whatever was needed to bring an instrument back to life. Sid had given her a violin when she was eleven. It was used and the wood was a little scuffed up in places, but it was a good one. She hadn't let it go since.

Her uncle was busy with a customer, so she gave him a quick wave and headed towards the back to find Audie, parting the curtain that led to their living space, strings of beads jangling behind her.

Audie must have heard the beads. She floated into the kitchen, followed by yards of lime green linen. Her dress fell across her pleasantly plump body in billowing ruffles, punctuated with about a dozen bangles and a big wooden necklace. Her glasses were too big for her face, and her hair was just a tad too long for her age.

"Hey there, Syddie," she said, wrapping Sydney in a noisy, jewelry-jangling hug. Her aunt held her tight, longer than she usually did.

Finally, she pulled back, and her aunt's eyes looked almost wet. She brushed a strand of hair behind her ear. "What brings you this way, dear?"

Sydney held up her fiddle. "Broken string."

"For the show tonight, I presume?" Audie asked.

Sydney nodded. "I can just get a pack from Uncle Sid," she said. "I just thought I'd come back and say hi."

"Nonsense," Audie said, taking the fiddle out of Sydney's hands. "Let me just see if he has a second."

Sydney didn't protest, and in minutes, Audie was back, the beads dancing around her, the kettle on the stove starting to whistle.

"It'll just take a few minutes," Audie said, clasping her hands together and nodding towards a chair. "Earl Grey or English Breakfast?"

"Earl Grey," Sydney said, sitting down. Her aunt smiled and popped teabags into two chipped cups. She grabbed the kettle and poured, and steam rushed up between them, blurring Syd's vision for a moment. Audie sat down next to her, an eager, earnest look on her face. She wanted to talk.

"Is that new?" Sydney asked, pointing to a wooden sign hanging above the stove. *Pie Fixes Everything.*

Audie nodded. "I found it at the flea a few weekends ago. You know I had to have it." Sydney did. Audie was Miss Baker Extraordinaire, among other things.

"It looks nice," Syd said, adding sugar.

"Thanks."

Silence for several minutes, apart from the clinking of the spoon against Sydney's teacup. The sugar had long since dissolved but she just kept on stirring.

"I'm thinking about painting the living room orange," Audie said.

"Really? What kind?"

"Deep, deep orange, like a pumpkin," Audie said. "I know you aren't afraid of bright colors." She ran her hands through Sydney's bangs.

More minutes passed while the tea steamed between them. Finally Audie took a sip and then opened her mouth to speak. Closed it. Opened it again. "Did I ever tell you that my best friend died?"

Audie stared at her, waiting for an answer.

"No."

"It was before you even existed," Audie said. "She was only thirty-two. We knew each other since high school. We were joined at the hip. She and her husband used to double with me and Sid. We played bridge together. The whole works."

Sydney was quiet.

"I still think about her every day," Audie said.

"So it never gets better then?" Sydney asked. "That's what you're telling me?"

"I'm just trying to tell you that I understand," Audie said. "And it does get better. It gets less," she said. "It's like a scar. Some days you barely know it's there. Some you find yourself running your finger over it. Seeing how it feels."

"Right now it feels like a big gaping bleeding hole. Not a scar," Sydney snapped.

"I know, dear, but—"

"How did she die?"

Audie paused a minute before answering. "A car accident. There was no reason for it. Just a bad intersection and two people driving too fast."

Sydney nodded. A car accident. It was a normal way to die—one that made sense. One that took lots of people. Like old age. Or cancer. She thought about Astrid's terse, emotionless description when she talked about her dad. Car accident. It was just one of those crazy things that happened. An easy way, a TV-show kind of way, to die.

"That's how Astrid's dad died," she said.

"Oh, I know," Audie said. "I remember."

Sydney's eyes widened. "You do?"

Audie nodded, a soft smile creeping up at the corners of her mouth. "He used to come in here often—with Grace. Had a saxophone, nothing fancy, just an amateur one. I think he used to play old jazz. Big hotshot that one—going places. It was such a shame."

Sydney shook her head. She'd learned more about Astrid's family in five minutes than she had in five years. "Astrid never talked about him."

Audie quietly took a sip of her tea. She took a deep breath, remembering. "You didn't know what love was until you saw those two—Robert and Grace."

Robert, she thought, turning the name over in her mind. She'd never even known his name.

Audie went on. "They were gaga for each other. I mean ga-*ga*. Couldn't keep their hands off each other, and Astrid, God, was she the cutest kid. I mean, hair like you wouldn't believe, a crown of ringlets. Some kind of Irish angel, she was."

Sydney shook her head, wishing she had moved here sooner, that she could have known Astrid as a tiny tot, shared a kiddie pool with her, swapped the toys of their Happy Meals. That their limited time had been longer.

"So what happened? Was it like a big wreck?" Thinking about it, *talking* about it now, it was nuts how little she knew. But it was the way Astrid had always said it. *Don't push. This is all you're going to get.*

Audie gave a shrug. "I don't know the exact details. They were up in West Virginia, I think, when it happened. He was alone in the car—a rental, I guess. The funeral was far away—I think he had some family on the West Coast."

"And that was it? Everyone just never spoke about him again?"

"It was what Grace wanted," Audie said with a sigh. "God forbid something like that ever happen to me and your uncle," she knocked on the table and proceeded to cross herself. "But who's to say what you'd do to get through it?"

Sydney nodded, but she wondered how Astrid had felt about that. If she'd just accepted it with nothing more than a sigh and a shrug.

Sydney thought about Astrid. Choosing to leave. Taking fate into her own hands. She almost wished it had been something as simple as a wreck.

"I'm really sorry about your friend—and about Astrid's dad," she added, her breathing quickening. "But it's not the same."

"What do you mean?" Audie asked, her mouth just barely hanging open. She almost looked hurt.

"Because it wasn't your fault," Sydney said. "Anything like that—it just happens. There's not a reason. There's no fault. It's not the same," Sydney said again. "It's just not." Her voice caught in her throat.

Audie slammed her cup down on the table so hard that Sydney almost thought it would break. "It's not yours either," she said.

Sydney just shrugged.

"Look at me, Sydney," Audie said. "You have to believe that. It's not yours."

"I don't know," Sydney stared down at her cup. She thought about the night at the party, Astrid almost ready to open up, how she'd just walked away. "She was my best friend, and looking back, it's like I barely knew anything about her. I didn't even know her dad's *name*. I should have done things differently."

"It's *not* your fault," Audie said. "Astrid was a quiet girl, a disturbed girl. Nothing you could have done would have changed that. It's a tragedy, just like what happened to her dad. It's just a tragedy." Audie put her hand on her cheek then, but Sydney couldn't even bear looking up. What if it was like that thing in psychology, the thing where all the people just watch a crime happening, and no one does anything because they think the other person will—bystander something? What if that was them—Astrid crying and crying for help and she and Ella just standing there, waiting for someone else to take care of it? She wished there was something stronger in her tea, something that would erase the thought.

The timer dinged, and Sydney felt herself jump. The moment was broken, and Audie moved her hand back to her lap. "Scones," she said quietly. "You'll stay for one?"

Sydney shook her head. "I should go."

"Wait," Audie said, ignoring the beeping timer. She shuffled over to the bookcase, grabbed the first one on the shelf. "I want you to take this," she said. "I think it'll help."

Her aunt pushed the book into her hands: *The Other History of Falling Rock*. It was Audie's pride and joy. A book that they now sold in town gift shops, the kind of shops that also sold hemp jewelry and postcards. It had taken Audie ten years to compile.

Sydney opened it to the first page: "What follows is a history which not all will believe . . ."

"The ghost book?" Sydney asked. "I don't really think—"

"It's not just about ghosts," Audie said. "It's about loss. It's about spirits moving from one world to the next. About how this one here is just one stop on the journey."

Sydney felt her stomach knot. The dead, spirits, whatever you wanted to call them, were a huge part of Audie's worldview. Guardian angels. Ghosts hanging out in old places. A whole other world full of specters and unusual sounds in the night. Most of the time

Sydney found it at least mildly funny, just another one of her aunt's quirks. Now was not that time.

Sydney scooted her chair back and stood up. She wasn't in the mood for any half-cocked philosophies or theories. Astrid had left. Astrid was gone. And she wasn't coming back. Maybe Sydney could have done something months ago, but now there wasn't anything that could help—especially not some bullshit book.

"Thanks for the tea," she said, but it came out as a snap. "I should go."

And she breezed through the beaded curtain before her aunt could protest.

Up at the front, her uncle was checking out a customer. Her fiddle, newly strung, was ready on the counter. "Thanks," she said quickly, as he counted change out of the register. She flicked her eyes to the large grandfather clock, though she still had plenty of time before practice. "I'll see you later."

Her Uncle Sid handed the customer his bag and then turned to her. "You stay longer next time, okay?"

Sydney nodded, walking quickly out of the shop.

It was only once she got to the car that she realized that she was still holding the book in her hands.

Max was a jerk at practice.

"Come on, Sydney," he yelled. "Focus!"

Sydney shot him a look but it didn't stop him.

"The show's tonight, the fair's this weekend, and you're all over the place."

In just days, he'd gone from supporting, loving, eager-to-hook-up Max to demanding dictatorial Max. She'd experienced the transition before, but she'd at least thought his good mood would last a bit longer this time, considering. It was like he was two different people. When he wanted her (whatever she was to him), he was sweet and comforting. When he wanted music, or more like a musical ideal that he (and only he) could understand, he was exacting, overbearing. In short, an asshole.

And yet in spite of herself, she still liked the way that his sandy brown hair fell around his face, just above his shoulders. He'd always have that on her.

"Alright," she said, taking a deep breath in an attempt to still her mind. "Let's just try it again from the top." She had her bow at the ready. Max, on guitar, started them off, softly strumming.

Eight counts of eight, she told herself. Eight counts of eight.

One. Two. Three. Four. Five. Six. Seven. Eight.

It wasn't a difficult song; it was one they'd played many times. Not the main crowd favorite, but well-liked. A bit moodier, still upbeat. On the demo that Max wanted to record, it would be the second track. He was serious about River Deep. Had been since they'd started three years ago. So was Sydney.

But the problem wasn't the music. It never was. It was Max. He hadn't said a word about them hooking up. Of course, she hadn't either, but that was beyond the point. He was the one who wanted space until he didn't want it anymore, for a few fleeting moments. He was the one who called the shots.

Three. Two. Three. Four. Five. Six. Seven. Eight.

She hadn't told Ella what had happened between them. She had a feeling that she wouldn't approve. Astrid was the kind of person she told those things to. Astrid was the one who never judged. It's not that she didn't love Ella—she did—but Ella wasn't the one that you ran to if you were ashamed of yourself. She was the one you celebrated with when you were proud.

Six. Two. Three. Four. Five. Six. Seven. Eight.

Astrid had wanted to tell her something, too. Her mind flashed back to that stupid party, Astrid getting drunk, her face right before Sydney walked away. What had she and her mom been fighting about? A boy? But Astrid never was all that into boys, at least not beyond the faraway crushes that everyone had at some point or another. Could she have been seeing someone and they hadn't even known about it? Had she tried to talk to her mom about her dad? Was she tired of never mentioning him, of practically pretending that he'd never existed? Sydney had never even seen a photo of him anywhere in their house. She'd always thought it was a little strange, but now that he had a name, now that she knew he played the saxophone, liked jazz—was wild for Grace—it just felt wrong.

And yet she'd never questioned it. Not once.

Now, Sydney wished more than anything that she'd stayed. Pressed her until she got it all out. But instead, she'd just let Astrid be Astrid. Open up one moment and shut back down the next.

That night, Sydney had known that something was wrong. God help her, she'd known. And she hadn't done anything to help.

Eight. Two. Three. Four—

The guitar stopped. Sydney looked to Max and Carter. Carter quickly stopped playing and looked at her bashfully, his face warm and nice like it always was. He felt bad for her. He always did.

Max just stared at her. "Can you not count?"

She thought of Astrid and all she felt was rage. At herself. At Max. At everyone.

"I guess not," she said, and she threw her bow across the garage as hard as she could. It hit a plastic sled and landed on top of a can of mineral spirits. She didn't throw her fiddle. Even she wasn't dramatic enough for that. And she knew that it damn well wouldn't do anyone any good.

She set it down instead, stomping out of the garage, cursing the pretty sunset that met her outside, bright orange and pink that really ought to be enjoyed. She had nothing else to do, so she sat down by the mailbox in front of Max's house. She put her hands at her sides, took a deep breath, and screamed.

No one turned, no neighbors or idle walkers, because there was no one there to turn. Max's house was the only one along this road. In another place, maybe someone would have thought that she was hurt, that she'd been attacked, but not here. She almost wished that she was hurt, really hurt, with a broken ankle or arm or even just a sprain. She wished that she could trip and fall and have a reason to scream and cry. She wanted concrete, physical pain, instead of this: the abstract, the questions, the guilt—hot and angry and empty and heavy all at once.

Carter came up to her shortly after. He sat down next to her, about an inch away without touching. He didn't say anything yet, but his presence, his tall lanky body and stupid curly hair, was almost comforting. Almost.

When he finally spoke, his voice was honest. "Max can be kind of an ass sometimes."

"It's not just Max," she said, without looking over.

"I know."

They didn't say anything more for a minute. The sunset was more progressed now. Almost purple. A mosquito buzzed by and landed on her arm. She swatted it away.

"I guess you want me to come back in there," she said. "And learn to count."

Carter looked back towards Max, and she followed his gaze. He was hunched over his notebook, probably working out another damn chorus, his back facing them.

"Max just doesn't know what to do with you," Carter said. "I know he feels bad about what happened, and he—"

"So that's how he's trying to help?" she asked. "By criticizing the hell out of me?"

"It's a lame tactic, I know," he said. He crossed his arms in front of him, then let them go again and stretched out his legs. Carter was all angles. He never knew quite what to do with himself. "What I mean is that he's scared," he said.

"Of what?"

"Of you, of things that are real. You know."

"We broke up a year ago," she said. "Why does it matter?"

"He still cares about you," Carter said. "And he knows that you need somebody, and he just gets freaked out and then starts shit and pushes you away."

She stared at Carter then, and he looked so open and honest and comforting. He was so good sometimes. Too good.

After a minute, she put her hand on his shoulder and forced a smile. He was so tall, she almost had to stretch. "Carter, babe. I think you've been listening to too much talk radio."

"My mom puts it on in the car," he said. "Not me. I only listen by proxy."

"Mmm hmm," she said, laughing. "Sure."

"Well tell me I don't have a good point, here," he said. "Just trust me on this one."

Sydney crossed her arms in front of her. "So you want me to come back in?"

He sighed. "Max will be Max," he said. "Just try not to let it get to you."

She uncrossed her arms and leaned back on her palms. "Whatever," she said. "Let's go."

Carter jumped up immediately, but then he seemed to change his mind and squatted down so his face was level with hers. Close.

"And Sydney," he said. "I'm really sorry."

"You didn't do anything," she said. "It's all Max."

"I'm not talking about Max," he said. "I mean, you know, everything else."

"Thanks," she said quietly. "You don't have to be sorry. It's not your fault."

"It's not anyone's," he whispered, shaking his head. He didn't wait for her to respond. "Come on," he said, jumping up again, grabbing her hands and pulling her with him. "Let's go."

"From the top!" Carter yelled, as they walked back into the garage. Sydney retrieved her bow quietly, avoiding Max's eyes. She picked up her fiddle and waited.

But Max caught her eyes. "From the top," he echoed, looking straight at her. "I'll try to be better with my cues this time."

And she knew that that was the only apology she'd get.

That night, she leaned against the back wall of The Grove with Max and Carter, adjusting her earplugs, pushing them in tighter, as the lead singer of Death Star let out a long piercing wail and strummed on an electric guitar with *way* too much distortion. The floors were dirty and the lighting dim, and the stale smell of sweat and Natty Light filled the air. Around them, the crowd of people, all twenty or so of them, looked about as bored as she was. Apart from a group of girls who must have been the Girlfriends. They banged their heads almost in perfect tandem with the three blond-haired, pock-marked boys of Death Star jumping up and down on stage. That was the thing about The Grove. It was her favorite, for sure, but they weren't always as selective as they could be in their lineups.

Max was standing there, arms crossed in front of him, in serious pre-show mode. He'd been nicer since her breakdown, nice for Max, at least. Carter turned to her, stuck his tongue out, and wiggled his head back and forth in a mock-Kiss tribute. She forced herself to laugh, doing a few head bangs herself. But she knew it came out as fake. She just couldn't help it.

River Deep didn't go on for another hour at least.

The Grove was the first place they'd ever played. She'd been fifteen, they'd just started the band, and she'd finally begun calling her violin a fiddle. Her hair was honey brown then, natural. Two tiny, generic holes in her ears were her only piercings. She barely even knew what makeup was, and Max was nothing to her. Just the nerdy guy in her English class who also hated Chaucer but liked Keats, and wanted to start a band. She was first-string violin in the orchestra, so it only made sense. Once they'd found Carter, the only one weird enough to try his hand at the mandolin (it still looked so strange against his stretched-out body, like it had been made for an elf or a fairy), they were set.

That first night, they'd opened for another local band who also had no following. Astrid and Ella and a few friends of Max and Carter were the only people in attendance. And yet, Sydney had been seduced by the colored lights and the feel of the stage and the excitement of the unexpected, the not quite knowing how it would turn out, how long she should hold the end note, the happy look on the faces of her friends when they heard something that they liked, the smile Max gave her when she got the riff just right. She'd been hooked on all of it ever since.

Astrid always loved their shows, and she especially liked their early stuff, all quiet and basic because they didn't really know how to write. Ella saw things more practically. She thought the new stuff was better, more complex, had a greater chance of getting them into the larger festivals, but Astrid didn't see it that way. She still had a thing for that first one that Sydney had written with Max, even though Sydney told her over and over that it was far from their best.

Now, two years later and so much had changed, sure. She had a whole list of things that just weren't as good and easy as they were back then. But the only thing she really wanted, the one thing that she really missed, was for Astrid to be out there in the crowd, just one more time.

"You okay?" Carter asked, waving a hand in front of her face. "You look a little dazed. Nervous?" he asked.

Sometimes Sydney wondered if he liked her. She wondered if things hadn't happened with Max, whether anything would have, could have happened with Carter. Her mom had always wanted them to date. So had Ella. She supposed that there was no reason why things couldn't happen still. But as the low lighting picked up his chocolaty eyes and the slightest smattering of freckles along his forehead, she knew for sure that they wouldn't. Carter always did the right thing, was always so good. She never seemed to like that.

"I'm fine," she said, and as she did, she saw Ella and Ben walking in.

Ella walked slowly towards her and gave her a hug, long and tight. Sydney could feel her arms shaking around her.

"Are you okay?" Sydney asked as she looked her over. Ella was pale. She almost seemed scared. "Did something happen?"

Ella looked down at her purse, fished around but then looked back up. "I'm fine," she said. "It's just that it's the first show since . . ."

"Since Astrid died," Sydney interrupted. "I know," she said. "You don't have to remind me."

Ella just stared at her—deer in the headlights.

Next to them, Ben and Carter started talking about football. The two had always been friendly—they'd been science partners in 8th grade or something—but in the past couple of years, their friendship had turned into a full-on bromance.

"Did you at least bring it?" Sydney asked.

Ella narrowed her eyes, and then it seemed to dawn on her. "Oh," she said. "Yeah."

"Sweet," Sydney said, trying to sound at least somewhat cheerful. "Bathroom break."

The walls were covered in Sharpie phone numbers, cracked paint, and Xeroxed flyers for shows that had already happened and beginner guitar lessons. Ella pulled the nail polish remover out of her purse, and Syd walked into the first stall, jerking on the roll of toilet paper and scrunching it into a ball.

She grabbed the remover from Ella, poured a little on the paper, and began to work on the X on her hand. It was a trick they'd cultivated long ago, after they'd fully pissed off the bouncer by covering the backs of their hands in so much Vaseline that his pen wouldn't even work. This way, they took their underage Xs with smiling, innocent faces and scrubbed them off when safely out of sight. You only had to be sixteen to go to shows at The Grove, and once the marks disappeared, no one gave you any trouble.

Syd scrubbed harder, and the paper in her hands began to turn black as her skin cleared, turning just the slightest bit red. When the X was nearly gone, at least gone enough to pass in a dark room, she poured some more remover and handed it to Ella.

"I don't know," Ella said, somber. "I'm not sure if I want to drink tonight."

Sydney crossed her arms. She knew that Ella would never adopt the party-girl persona that she so readily embraced, but still, Ella had always had fun at her shows. When their set was done, they'd all drink a beer together and imagine that Sydney had finally made it big, trading fantasy stories of cute, bespectacled groupies and sketchy tour buses that would inevitably come along with fame.

"Geez, El," she snapped. "What the hell happened?"

Ella looked down, then shrugged. "It's just been a rough week," she said.

"I know," Sydney said. "All the more reason to drink." Sydney forced a smile and held the wad of paper out to her.

Ella shrugged again. "I don't really work that way, Syd."

"It's been hard for me, too," Sydney said. "Obviously. But this is our first show of the summer, and it's our only show before the fair. I just want to have a good time. Please."

Ella hesitated.

"*Please*," she said. "I need this."

"Okay," Ella said. "Alright." And she took the wadded up tissue. "You're going to be great," she said, as she scrubbed her hand. "I know you are."

"I hope so," Sydney said, and after a moment, they walked back out. They headed straight to the bar and ordered their first beers.

It felt good to be up on stage again. The three of them were six songs in; they had just a couple more to go. Sweat beaded on her brow, and her heart felt like it was beating right along with the strumming of Max's guitar. The lights were bright on Sydney's face, red and blue and shining strong so that the crowd in front of her became one mass of swaying, vibrating bodies, and she could tell that they liked what they were hearing. Sydney wasn't drunk, really. She wouldn't be until later, after their set was over. But she'd had just enough to make her blood pulse fast and her body feel warm and light, the music natural and *alive*, as if her bow were simply an extension of her hand.

The problems she'd had in practice seemed to disappear beneath the lights. She didn't need to count; she just felt, whipping her bow back and forth, back and forth, faster and faster and faster across the strings, until powerfully, and with a final quick stride, the song was over, and the crowd burst into applause, Ella's cheering voice among them.

"Thanks," she said into the microphone, between big gulps of air. She looked over to Max, and he was smiling right at her, bright and wide. "Perfect," he mouthed, and it was moments like this that proved to her that she'd never quite be over him. When he smiled at her like that, when they were up on stage, when he kept up with the rhythm of her movement. When he let her lead, when he followed faithfully behind, when he really believed in her, as she knew deep down that he did. It almost felt like the two of them were the only people in the world.

Max leaned in towards the microphone. "Let's hear it for Syddie," he said, to more applause, and in spite of the sweat on her face, the heat in the room, she swore that she blushed, beamed hotter.

The crowd stilled, and there was a moment of pretty silence. Max broke it.

"Now we're going to slow it down a bit," he said, turning to her. "This one's the first song that we ever wrote."

Sydney took a breath to steady herself. Here it was: Astrid's favorite. It certainly shouldn't be hard. She and Max had written it in a couple hours one night when they'd first started the band. It was quiet and slow, unlike most of the others. Simple rhythms; the chorus just the melodic coo of her fiddle. It had never been anybody's favorite but Astrid's. But they almost always squeezed it into the lineup just for her.

Now, in the midst of the lights and the set and the crowd and the real, actual night, Sydney wished that she'd asked Max to leave it out. Astrid wasn't here to hear it. She was far away, away from them, away from all that she'd loved, all that they'd loved together.

But Max's guitar was already strumming slow. In a few seconds, his voice rang deep.

Spring left quickly; summer's all around.
Sydney leaned towards the mic.
The sun shines brightly on the ground.

Max took a quick breath, glanced over.

You and I will swim through creeks.

Syd trilled back, light, careless. Trying to sound that way, at least.

Thirteen happy, pretty weeks.

Sydney pulled back and Max kept strumming. The chorus was just her and her fiddle: slow, melodic. No words necessary.

She pulled her bow across the strings, feeling it move, vibrate. Hearing it ring. This was harder, this playing quietly. She wished she could go back to the ones from before, angry and energetic and fast, but instead, she moved slowly, easing her bow back and forth, staying legato, dark, sad. Just like she was supposed to. Just like Astrid had liked.

She held the last note until Max's voice was back.

Autumn leaves crunch beneath our feet.

Sydney leaned forward again.

Though we fight, you still seem sweet.

Max looked right at her then.

I don't want to let you go.

And for once, it wasn't him that she thought of.

Stay with me through winter's cold.

Sydney tugged on the bow, and it made a quiet, low moan. Back and forth. Up and down. Ella's eyes caught hers and she knew that they were on the same page. She wished that Astrid could be there, too. She wished that the song didn't have a different meaning for her now. She felt the heat rise up through her cheeks, and she couldn't do this now, not during their first show, not in front of everyone. She had to show them that she was okay.

She held back all she could, and Max went on.

Murky snowdrifts, frosted windowpanes.

She only had to get through this. They were almost done.

Tell me why we had to change.

Max's voice got louder, right on cue.

I wish I hadn't let you go.

Syd leaned close, sang almost in a whisper.

Now we're broken. Winter's cold.

She pulled back for her final notes. She moved into the upper octaves, but she still stayed soft. Climbing higher, her fiddle seemed to weep. She was almost done.

Her eyes caught Ella's once again, but she looked away as soon as she could. She willed herself to get through this without breaking down.

In moments the fiddle solo was over. She let her arms fall. She leaned into the mic again. She and Max would sing the last two lines together.

Every season, every day, I will hold you dear.

Even though you're far away, I will hold you dear.

The strumming stopped, the crowd quiet for a minute, and before the applause even started, before they even knew it was over, she felt a tear tip over the edge.

She wanted to run, she wanted to flee the stage; she didn't want anyone to see her like this. She hadn't been able to cry since Astrid died, and now here they were, her first tears falling, right up on stage.

Not now, she thought. Not now.

But it was no use. She felt more tears coming, strong.

Before she could move, the lights cut out. She was bathed in darkness. She couldn't see a thing. She couldn't help it, she let her shoulders fall as the sound of movement rung around her, the impatient yells of "What the hell?" from the crowd.

She let them come; she let her body shake. She felt an arm around her shoulders, and when she turned she could barely make out Max's face.

A gruff voice rang out on the intercom. "We are experiencing technical difficulties. Please wait patiently, and do not try to leave."

Max's arm squeezed her tight. "It's okay," he said, rubbing his hand down her arm. "You were perfect," he said. "You were great."

And she felt his finger underneath her chin, tipping her face up to his. He pressed his lips to her lips, and she tasted the salt of her tears when she parted hers.

He pulled back in a second, and he wiped his thumbs beneath her eyelids, along her cheeks. "I'm okay," she said, turning towards the back, rushing to get the last bit of tears off her face.

And then she heard the crackle, followed by a long buzz, and in a minute, the bright red lights were on her again. Carter looked at her, his eyes serious and sad, and mouthed, "Are you okay?"

And she nodded, because she was. She felt a chill run down her spine as she realized that no one had even seen.

Max leaned into the mic. "How's that for a dramatic end?" he called with a swagger. "Stay put. We still got a couple more for you."

Before she knew it, he was strumming again.

But she couldn't help feeling that someone was looking out for her.

CHAPTER FIVE

Ella was trying to pull herself together. River Deep's set was done, Sydney was busy with Max, Ben was deep in conversation with Carter, and Jake hadn't even shown up (not that she'd expected him to after her dramatic exit). Now it was just her and her thoughts.

I miss you, too.

All she wanted to do was go home.

Ben turned to her and gave her a quick smile, the, *I'm having a great time, I'm not ready to leave yet,* smile. She briefly considered pulling him aside, telling him it was time to go, telling him what had *happened.* But she didn't know how. She'd double-, triple-checked, but the message was gone. Like it had never even been there. How could she explain that? So she smiled back in spite of herself. His beer was already three-quarters gone. Maybe he'd be ready soon.

There was an empty stool beside her, and she felt a pang in her stomach, because she could almost see Astrid sitting next to her, twirling a lock of hair around her finger. The two of them could have been talking now, Ella making up stories about the people around them, Astrid acting as the listening board.

"That couple in the corner," she'd say.

"Which one?"

"The blond with the boy who looks like he could be her brother."

"Maybe they are brother and sister."

Ella would laugh, smile. "They're not."

"So what about them?"

"She tried on six outfits before she settled on a dress that looks like my grandmother's sofa. She showed her cheerleading friends each one of them, sending them pictures from her iPhone. Her favorite band is something awful like Coldplay or Dave Matthews. Her name's generic yet uncommon—Debra."

Mainly she'd just listen, but sometimes Astrid would help out, too: "The guy asked her to come to The Grove, and she asked him if she'd need her hiking boots."

Laughter: "Not that she has any."

"Of course not."

Astrid would never let Ella get too far. "Maybe she's cool," she'd say with a shrug. "You can never know what people are really like." That was one of the wonderful things about Astrid. She always managed to keep people good and honest. For the first time, Ella wondered if she'd ever been able to see how good and honest she was herself.

They'd talk about the real things, too. Astrid was always good at advice: "What is going on with Sydney and Max?" Ella would ask. "Should we try to distract her?"

Now, Ella glanced over to see Max leaning in towards Sydney, talking close. She couldn't decide if it was bad or just harmless band bonding, or if it was even her place to give an opinion. And Astrid wasn't here to give her advice.

I miss you, too.

Ella jumped when she heard a voice behind her. "This seat taken?"

Startled, she turned around quickly, her elbow knocking over a half-empty glass on the bar.

"Shit," she said, as she saw Jake standing right in front of her, quickly grabbing a few napkins to sop up the mess. Stale beer ran down the side of her dress.

"Here you go," he said with a nerdy smile, handing her a stack.

"Thanks," she said, and she immediately started dabbing even though it was no use. She'd smell like beer for the rest of the night. "What are you doing here?" she asked.

"Besides helping you clean up?" he asked. "I'm pretty sure you invited me."

"I know, but I didn't think you'd come. Especially after—"

"You walked out on me without an explanation?"

"Sorry," she stammered, even though she still wasn't going to give one. She hoped that's not why he'd come. "It's late," she said. "I just didn't think you'd be here. The show started awhile ago."

Jake almost looked annoyed, but he gave her a grin. "Well you didn't tell me when it started—or where it was. You booked it out of there before you got to those minor details."

"Oh," she said, and she felt like an idiot. Hoping he would come when he had nothing to go on—when she'd given him every reason not to. And yet, he had. "So how did you know?" she asked.

"The beauty of the Internet," he said, flashing another smile. "You want a beer? Now that you've knocked the other one over."

"That wasn't even mine—" she started to say, but he was already flagging down the bartender.

She glanced back at Ben while Jake ordered. He was fully turned towards Carter and hadn't even noticed the spill—or her new friend.

In minutes, a can was sitting in front of her. Sweating. Ice cold. Surprisingly appetizing. She grabbed it, taking something between a sip and a gulp.

"Hey," Jake said. "We didn't clink. It's bad luck."

"According to who . . . *whom?*" she said, correcting herself.

"The entire world? Come on," he lifted his can. "We have to toast to something."

Ella shrugged. "There hasn't been a lot for me to toast to lately."

"Well," he said. "Then we toast to each other. To new friends."

"Okay," she said, even though it felt strange. Wrong, in a way. Lose one friend. Gain another. "To new friends." They smashed their cans together so hard that beer splashed out the top. That finally got Ben's attention.

"Hey," she said, catching his eyes and setting down her drink. "This is Jake. He's working at the café now. He was Astrid's cousin."

Ben stared at her for a moment. Then he looked back to Jake. He seemed surprised. He knew all of her friends, after all. He pretty much knew everyone in this room. "Ben," he said, reaching out to shake Jake's hand. "Ella's *boyfriend.*" He said it as if it were a fact that couldn't be contested. She'd have introduced him that way if he'd only given her a chance. "I didn't know Astrid had family here."

"She didn't," Jake said, shrugging his shoulders. "I'm in music school in Chicago. But it doesn't start back until August. I was just going to spend the summer with my parents in West Virginia, but . . . well, you know."

Ben nodded. "Cool." And then he just stood there. No, *I'm sorry about your cousin. How's it going so far?* Instead, he turned away from Jake and looked right at Ella. "We're going to get another round," he said, nodding over to Carter and the crew. "You want me to get you anything?"

"Jake just got me one," she said, motioning to the beer in front of her.

"Alright then," Ben said. "I'll leave you alone."

"What are you talking about?" she asked, but he just turned back to the bar to order more. Ella sighed and took a sip of her beer. He was the one who'd barely paid attention to her all night and now he was the one who was mad. She turned towards Jake, who was politely looking at the stage, pretending not to notice.

She racked her brain for something to say that wasn't about Astrid. "Music school," she finally stammered. "You never said anything about Chicago."

"You didn't ask."

"I know. I just figured—"

"—that I work at the 7-Eleven and live at home like a true West Virginian?"

Ella laughed, looking at his thick glasses. She couldn't explain to him that that's about the last thing she'd thought. "No," she said. "I don't know. I didn't even know you were older. I told you, Astrid never told me about you."

"I'm barely older," he said. "A and I were only a year apart. I graduated last year."

Ella nodded. "Music school in Chicago. You must be a proper music snob then."

"Card carrying," he said with a smile.

"So you're one of those kids who 'goes to shows.'" She made the fake air quotes and then took another sip.

"May I remind you that you invited me to a show. Perhaps you're one of those kids as well."

"I go to Sydney's," she said.

"Pretty sure that counts."

"Maybe," she said. "I've never been much of a music person. I leave that to her."

"Oh come on, everyone's a music person. Who do you like?"

Ella raked through her musical repertoire, trying to find something that would sound at least mildly impressive. "The China Dolls," she said, remembering a band that had come up on the Internet once that was decidedly not top-forty.

"Nice," he said. "Not a music person and the first band you name is like one of my favorites. You like The Black Rabbits?" he asked.

"Uhh . . ."

"They sound a lot like The China Dolls, but I like them better. They're actually from North Carolina." He smiled.

She smiled back. "How did you decide on music?" she asked. It felt good to carry on a conversation. Like normal things could happen—even now.

Jake shrugged. "I'm pretty good at math so I figured I could be an accountant and hate my life or compose music and probably be dirt-poor but maybe be a little happy . . . so long as I can eat," he added. "It's the thing I like. It's hard to say no to that."

Ella nodded, taking another sip.

"Do you know what you want to study next year?" he asked.

Her heart beat faster, anxiously. No, she didn't know. And she didn't want to think about it. She'd been thrilled about college a few weeks ago, and now she dreaded it. She almost wished she weren't going at all.

Ella had been convinced they'd all be together—she and Astrid both applied to State, the university down the street, Sydney would be at the community college in town until River Deep got their big break, and Ben had a football scholarship to one of the schools just an hour away. It was perfect.

Even when Ella got in and A told her she was wait-listed, she was sure it would work out. They could room together and they could go to parties and pull all-nighters and do all the things two best friends would do.

Despite what everyone said about losing touch with your high school friends when you got to college, *they* would be the ones to make it work. She'd been sure of it.

But then everything had changed. Sure, Ben and Syd would still be around, but she'd be alone—no matter how many new friends she made—she'd be completely alone.

She realized Jake was still looking at her—waiting for an answer.

"Not really," Ella said, holding back tears, because she knew that when she went to school in the fall, she'd only be reminded of what she'd lost—the space on the bleachers, the empty seat at the dining hall, the extra-long twin bed filled with someone who wasn't—who could never be—Astrid.

I miss you, too.

Up onstage, the next band was doing sound checks, setting up their instruments.

Jake took a long gulp and set his beer down. He shoved his hands in his pockets, took them out and let them hang at his sides, then shoved them back in again.

"So, uh, are you okay?" he asked. "From before, I mean?"

"Yeah," she said, nodding quickly, even though she didn't believe it. "I'm fine."

The boys on stage tapped at the mics. Feedback rang through the room. He was waiting for her to tell him more. She wasn't going to.

"How's Grace," she asked instead.

Jake took a long sip. He stared at the guys on stage for a minute before answering. "Grace is Grace," he said. "She does everything her way. This is no different."

Ella thought that she understood. Grace had always been unlike anyone but Grace. But she just couldn't help but ask. "What do you mean?"

Jake looked at her for a minute. Then he took another sip, looked back out in front of him. "I don't know," he said. "Like she keeps the door shut all the time. No one's allowed to go in there at all."

"The door?"

Jake gave her a look, like, *Are you going to make me say it?* and that was when it hit her, when she felt a shiver from head to toe. Astrid's room. The bed where she'd lain her head not all that long ago. The room where Ella had slept over maybe a hundred times. The walls that they'd decorated together with cut-outs from *Tiger Beat*, then taken them down again when they'd gotten old enough to be embarrassed about it. God, that room.

"Does she say why?" She felt her voice catch at the back of her throat, and damn it, she would not cry here in front of Jake, not when she was actually having a semi-pleasant conversation for the first time in days.

Jake shrugged. "I guess she doesn't want us messing anything up."

Ella waited a second before posing the next question. She tread carefully, afraid of throwing off the balance between them and ruining this new friendship before it had a chance to start. "But have you ever opened it, just to see?"

He hesitated. "I wanted to, but—" his voice trailed off.

"But what?"

He looked at her, almost like he had something else to say, but then he just shrugged. "It's not really my place," he said. "I mean, Astrid was her daughter and whatever she wants to do is what she should do. I'm just here to try and help."

Ella nodded. She stared at the stage in front of her. Three bearded guys looked like they were about ready to start. She took another sip and she realized that in minutes she'd downed her beer.

"I wish I could see it again," she said, but as she did, there was a crash of drums, and then the sound of the electric guitar, and the band began to play, and she didn't even know if Jake had heard her. But she knew that they didn't have to fill the empty spaces anymore.

Ben drove her home. They left halfway into the next act, and Jake stayed—he figured he might as well hear some music. She didn't know if she could do that, stay at a show alone. She looked over at Ben. She guessed she didn't really need to. That was the nice thing about him. She knew she'd always have someone to count on—even if his attempts at understanding left a little to be desired.

They bumped along the windy mountain road that led from The Grove back towards their houses. It was extra bumpy in Ben's Jeep.

"So Jake seems cool," Ben said, as he turned onto her street.

"Yeah," she said. "I wasn't sure at first but he seems cool enough now. I like him."

Ben was silent, and Ella looked over. He was looking straight ahead and still wore a slight grin, but against the wheel his hands were ever-so-slightly clasped tighter. After three years of dating, she'd learned to notice those things.

"What?" she asked.

Ben shrugged. "Interesting choice of words is all."

"What, cause I said I like him?"

"Well he certainly likes you."

Ella laughed. "I'm like the only person he knows in town. He's kind of forced to like me."

"Well isn't that convenient?" Ben said as he pulled into her driveway.

Ella fumbled for her purse on the floor and then looked back up at Ben. He'd put the car into park, but he still looked tense. Beneath his t-shirt she could see that the muscles in his arms were taut. "You're not serious, are you? You're not actually jealous?"

"I'm not jealous," Ben said. "I just thought it was interesting that he came only to see you, bought only you a drink, and talked to only you the entire time."

"You were talking to Carter," she said.

"I thought you didn't want to talk to me."

Ella just stared at him. At first she'd thought it was just funny, but now she felt anger bubble in her stomach. Of all the stupid things to worry about—as if she didn't have enough going on.

She put her hand on the car door. "Thanks for being there for me, Ben."

But he reached out, put his hand on her shoulder. "What does that mean? You know I'm here for you."

Ella shook it off. "No, you're just worried about who I talk to and where I get my drinks. You don't think that it might be nice to have someone to talk to from her family? You don't think that Jake might understand a few things that you don't? Oh wait, you were too busy talking about football and being irrationally jealous to actually think of me."

"Ella," he said, reaching for her arm, but she pushed open the door, slipping out of his grasp.

She stood there, facing him, one hand on the door. "I know you're a dude and all, but I thought that you might be able to put your stupid macho ego aside for a minute while I deal with the fact that my best friend is gone." And she slammed the car door before he could get in another word, and ran up the steps of the porch and inside before he could see her start to cry.

Ella dreamed about Astrid that night. She was following the same path she'd followed the day they'd found her. But now it was night. The sky was dark, purpley, and the moon was bright. That was what a dream could do. Take your real-life nightmare and make it even worse.

She was walking through the woods, ducking under branches, and avoiding snares. She could feel that she wasn't alone, that Grace was just behind her, but even when she tried to turn she couldn't.

She wanted to run, but she couldn't do that either.

Finally, the cabin was before her, splashed in shadows. She walked up to it, and she knew that there was something, something so unimaginably bad behind those doors. She felt her body break into chills and a heavy weight in her stomach.

She opened the door in slow motion, and things were all out of order now. She heard Grace's gasps and cries behind her, and she saw Astrid lying on the floor. Ella ran as fast as she could—but now her vision was foggy, her legs were like rubber—she knelt down beside Astrid.

Maybe this time she wasn't too late. Maybe this time she could actually save her, but then the room began to spin, and there were the pictures, all of them, staring at her, teasing and taunting her, Astrid's face in every single one.

The room spun faster, and she tried desperately to focus, to see Astrid in front of her, and eventually she could. Her skin was pale. Her hair was spread out in tangles. Her neck was bare. But her eyes weren't open this time. Her eyes were shut tight.

Ella tried to touch her but her hands wouldn't move.

And then it happened: Astrid's eyes flickered open, but they weren't blue; they were black. Deep, gaping holes.

Her mouth formed a soundless shape. "Help."

Ella woke covered in a cold sweat.

She sat up, her chest heaving, and shook her head back and forth, trying to get rid of the horrible image. She was surrounded by darkness. If someone had been two feet in front of her, she wouldn't have known. She fumbled her way out of bed and opened the blinds just to get some light, but the shadows were almost worse.

She walked across her room and flipped on the light. There was nothing there. Just her room. Just her boring, safe old room. But God, did it feel like so much more.

Ella sat down on her bed, drew her legs up beneath her arms, trying to get back to reality, the slamming of the car door, the anger she'd felt at Ben, the feedback from the band up on stage. Not the message. Not the dream. But all of that felt like a whole different world altogether.

She didn't want to go back to sleep—she knew that Astrid's black eyes would be waiting for her when she did—but her own eyelids pulled heavy at her. So she lay down, the lights still on. She wouldn't sleep. She'd just lie there.

God help her, she wouldn't go back to that place.

She felt like a zombie the next morning. She had slept—of course she had—even with the lights on. The dream had been there, waiting for her. It seemed like every time she shut her eyes she was back in those damn woods, with Astrid to jolt her awake.

At some point in the night it had stopped, though, and she'd caught a few minutes sleep without Astrid's face right in front of her. Of course, then she woke and realized that she'd overslept.

Jake barely looked up when she got to Trail Mix half an hour late. The line of customers was almost out the door. Looking down at her watch—she was usually never late—she squeezed through the crowd and grabbed her apron off the hook, tying it behind her as quickly as she could.

"Hi," she said. "Sorry I'm late. What are these?" she asked. The espresso machine was littered with two carafes half-full of milk, a turned over espresso glass, and three empty paper cups.

Jake quickly shoved the money in the register and turned to her. "You okay?" he asked. His face looked genuine, his eyes open wide. "You look awful."

"Thanks for letting me know," she said. And she felt awful. Her head hurt, her eyes seemed to be begging her to let them shut, she'd woken too late to have even a drop of coffee or a handful of dry cereal, and it was hot as Hades in the café. "I couldn't sleep."

A grumpy man crossed his arms at the front of the line, and she repeated the question, even though all she wanted to do was lie down. "What are these?"

"Oh," Jake said, as if he had forgotten the whole line of people out of concern for her. "Two lattes, one skinny, one with soy, and a red-eye—two shots," he rattled off.

Ella nodded. She slowly tamped down the espresso and began to pull the shot.

It was hard to focus, and her mind wanted to wander. She thought of the first time she'd been here as espresso started to drip, the smell of the beans strong and bitter.

She hadn't liked the smell then—what self-respecting eleven-year-old did like the smell of coffee? Her mom had just gotten a job teaching art at the university, and they were moving out of her grandparents' house for the first time, driving down from New Jersey and starting their new life together. Their van was full of boxes—it was the cheapest moving truck they could get, and the AC was barely working, the North Carolina air almost suffocating them, it was so humid and thick. Ella wanted a lemonade, her mom wanted coffee, and Trail Mix, tucked among the trees along the main street in town, seemed like the best bet.

Ella began to heat up the milk as the shot continued to drip.

Some of her memories were clear, like pictures. And maybe they weren't really memories—maybe they were creations of her mind, drawn and fleshed out from years of loving Astrid and Grace, but what she remembered so deeply was the shock of red hair—on the both of them. It was the first thing she saw when she walked in.

"What can I get y'all?" Grace had said, flashing a killer smile. Astrid stood there next to her. She was gawky and tall for her age—just like Ella.

Astrid smiled at her while her mom ordered a latte and a lemonade and talked about the normal adult things with Grace—weather and where to find the drug store.

"You new here?" Astrid asked, as she carefully counted out the change. Her hair was wild and curly, and she had a vintage-y key tied around her neck.

Ella nodded. "Just got here today."

"What grade?" she asked.

"Fifth," Ella said.

"Me too," Astrid said.

"What school are you in?" Ella asked.

Astrid just laughed. "There's only one school here. Falling Rock Elementary. Who's your teacher?"

"I don't know," Ella said, as Grace handed her the lemonade, and her mom started towards the door.

"Maybe I'll see you in school," Astrid said, smiling as they walked out the door. And even then she knew that she liked her. Even then she hoped that they'd be friends for a long, long time. So much for that.

"You okay?" Jake asked, snapping Ella back to reality. Espresso was spilling over the shot glass. She'd accidently brewed a double-shot.

"Sorry," she said, setting the milk down and attempting to pull it out, but as she did she just knocked over one of the other carafes.

"Whoa," Jake said, pulling her by the arm as the bubbling milk spilled down the side of the counter. "That's hot," he said.

She heard muttering in the line. "I'm sorry," she said. "I don't know what—"

"Don't worry about it," he said. "Just grab the register. I'll take care of this." And he led her by the arm, his fingers hot against her skin. "Okay," she said, because she was starting not to trust her judgment.

And then his touch was gone, and he was grabbing a rag and starting at the mess. Ella looked down at the buttons, and they were the same buttons that had rung her up that first time, that she—and Astrid—had pressed about a million times since, but it was hard to focus on anything now. Just like in the dream. She felt the room starting to spin.

"Can I help you?" she asked, but as she did she grasped the counter with both hands and she leaned into it, and her head felt so light—maybe from the lack of sleep or from the heat—and she heard herself stammer, "I need to sit down," and she didn't want to fall because she knew that the dream would be right there, waiting for her, as soon as she closed her eyes.

But she felt Jake's arms behind her, and she knew it was no use.

❧

The first thing she saw was Jake, blurry, with two big brown spots where his eyes stared down at her. "She's awake," he said, but it sounded like he was talking through a tunnel. She blinked her eyes, and Jake came into focus, and then there was Claire's prim and proper face, looking at her, too.

She felt hands behind her shoulders, and she was being lifted up. She was sitting on a bench in the back office of the café. Claire pushed a glass of water at her.

She took it.

"What happened?" Claire asked. Everything still sounded kind of tunnel-y.

"You were just standing at the register, and then you fell," Jake said, and she remembered, and she felt the whole night full of dreams, and then there was Astrid, peeking at her, from the back corners of her mind.

"How do you feel?" Claire asked.

"Alright," Ella said.

"You should go home. Becky's here now, and Jake can drive you."

❧

It was the second time in two days she left Trail Mix early.

"Have you ever fainted before?" Jake asked as they pulled out of the lot.

"No," she said, shaking her head. The music in the car was soft and melodic—meandering. She'd expected something different, more like the stuff Ben listened to. Old classic rock or new hip-hop or country. Like most guys she knew listened to. This actually sounded like something Sydney would have liked.

"Huh," he said, drumming his hand against the wheel. "You just like wiped out in there."

"I'm aware," she said, scooting herself down further in the seat. Her head still felt a little woozy.

"I'm sorry," he said. "I'm not trying to make you feel bad. I'm just worried about you."

"You keep saying that," she said. She tried to laugh but it didn't come out right. "You barely know me."

Jake turned the music down. "Well I haven't known you that long," he said. "But under intimate circumstances, to say the least."

"Yeah," she said. "I guess."

In moments they were at her house. Jake pulled into the drive.

"You want me to come inside for a bit?"

He looked so warm and open, and he was right, they did know each other in the most unusual, intimate, horrible of ways. She almost wanted to say yes. He could prevent her from going to sleep and going back into the cabin for the hundredth time.

But her mom must have heard the car. She was already running out the door and up to the window. "My God, baby, are you okay?"

"I'm fine," she said. She opened the door and stepped out slowly. Her mom's arm was instantly around her, leading her to the house. Behind her, she heard Jake's car start. She turned to say thank you, but he was already backing up and pulling away.

Her mom had ordered bed rest, but she couldn't bear the thought of sleep. So she opened her computer, went to Astrid's page, checked her post for the millionth time. *Nothing.*

Even lying down she felt dizzy, from the heat or the dream she couldn't tell.

I miss you, too.

She wouldn't post again—it was too public. Too desperate. She hadn't told anyone what she'd seen, and she didn't want to until she had something more—something to show.

So she clicked on the message button on the top of the screen.

The little box was there in an instant, beckoning her.

Hi. I'm here.

It was silly—childish—crazy to think that Astrid would, that Astrid *could*.

Ella stopped. She could hit cancel now, forget about the rest of it. She could party with Sydney and make out with Ben and cry and grieve and just try to move on.

But she didn't want to.

So she held her finger over the button, took a deep breath, and clicked send before she could lose her nerve.

CHAPTER SIX

When Sydney woke up the next morning, she could smell the strong aroma of veggie bacon coming from downstairs. She wiped her hands across her eyes and stretched. She hadn't slept well. She hadn't *been* sleeping well. There'd been no dreams, at least none that she could remember. But she'd tossed, waking up what felt like every few minutes.

Now she was fully awake. She was tired. And everything was inescapable. She wanted to go back to sleep and forget about things, but even sleep seemed like work.

She couldn't stop thinking about Ella. She'd fainted at Trail Mix. Ben had called to tell her as much, but she still hadn't gotten a chance to talk to her.

She was upset about Max. They were on a whole other plane of messy.

She was worried about next year. Would things actually happen with River Deep, or should she just suck it up at a community college and try to transfer after one semester?

But the worst thing was the one that was ever-present now. The fact that Astrid was gone. The fact that maybe, just maybe, she could have done something to help her. That was the one that hit her every time she woke up.

Sydney ran her hands through her hair and threw a bra on under her tank top. She was required, of course, to make an appearance downstairs. Happy family time! Let's all eat breakfast together like on TV! We'll make it organic so we can not only save the environment but offset our inherent white guilt! *Composting!*

She hobbled down the stairs and was met immediately by the piercing giggles of Darcy, and the uber-long ponytail of George, her stepfather.

"Morning, sunshine," her mother said, leaning over to kiss her cheek, as Sydney grabbed a plate. "Sleep well?" she asked.

"Not really," she said. Her mom just turned back to Darcy, pouring her more orange juice.

"It's that pillow of yours," George said. "It's no wonder you can't sleep."

Sydney just shrugged and headed straight to the stove. George had one of those alignment pillows that you had to order on TV. He was always going on and on about how it had changed his life. Like, even when they had people over for dinner. She liked feather pillows, like normal people. George gave Sydney a friendly pat on the shoulder and headed to the table, kissing her mother on the lips and Darcy on the forehead before he sat down.

She filled her plate with grits and lots of butter, eggs, and a slice of facon. It's not that she was against breakfast, per se, or composting, or George's Chaco sandals, it's just that it wasn't her mother. Or at least it hadn't been. When she'd been with her dad, the best breakfast Sydney could look forward to was an Eggo waffle with syrup while her mom munched on a granola bar before she headed to the office. Her mom and her dad had both been accountants. They'd divorced when she was ten—he lived only thirty minutes away and she saw him enough to feel like they still had a relationship —but she still couldn't help but feel that her mom was on family #2. While the ink was still wet on the divorce papers, she met George and they moved to Falling Rock, and within a couple of years they had Darcy, veggie bacon, and a membership at the local co-op. Plus, no more work for her mother.

George was some kind of technology whiz, and this time around, at least, she was spending her time doing what mattered. Her mom just hadn't felt that way when she was five.

Sydney was almost done with breakfast—the grits were salty and greasy, just like she liked them—when she had an idea. "George," she said, setting her fork down.

"Yes dear?" He had this habit of calling her dear at family gatherings, like breakfast. It annoyed her—it fell somewhere in between trying to be a father and trying to be a friend, and she didn't really need either. "You've been in Falling Rock a long time," she said.

"Thirty years," he said with a smile.

She cleared her throat. "Did you know Astrid's dad?"

He didn't look up as he answered. "I did," he said. "Good man. It was a tragedy."

Tragedy. There was that word again. Like you could just say it and somehow everything suddenly made sense.

Her mom gave her an understanding look—it was like she was studying to be a grief counselor—and she kept going.

"How come you never talked about him?" she asked. "Like to Grace or anything."

He looked at her then, narrowing his eyes. Then he paused. "He's been gone a long time," he said. "Since before I even met your mother. I guess I just don't think about it that much. Why?"

The doorbell rang and her mom quietly got up to answer it.

"I don't know," she said. "I guess I just think it's weird that no one ever talked about him."

"It was a long time ago," George said again with a dismissive shrug.

That's when her mom called her, her voice so happy and light that it could only be Carter at the door. Everyone wanted the two of them to get together. It was the smart, responsible thing to do. Maybe that's why she'd never been so into the idea. She didn't exactly do smart and responsible.

George was obviously a dead-end, so she grabbed her plate, set it in the sink, and headed to the door.

"Hey," she said. Carter was all smiles. "Wal-Mart?" he asked. "I need socks."

"I don't know," Sydney said. She pulled her phone out of her pocket. Still no response from the, *Are you okay? Call me when you can*, text that she'd sent Ella last night.

"You should go," her mom urged. "What else do you have to do? It might make you feel better."

"Alright, alright," she said, rolling her eyes at her mother and forcing a smile for Carter. "Let me just get my shoes."

She and Carter often went on little excursions like this. She didn't even know if he truly needed socks. Or if he just wanted to get out of the house. Or if he just wanted to hang out with her.

"So what happened with you and Max the other night?" he asked. Sydney sighed as she realized that the latter was probably the case.

"Nothing," she said, even though it was a total lie. She knew it. He probably knew it. In reality, she and Max had made out in a corner of The Grove through the entire last act before fooling around in his car before she decided that it wasn't a good idea and demanded, perhaps a little drunkenly, to be taken home.

Carter just gave her a look. He'd probably seen them pawing each other in the corner.

"What?" she asked. "You want me to give you every gory detail?"

"No," he said. "I just want to be your friend."

"We *are* friends," Sydney said. "It's just weird to talk about Max with you."

Carter didn't answer that. Instead, he pretended to be distracted by the fishing aisle. "Look at this," he said, turning back to her, but it looked like his smile was painted on. "Maybe I should get this for the fair."

He pulled an electric orange vest around him, and it totally didn't fit across his shoulders. He crossed his arms in front of him anyway and posed, and in an instant the awkwardness between them diffused.

"Hot," Sydney said. "Should I take a picture?"

"No, just immortalize me in your mind."

Normally she would have thought it was funny, she would have pulled on a vest herself. But she couldn't get Ella out of her mind. The girl had *fainted*. It was so un-Ella in every single way.

"Didn't you need socks?" she asked.

"I'm getting there," he said. "It's about the journey, Sydda-Lee, not the destination."

"You know I hate that name."

He ignored her and took off his vest and put it carefully back on the hanger. He grabbed two camo fishing hats: one for him, one for her. He put his on and then tugged hers over her head.

"We should go fishing sometime," he said. "This look suits you."

She smiled a fake smile.

He shifted his weight from foot to foot. "Why is it weird to talk about Max with me?"

"I don't know," she said, shrugging. "It just is."

He nodded, but he looked a little disappointed.

"Where should we head next?" he asked.

"I thought you wanted socks?" she said. All of a sudden she was tired of messing around here. She didn't want to go bounce on the exercise balls until an associate inevitably told them to stop. She couldn't keep her mind from going back to Ella.

She tried to imagine what had happened. Had she just fallen right over in the middle of Trail Mix? Was she making a latte? Was she sweeping up the floor? And then she'd just collapsed?

But the weird thing about it was that this part of her, this teeny tiny part of her, was almost a little bit jealous. Ella was so consumed with grief that she was falling over, while she was out here shopping for socks. She was drinking and partying and carrying on with summer.

Almost as if nothing had happened at all.

What would Astrid think if she could see her? Would she think she didn't care?

"Uh, Syd?" Carter asked. "You coming?"

"Sorry," she said, his voice startling her, breaking her train of thought. "Yeah," she said, and she slowly followed him down the aisle.

Sydney called Ella as soon as she got home. She answered on the fifth ring.

"Hey," Ella said. She sounded groggy.

"Did I wake you?"

Ella cleared her throat. "Kind of," she said. "I was just lying here."

Sydney looked at her watch. It was almost noon. It wasn't like Ella to sleep late. Of course, it wasn't like Ella to faint, either.

"Ben told me you fainted, so I called yesterday, but—"

"I know. My mom told me."

"And I texted you."

"I know," Ella said. "I just—"

"Don't worry," she said. "It's okay. Are you feeling better?" Sydney asked.

"I guess."

"Do you want me to come over?" Sydney was desperate to do something. She knew she hadn't been there for Astrid. She knew it deep in her heart—it had cut her to the bone every day since. She needed to help Ella if she could.

"I'm okay," Ella said, but her voice was anything but convincing.

"What happened?" Sydney asked. "I mean, how did it happen?"

Ella sighed, as if she'd already told this story one too many times. "I was tired. I didn't sleep much the night before. I was having bad dreams."

"What kind of dreams?"

"Bad ones," Ella snapped. "Sorry. I kept dreaming I was in the cabin, you know, like I was."

"You mean when you found her?" Sydney felt nauseous. Yet another thing she hadn't done. She hadn't been there with Ella when she'd discovered Astrid.

Ella's silence was a confirmation.

"Oh God," Sydney said. "Oh God, I'm so, so sorry. I'm coming over."

She heard her friend's words break. "No," she said. "Ben's going to come over later, and my mom's here, and I just don't—"

"I'll be there soon," Sydney said.

"No," Ella said. "No. It won't help. Just leave me alone today. Please."

"Okay," Sydney said. "Okay." She felt like she might cry herself. Ella didn't want her to help. Ella just wanted to be left alone. Is that what she should want, too? To just curl up in a ball and think about Astrid?

"I'm sorry. I'll talk to you later," Ella said, her voice shaking, and she hung up the phone.

Sydney lay back on her bed. She closed her eyes and thought of Astrid and tried to cry. She'd still only done it the once, when she was up on stage.

But it was no use. The tears weren't coming. She didn't want them to anyway. She whipped her eyes back open, and the first thing she saw was the book that her aunt had given her the other day.

Maybe it will help you understand, her aunt's voice rang in her head.

She knew it wouldn't, but she picked it up anyway. She couldn't help but feel a deep curiosity. She couldn't help but wonder what it was that Audie wanted her to see.

So she flipped to the first page and she started to read.

She was only on chapter three, but she could not understand how people could actually believe all this. Spirits left behind. Bodiless specters. The voices of the woods.

She flipped the page.

"The Afterlife of Alexa Coleman."

The face of a teenage girl stared prettily back at her. She could have been about Astrid's age. It was hard to tell from the photo. It had obviously been clipped from a newspaper.

Sydney read the words below: "Nobody saw it coming . . . jumped from a cliff above the river . . . just sixteen."

Her aunt went on to describe the "mysterious" events that transpired after her death—visions of a nightgowned young girl, roaming through the woods, how the ivy stopped growing on the ledge where she jumped—paired with quotes from neighbors and friends and family—"She was too young to really leave us," "I swear she's still out there somewhere, watching us through the trees."

Jesus.

Sydney shook her head. The poor girl had died more than twenty years ago. She wondered if the girl's real friends bought all this, if they liked the young girl being kept around on supernatural life support.

Sydney read over the name again, running her finger across the words on the page.

And then she saw it. A quote that startled her. From one of the girl's childhood friends. "I keep dreaming about her. I keep seeing her in those woods. I keep seeing that cliff. I go there still. It looks just like it did when we were younger. And sometimes I can feel her, watching me."

Sydney flipped the book shut. She knew that all this wasn't real; she knew that it was just imagination, grief, too much time on her aunt's hands, but she couldn't help it; it still gave her the creeps. Like a scary movie. One you know can't be real. But one that frightens you just the same. That gives you that sinking, that heaviness, that bad feeling right in your gut.

A young girl. The woods. There were too many parallels.

She thought about their cabin, sitting there, just like it always had been.

And she decided that something needed to change.

CHAPTER SEVEN

Was it horrible to not want to see your best friend?

Ella hung up the phone with Sydney feeling spent—*guilty*. Maybe she should have just let her come over, but she had a feeling that she just wouldn't quite understand. Sydney wouldn't want to talk about Astrid. She'd want to talk about anything but. She'd want to distract her. She'd ask her to go shopping or something, but at the moment, the thought of a new pair of wedges—or weighing in on Syd's stage-makeup choices made Ella cringe.

So she stretched, looking out the window. It was a nice day out—so far, at least. In this town, a storm could come in a matter of minutes. She knew she should get up—do something—but she wasn't ready to move. So she pulled her computer onto her lap.

She checked her messages first—like she had every hour since she'd hit send—nothing. Then she went to Astrid's page. It was habit now, a nervous tic. She wanted something to happen. Maybe if she waited long enough, it would.

Ella clicked through the photos. She found one that she'd added, not all that long ago. Astrid smiled at her, showing her teeth, her hair draped across her shoulders. Her eyes were wide, and more than anything, she didn't look sad. A blue sky stretched behind her, and round, pebbly rocks. On her shoulders, Ella could see the skinny straps of a swimsuit beneath a tank top.

They'd gone to the lake, the three of them. Ella had snapped the photo of Astrid before she'd gotten in. Astrid had been slathering on sunscreen. She had that perfect Irish coloring. Her skin was always so pale. Ella was going without. Her skin was pale, too, but it was olive.

The sun could turn her around, even her imperfections, lighten her hair. She wanted to get burnt. At least a little.

"Shouldn't you do that after you take your clothes off?" Ella asked. Sydney was already in the lake, splashing away.

Astrid shrugged. "I don't really feel like swimming."

Ella put her hands on her hips and dipped a toe into the water. "So what, you're not going to swim at all?"

"I'm so disgustingly pale," Astrid said. "Not like you guys."

Ella just rolled her eyes. Astrid was gorgeous. It was impossible not to see. "Well you're never going to get a tan if you keep slathering on that stuff." She looked at the bottle of SPF 60 in Astrid's hands. "It's like a body suit."

Astrid didn't look up. She just kept massaging it into her leg. "My mom says I'll get cancer if I don't."

"Oh, come on," Ella said. "You won't get cancer from a *tan*."

"That's what she says."

"Well, she's not here, is she?"

Astrid looked up at her then. "She'll know when I come home," she said. "Why do you think I don't just whack my hair off because she's not here? She'd see it as soon as I got home. It's impossible to hide."

Ella sighed. Sometimes Astrid could be so weak. "If you want to cut it, just cut it."

"She'll kill me if I do," Astrid said. "She'd ground me forever."

Ella shook her head and bounced into the water, running forward to grab the rope swing that they always used for the first plunge. She looked at Astrid as she walked the rope back. "Well you know, she's right," she said. "You'd be crazy to cut your hair. It's gorgeous. It's perfect. People hire Hollywood stylists to get theirs to look like that."

"I hate it," Astrid said, her face serious for a moment. "It's not me."

"You're nuts," Ella said, and she grabbed the rope, felt it rub, scratch against her palms, lifted her feet and flew, higher, faster, 'til there was nothing but her and the air, a cloudless sky, and openness all around her. She let go, and the water hit her feet first, washed up her legs, surrounded her as she held her breath and plugged her nose, struggling to readjust her swimsuit bottom as the water bobbed her up.

"Nice," Sydney said when she was barely out of the water. "A, you coming?"

Astrid glanced at the rope, and then back at her friends. "No," she said. "I'm not ready to go in yet." But it was the same song and dance, because they all knew that she wouldn't, that she'd dip her toes in the water, walk 'til it hit her knees, but then amble back, sit on the rocks at the edge.

And she never ever took that plunge.

And she never let herself get burnt.

And she never cut her hair, either. Ella had never thought a thing of it, but now she felt almost sick. Had Astrid really hated the way that her skin looked? Had she really detested her long, beautiful hair? Had she really been so fearful of disappointing her mother that she couldn't be herself?

How many other things like that had Ella missed?

Ella shook her head and kept on going through the photos. Nights in the cabin. Afternoons in front of lockers. It was a while before she found one she didn't recognize—a picture of a darling girl with red hair, so tiny and so young. It must be Astrid, when she was only five or six. Young and innocent and happy and *alive*. She looked to who posted it, and the name caught her eye: Jake. It was put there by Jake.

Ella couldn't help it. She clicked. His photo was of him at the piano. So that's what he must be studying in school—she'd never even asked. She scanned his info—college, Chicago School of Music; hometown, Charlottesville, West Virginia; relationship status . . .

Single.

Ella jumped when she heard her phone ring.

She pushed the computer aside and looked down at her phone. It was a number she didn't recognize. Reluctantly, she clicked answer.

"Hello?"

"Ella?" The voice sounded friendly. Familiar. "It's Jake."

"Oh, hey," she said, her eyes flicking back to her computer screen. She felt like she'd been caught. "How do you have my number?"

He laughed. "You do work for my aunt, you know. I have my ways."

"Oh," she said. "Yeah . . . what's up?"

"I was just calling to see how you were."

"How I am?"

"You fainted, remember?"

Ella shook her head. It was like she'd taken a course in valley girl. "Yeah," she said. "I'm feeling okay."

"Good enough for dinner?" he asked.

Ella's heart raced because for a second, she thought he was asking her on a date. Even though he couldn't be. Because now he'd met Ben . . . and Ben had made it clear as day that he was her boyfriend, and . . .

"Uhhh . . ." she stalled for time.

"Grace, I mean—*we*—were all thinking that if you were feeling up to it, it might be nice for you to come over for dinner. To the house."

"Oh," she said. And it all made sense then. Of course he wasn't asking her out—what was wrong with her? He was just asking her over to the house. To Astrid's house.

"I mean, only if you're feeling up to it," Jake continued.

"Yes," she said, eagerly. "Yes, I am."

"Great," he said. "I'll tell Grace. She said you could come over around seven."

"Okay," Ella said. "That sounds good."

"Oh, and Ella," he said.

"Yeah?"

"I really do hope you're feeling better."

"I am," she said.

"Good," he said. "I'll see you tonight."

"See you tonight," she echoed, and she hung up the phone and set it down on her bed. She felt better. Truly. She was going over to Astrid's house. She was going to be there again, she was going to see what it was like, and she was going to finally get to spend some time with Grace.

But it didn't last.

In seconds her phone was ringing again. Ella picked it up and her heart stopped, because there she was—staring right at her. She heard herself scream, saw the phone drop from her hands. One smiling face and six little letters.

Astrid.

CHAPTER EIGHT

The sky was clear when Sydney got to the cabin, and the caution tape was gone. It looked like the Falling Rock police had actually come through for a change. It was better this way. Not so scary. With the cloudy blue sky above it, it almost looked quaint. Almost.

Sydney stepped up to the creaky old porch, stomping hard to get the clay off of her combat boots. The ground was damp today because it had rained last night—she hoped to God it wouldn't rain again.

The door was shut—tight. It was funny how the police had done it that way, as if it actually mattered at this place. Sydney slowly placed her hand on the doorknob and turned. She knew that it wouldn't be locked.

She stepped inside, and the faint scent of oranges hit her—it smelled like her house after her mom had cleaned. The books and yearbooks were no longer scattered across the floor. Neither were the blankets. Sydney walked up to the old armoire and opened it—there they were, neatly stacked, probably just as they had been when A had come here herself. Perhaps she should give the FRPD more credit than she had in the past. Altogether, the place looked better now, more like it used to. Less like death.

Her phone buzzed in her pocket, and she pulled it out. It was Max.

Hang tonite?

Sydney rolled her eyes. What the hell did he want anyway? They hadn't even talked since she'd drunkenly demanded to be taken home. And now he wanted to "hang." She would have called Ella for advice, but the girl was in post-faint mode, and she didn't want to bother her. Plus, she knew what Ella would say. "You are *too good* for Max. Tell him you're busy and you'll see him at practice."

But she couldn't help staring at the center of the room where the three of them all used to sit—where they used to talk about these things. What would Astrid have said? Would she have tossed her hair over her shoulder and echoed Ella? Maybe.

Or would she have looked at Sydney with those eyes that always seemed to know everything about you, everything you truly felt, and would she have said that it was okay. That we all couldn't be perfect. That she knew what it was like to feel lonely.

Sydney startled because it came so fast she could almost see it, this memory, playing out in her mind. It was one of those nights that they'd all met here, just a couple months ago, when the weather had finally gotten nice as Falling Rock welcomed spring. It was before some party—she couldn't remember whose.

Sydney had come in and the candles were already lit and the blanket was out, but Astrid was sitting there, just staring out into space. Her journal was open and she gripped a pen in one hand, as if she'd been writing. She slammed it shut as soon as she saw Sydney.

"Sorry I'm late," Sydney said, tossing her bag in the corner and pulling out a bottle of wine. "I found this tucked in the back of my mom's cabinet—she won't miss it for awhile at least. She'll probably just think that George took it to one of his nerdy pretentious math parties."

Astrid didn't laugh.

"You okay?" Sydney asked, sitting down next to her and fiddling with the corkscrew.

"I don't know," Astrid said. "I feel weird."

"What do you mean?" Sydney asked. "Like you're sick?"

Astrid looked up at her then, and she half smiled, but it wasn't one of those nice smiles. It was a smile that said, *There's something I'm not saying.* "No," she said. "I don't think I'm sick."

Sydney narrowed her eyes at her friend. "You have another fight with your mom?"

Astrid shook her head. She tucked her journal into her bag. Sometimes Sydney wondered what it said. "My mom only fights with me when . . ." her voice trailed off.

"When what?" Sydney asked.

Astrid just shook her head. "Never mind."

"A," Sydney said. "I know. Sometimes I swear my mom's crazy. I mean, she just fell for George in like five minutes and sometimes she's nice to me and sometimes she's such a bitch and she just looks at me like I'm like not even her daughter. Everyone's parents are a little nutso."

Astrid nodded, but Sydney could see that her eyes were starting to water.

"Hey," she said, putting her hand on Astrid's shoulder. "You can tell me. It's okay."

"Sometimes I just feel alone," Astrid said. Slowly. "Completely alone."

"You have me," Sydney said, but she couldn't say more because then Ella was walking through the door, and Astrid was quickly wiping her eyes and saying "hey" like nothing in the world was wrong.

And Sydney let it slide, like she always did. She always figured that Astrid would talk to her when she felt ready. When she really needed to. Of course, she'd been completely, terribly wrong.

What would she have said if Ella hadn't come in? Hell, what would she have said if Sydney had asked? If she had grabbed her, shaken her, gotten the wild truth out of her.

No one would miss me if I was gone.

Sydney could have reasoned with her, held her. *Helped* her. Astrid's death was shocking, yeah, but in hindsight, was it really even a surprise? Sydney could have saved her. She'd had more than one chance.

Sydney slammed the door behind her and rushed to the wall, tearing one of the photos down. It ripped in two, half of it sticking to the wall, half of Astrid's face in her hand.

Why the hell had it been so hard to just *ask*?

She had to change this place. Take the chills out of it. Make it so it wouldn't be The Place That Astrid Died. So her aunt wouldn't write about it in her next edition of town haunts. And the only way she knew how to do that was to erase their marks on it—to make it like they'd never been here at all. Maybe she couldn't cry and she couldn't faint and she couldn't grieve like Ella could. Maybe no matter what happened, no matter how many days and weeks and *years* passed, she would always know that it was her fault—that, God help her—she'd all but killed her friend. But at least she could do this.

She stared at the torn photo and her heart broke all over again. She wanted to change this place, not destroy it. She carefully peeled off another photo, slowly, so it wouldn't rip. It was one of Astrid, sitting in a tire swing that used to hang in Sydney's yard, before the tree fell in a storm. She flipped it over and removed the scotch tape from each corner, crunching it into a wad.

She couldn't fix it, she couldn't make it so this place wasn't awful, so it wasn't the place that A had chosen to die, and hell, she sure couldn't save Astrid—or even herself—but she could make it a little better at least. She could make this just a run-down cabin in a mountain town. Not a grave. They could divide the photos between them—they could even put them in a box or a book or something that they shared. It'd be better than having them stuck here.

The process wasn't a quick one. There were hundreds of photos to take down, and even though Sydney tried to pull them off without looking, without remembering, she still had to move slowly so they wouldn't tear.

Sydney's fingers were sticky, and she was almost done when she felt a cool rush, when she realized that she could hear the crickets and cicadas echo louder than they had before. When she turned she saw that the door had creaked open.

The gust came through before she had a chance to close the door. It swept through the room, rushing through the open slats on the back wall. This place seemed ready to fall apart any minute. On the way through it ruffled her pile of photos, scattering them across the floor.

She ran forward and slammed the door, and as she did, she heard a clap of thunder and the early patters of a rainstorm.

"Shit," she said, running to the window. The sky was gray and the rain was already starting to come down. Thunder crackled again. In moments, the rain would be everywhere, surrounding the cabin on four sides, pelting against the windows, turning the clay to mud.

"Damn it," she said, because she knew if she didn't leave now, she'd be soaked. She looked at the photos scattered across the floor, trying to avoid Astrid's eyes staring back at her from almost every one. Ella would have brought a box or a binder, but she hadn't, and if she tried to take them with her, they'd get soaked, too. She'd just have to get them later. So she grabbed her bag and rushed out the door, closing it tight behind her so that the photos wouldn't get wet.

Maybe if she ran fast enough she could beat the storm.

CHAPTER NINE

Somehow, Ella had managed to pull herself together for dinner. She hadn't answered the phone call—by the time she'd gotten the nerve, the ringing had stopped. She wanted to call back, but she couldn't bring herself to do it. So she'd shut her computer with shaking hands, tucked it under her bed. Turned off her phone. Tried to pretend that things were somehow okay.

There had to be some explanation, after all. Maybe she was seeing things. Maybe she was imagining things. Did people do that? Did people actually go nuts because someone close to them died?

But she knew that she'd imagined nothing. She knew what she'd seen. Her scream had been real. The terror, the pain she felt right now, was just as much so.

So she'd showered. She'd watched bad TV. She'd told her mom that no, she didn't want to go shopping for her dorm bedding. School seemed so far away. A completely other world. Eventually, seven would come. And it did.

Ella's mom dropped her off at Astrid's right on time. She hadn't been there since that most horrible day. It was small but quaint, with creaky floors and plenty of crannies to play hide and seek. Astrid used to claim that the place was haunted. It certainly had seen better days—the paint peeled on the edges, and the posts of the front porch were rotted in parts—but that had always been part of its appeal. It was like a fairytale cottage, their favorite spot to meet besides the cabin. Now, it's once-charming façade just looked sad and lonely.

"Just call me when you want me to come get you," her mom said.

She'd have to turn on her phone for that. She didn't want to. "I'm sure Jake can drive me home."

THE AFTER GIRLS

"Okay," she said. "Just let me know if you need me." Then she put her hand on Ella's shoulder. "You feeling better, baby? I know you had a rough day."

"Yeah," Ella said, lying, and she gave her mom a hug and stepped out of the car.

"See you later," she said, and then she ran up the drive, straight to the door. Most of the rain had stopped by now, but it was still drizzling and the sky was super gray. Behind the house, the mountains were so dark that Ella could barely make them out; they looked like black splotches against the drab sky.

Claire answered the door, almost as if she belonged there. Which she didn't. She so didn't. She was so proper and pulled-together. She wasn't like Grace at all. It was hard to believe that they were even sisters. She pushed open the screen door, and Ella stepped inside.

"Hi Ella," she said, wrapping her in a quick, sterile hug. "Thanks for coming."

"Of course."

Jake poked his head out of the kitchen and waved. "Come in," he said. And so she followed Claire to the kitchen, and she couldn't help it, she turned her head as they passed the hall that led to Astrid's room, and she felt almost sick as she thought of the message, the dream, the phone call—everything.

Grace was there, one hand on the counter, bracing herself, and one slowly stirring a pot. She turned her head slowly. "Hi Ella," she said, and she sounded tired. Then she just went back to stirring. She didn't say anything else. No, *How are you? I'm glad you came.* No hug. No nothing. But she stirred that pot as if her life depended on it.

Jake led Ella to the table.

"Can I help you?" she said to Grace as she passed her, but Grace didn't turn, and Claire took over. "We've got everything under control," Claire said. "You all just sit down." She touched her sister's shoulder and, almost on cue, Grace stopped her stirring, dropping the spoon deep into the pot. It made a splash, but she didn't say anything. She just turned the way that Claire had pointed her. Almost

106

like a zombie. Where was the woman that Ella had grown up with? Who was this person here? It was like someone else altogether.

Claire fished the spoon from deep down in the pot, Ella took her seat, and Jake sat down next to her. From her usual place, she could see into the big living room, the couches, where she and Astrid and Sydney had stayed up late watching movies, the bookshelf, where they'd read aloud the more scandalous scenes from *Lady Chatterley's Lover*, but Ella's eyes stopped on the desk—the beautiful antique wooden desk where they'd played office and written their papers—the one whose key Astrid always wore around her neck (Ella had always wished that *her* mom's furniture had come with equally cool jewelry)—but something about it looked different. And in an instant she realized. It was a roll-top, and it had been pulled shut. In all the years she'd known Grace and Astrid, the desk had never been shut before.

But Ella didn't have time to think about it, because her eyes locked on Grace, who was taking her seat now, but she wasn't taking *her* seat at all. She was taking the wrong seat.

She was taking Astrid's.

Grace sat down like it was the most natural thing in the world. But it didn't feel natural to Ella. It felt wrong. Like Astrid was somehow being replaced. Forgotten.

"You okay?" Jake asked, nudging her with his elbow.

She turned to him, realizing that she must have been staring. She nodded and plastered on a smile. "I'm fine."

Claire brought their bowls over two at a time. It was chicken and dumplings. Astrid's favorite. *Great.* As if this day couldn't get any worse. Ella stared down at the salty broth in front of her, but she'd completely lost her appetite.

"Can I have some wine?" Grace asked when Claire set her bowl in front of her.

"Sure," Claire said, although she looked hesitant. She poured a glass and brought it over to the table. Ella noticed that Grace's lips were already kind of purple.

Jake dug in, slurping loudly. "This is great," he said, and he smiled that Astrid smile. The corners of his lips turned right up at the edge.

"Thanks," Claire said, and she began to help herself.

Grace took a gulp of wine, and then a big spoonful of soup.

Ella just stared at the bowl in front of her. Maybe it was the message or the phone call or the fact that she was back in Astrid's house, her favorite meal in front of her, or maybe it was that desk shut tight or Astrid's mom, sitting in her daughter's chair, but Ella just couldn't bring herself to eat.

"Too hot?" Grace asked. She was looking straight at Ella.

Ella shook her head, looking down at the soup. "No, I just haven't had this in a long time."

"I thought you liked it," she said.

"I do," Ella said, her eyes meeting Grace's. "Not as much as Astrid did, though."

Grace's eyes narrowed, and she just took another sip of wine. "Sometimes it was the only thing I could get that girl to eat," she said. "She always was so picky. Nothing I did was ever good enough for her."

Ella's eyes narrowed. She'd never heard Grace talk about Astrid like that. What did she mean that nothing she did was good enough? Astrid loved Grace. They were so close they were like sisters. Maybe Grace wouldn't let her cut her hair, and maybe she made her wear sunscreen, but they were still friends. Weren't they?

"I didn't think she was picky," Ella said.

"Well you weren't her mother," Grace said, lifting the wine glass to her lips.

"*Grace*," Claire said. "Let's just eat. Please."

Grace looked at her sister and must have decided that she had a point, because she took a sip of her wine like everything was alright.

But it wasn't alright. It wasn't alright at all. Astrid was gone, and her mother, her very own mother, was actually sitting here criticizing her. "Excuse me," Ella said, pushing her chair back. "I have to go to the bathroom."

She could feel everyone's eyes locked on her as she walked through the kitchen and ducked, out of sight, into the hall. She just needed to be alone. Just for a few minutes.

I miss you, too. The words flashed into her head, unnerving her.

She walked as steadily as she could, and her heart sped when she reached Astrid's door. It was shut tight. *Do Not Enter. There's Nothing For You Here.* She took a deep breath and kept going. Jake had told her that the door always stayed shut.

Ella closed the bathroom door behind her. She leaned down to the sink and splashed water on her face. Her head felt like it was spinning, and she hadn't had a drop to drink. Her stomach felt heavy, even though she'd eaten nothing. As she dried her face off, she saw it: a trickle of blood on her thumb around the cuticle. She must have been picking at it all day. It was an anxious tic of hers. One that she'd kicked a few years ago. One that apparently was back.

Ella opened the medicine cabinet in search of a Band-Aid. There was a stack of them there, and she opened one, wrapped it around her thumb. She should have shut it back right away, but she didn't.

There were bottles, tons of them. Some of them were empty. Some of them were full. Clear orange ones, white labels. Big words.

Just like the one she'd seen in the cabin.

Most of the words didn't mean anything to her. They were medicine words: Mirtazapine. Fluoxetine.

But one jumped out at her. Klonopin.

She recognized the harshness of the big K in the front. Even the way its name sounded was off—wrong.

She grabbed the bottle, and it rattled in her hand. The name GRACE ALLEN was printed in tiny, neat letters on top.

Strangely enough, she had never questioned how Astrid got those pills. There were too many whys to focus on how.

But now she knew it clear as day. She had gotten them from her mother.

She forced the bottle back onto its place on the shelf. She didn't want to touch it anymore. But she stared at the orange containers.

Had these really always been here? Surely she'd opened this cabinet before. Had she never been looking? Had she never been aware?

How much had Astrid tried to tell her that she'd refused to listen to?

Ella slammed the cabinet shut and dried off the rest of the water on her face.

She stumbled out of the bathroom, and she found herself standing in front of Astrid's door.

I miss you, too.

What if she were trying to tell her something now? What if Astrid wanted her to go inside?

Ella's heart beat faster and the hairs on her arms raised—goose pimples—she turned the knob slowly and opened the door, wincing at its quiet moan, and took the first step.

The space was largely unchanged. The bed was unmade, as if Astrid had just slept in it. Her graduation gown was draped across a chair. The cap lay at its feet, the tassel splayed out as if to say, "Yes, she threw me. She really did."

There were other clothes on the floor. Floral sundresses. Long hippie skirts. A "going-out top," a black sparkly halter that Astrid only wore to parties. One that Ella had even borrowed once herself, one of the few times she'd drunk liquor. She'd thrown up before ten and had spent the rest of the night crying about how she'd ruined Astrid's sparkle shirt.

Every piece had a story, a memory. Little reminders of good times and bad, but mostly good, so good that it broke Ella's heart that there wasn't a body—a living body—to fill these anymore.

Ella walked closer to the bed. The night stand was littered with a bowl that Ella had given her once and a movie ticket to this horrible action flick that they'd seen in 3-D. A used water glass sat next to it, printed ever-so-lightly with lip gloss. God, had that been there all this time, just sitting there?

And the bed. The bed was maybe the worst. It looked like it hadn't ever been touched again since that most horrible of days. It lay open, undone, as if Astrid had just hopped out. Just dashed out into the world. Out into the last bit of sunshine she'd ever see.

Ella's eyes stopped at the pillow. It sat there, depressed, as if saving a space for Astrid's head—*should it really still be that way, now?*—and Ella couldn't help herself. She closed her eyes and leaned down. She buried her face in the pillow, and she breathed in deep. She wanted to smell her friend, the scent of her coconut shampoo, the cheap stuff that came in the 99-cent bottle, and it was there, smelling all sweet and tropical like summer vacation, like Astrid, and the pillow was warm, and the fragrance so strong, like her friend had just been there, only moments ago . . .

Ella whipped her head up. She jumped back. Why oh why, why on earth was the smell so strong? Why did it all feel so real, so . . . here? Why had she gotten a call from her friend, just today? What did it all mean?

Her head felt light, just like it had at the café. The room was starting to spin.

She didn't know what to think, what to ask, what to believe.

But then she turned her head, and on top of the dresser was Astrid's journal, her pride and joy, her beloved, just begging to be read.

But she forgot it in an instant because, there, right next to it, flipped open like she'd just set it down, was Astrid's phone.

Ella picked it up, her hands shaking. The screen was dark—blank. She pushed the power button, trying to turn it on. Nothing. It was dead, as it should be, without Astrid to use it.

Totally, irrefutably dead.

That was when she heard footsteps, noise. The banging of the phone falling onto the dresser. The opening of the door.

"What are you doing?" Grace screamed, rushing towards her. She'd never seen Grace like this. Never seen such anger. Never seen her eyes, her eyes so wild and manic and terrifying, absolutely terrifying.

Ella stepped back, shaking her head. "I'm sorry—" she started.

"What the hell do you think you're doing?"

"I was just—"

"Get out," Grace screamed. "Get out of here."

And that's when the tears came.

"Get out," Grace screamed again, and Ella started running, without looking back. She couldn't face Jake and Claire, so she ran out the front door, shutting it tight behind her.

But in an instant, Ella heard the door open again, footsteps following her down the drive. She was out of breath and she knew that her face was wet, covered in tears, and she almost wanted to turn, to face Grace. To scream right back. To tell her that she wasn't doing anything wrong. That she'd just wanted to see her room.

That she just missed her friend.

"Wait."

Jake. Ella whipped around.

"What?" she asked, and her tears were streaming down now. He was pushing something in front of her, but her vision was blurred and fuzzy. Wet. It was red and round. Her bag. It was her bag.

And she stared at him through blurry eyes, because she realized that he was shoving her out, too. He was just like Grace.

"Thanks," she said, the tears catching in her throat so she sounded wild, deranged. "I'll get out of your life. I'm sorry."

"No," he said. "No. I didn't mean . . . What happened? I heard yelling, and then I saw you running out, and—"

"I'll leave," she said. "I'm going. Tell Grace thanks for dinner."

But she decided not to take the road. Instead, she turned and ran across the grass and towards the woods. If she couldn't find her friend here, maybe she could find her friend in there. Deep in those woods where she'd left them.

The rain was coming down now, and the sun was nearly set. It would be hard to see in the thick woods, so she pulled out the flashlight connected to her keys and clicked it on.

She stepped into the woods and onto the path that led to the cabin. The trees, the leaves, the twigs, and a cacophony of owls and insects, pushed at her from all sides. Her hair was wet.

Ella's toe caught on a rock, and she fell, her knees sinking deep into the mud, but she didn't care. She pulled herself up and kept going. Tall trees surrounded her, lush in the beginning of summer. She followed the muddy path, spattered with branches and rocks and crawling roots that formed a makeshift stairway. She stepped up carefully, slowly now. She didn't want to fall again.

Finally, she pushed through the trees until she felt the familiar scratches on her arm and the tiny thorns and burrs on her ankles. Almost there.

In the dream, Astrid had asked her to help, but if she could have, she would. Wouldn't she?

The door was shut, and the caution tape was gone.

Ella ignored the wind and rain and pulled the door open, stepping inside.

She didn't know what she wanted, to look at the pictures, to read through the books, to sit here and cry?

But whatever she wanted, it wasn't here. Ella shone her flashlight around the room and nothing but bare walls met her. She stepped forward and she felt something crumple beneath her. And then she looked down, and there on the ground, a million of Astrid's faces staring up at her.

She screamed.

CHAPTER TEN

Max arrived just as the sun was setting.

Sydney had told him to come over after all. Maybe it wasn't the best idea, but she'd at least chosen her house as the meeting point. That way nothing that shouldn't happen could happen. At least not for a few hours.

She was busy painting her nails when he showed up on her porch. He was a backdoor kind of guy. He never rang the doorbell. Yet another reason why her mom, et. al., had never liked him that much.

"Hey," he said, and he looked down at her fingers. "Black. I like."

His hair was pulled back into a short ponytail. It was just a little greasy, messed up. He was one of those guys who could go days without showering and only get hotter.

"What's up?" she asked.

"Nothing." He sank down next to her so the porch swing rocked and rattled. He didn't leave her any space—their arms were touching—but she didn't move either.

"You want a smoke?" he asked, pulling out his pack of Parliaments.

"Gross," she said, even though she knew that she might say otherwise if she were drunk. "And you can't, either."

"Oh, come on," he said, looking back through the window and into the living room. He gave George a half-assed wave. "We're outside."

"Not until they go upstairs at least."

"That won't be for hours," Max said, shoving the pack back into his pocket.

"Well, you'll just have to settle for the pleasure of my company," she said, shooting him a mock-smile.

"Fine." He pulled his iPad out of his bag. Max always had the newest everything. It was his parents' restitution for never really being around. He clicked onto YouTube and started looking for stupid videos.

They were so close that she could feel him breathe as he watched an SNL skit and she finished off her nails. When she was with him, she didn't have to talk about Astrid—she didn't really have to think about Astrid. Things were so easy and comfortable.

But she knew that it couldn't work out. He wanted everything from her and nothing all at once. He'd want it all from some other girl once he got a few swigs of Jack in him.

Sydney looked over, and his eyes were glued to the screen, and she wondered what it was about her that wasn't enough to keep him. She wondered what it was that he was looking for in everyone else.

She blew on her nails to help them dry.

They sat like that, rocking slowly, half-watching the videos, with few words between them. The sun fully set and the crickets began to hum, and for awhile, she almost felt some kind of twisted, messed-up peace . . .

Then she heard the thudding of footsteps, running footsteps, and in a second there was Ella, banging on the door of the screen porch, covered head-to-toe in mud. She looked like a nightmare.

Sydney got up and pushed the screen door open. "My God, what happened to you?"

Even Max managed to look up from his iPad: "Jesus, are you okay?"

In her state Ella didn't even seem to care that Max was there. Her words came in gasps . . . "I'm sorry . . . I saw a light on . . . I ran here . . . she talked to me . . . she tried to call me . . ."

Sydney pulled her friend onto the porch. She looked back—luckily, her mom and George weren't in the living room. They were probably putting Darcy to bed. "Come here," she said, sitting Ella down on the swing. "Calm down," she said. "Tell me what happened."

"I can't," Ella said, getting hysterical again. "I can't. I don't know what happened."

"Well, something had to have happened to make you lose it," Max said, and Ella just burst into sobs.

"You know, you're not helping," Sydney said, turning to Max.

Max flipped his iPad shut and stood up. "Fine," he said. "I can tell when I'm not wanted." He expected her to stop him. To tell him he was wanted, and that what he'd said was no big deal, to coddle him, to plead with him to stay. But she didn't have time for that right now.

"Good," she said. "Just go."

He looked at her like she'd totally lost it. But when she didn't say anything else, he finally got up and stomped off, slamming the screen door behind him. He was such a dick. Such a self-involved cocky heartless dick. Sydney waited until she couldn't hear his footsteps anymore to speak.

She sat down next to Ella and put a hand on her shoulder—one of the few areas not caked with mud. "I'm sorry," she said. "He's gone now. Now tell me what happened. Tell me what's wrong."

Her friend's words came out like vomit, in heaving spurts. "I don't know what's going on," she started. "Something bad is happening. None of it makes sense. She talked to me. And her mom screamed at me. And—and the cabin. The cabin, it's destroyed. I don't know what happened, but it's destroyed." Ella's chest heaved up and down as she spoke.

"Whoa," Sydney said, rubbing her friend's shoulder. "You mean the photos in the cabin?"

Ella nodded, tears spilling down her cheeks.

Sydney put her hand on Ella's cheek, turning her head to hers. "Ella," she said, but Ella was still sobbing. *Ella.*

"Yeah?" she said.

"That was *me*. I took the photos down."

Ella narrowed her eyes. She looked at Sydney like she didn't know her. Like she'd been betrayed.

"Don't worry," Sydney said again. "It was just me."

Ella just shook her head. "But, but, but why?" she asked, her words still shaky, but a hint of anger in them now. "Why would you do that? It was our *place*."

Sydney took a deep breath. This was certainly not how she'd wanted it to go down. She didn't know why in God's name Ella had gone there tonight anyway. She'd planned on getting the photos tomorrow, going over to Ella's, dividing them up, putting them in a book, whatever. It was supposed to be *cathartic*. So much for that.

"I know," Sydney said. "I know, but I just thought that after all that happened, it would be better for us to, you know, find a *different* place."

"A different place?" Ella asked, sobs overtaking her again. "A different place? What's wrong with you? How can you even say that?"

"Ella," Sydney said. "She died there. How can you want to constantly go back?"

"I *know* she died there," Ella snapped. "I was the one who found her. Remember?"

There was the punch of guilt again, right in her stomach. "I'm sorry," Sydney said, throwing up her hands. "There's nothing I can do to make that different," she said, and her voice was shaking now, too. "Don't you think I feel bad enough already?"

"Well you could try not destroying it," Ella said. "They were all scattered across the floor like a hurricane had hit. I walked in there and it was so dark, and I had my flashlight, and she was there . . . all those pictures of her just staring up at me."

"I'm sorry," Sydney said. "I was going to get them tomorrow. It started raining halfway through and I didn't want them to get ruined."

"You had no right," Ella said. "You had no right to do that without me."

"I'm sorry," Sydney said again. "I didn't think it was that big of a deal."

Ella just glared at her, but Sydney wrapped her in a hug, pulling her head underneath her chin. Ella let her, and they held each other like that for awhile, and it felt like Ella's anger was waning. She had to understand. She had to see that Sydney was only trying to make it better—for both of them.

But then Sydney looked up, loosening her grasp on her friend. "Ella," she said. "Why did you go there? After the dream I thought you wouldn't want to go back."

Ella's breathing started to quicken again, but Sydney had her hand back on her shoulder in an instant. "It's okay," she said. "You can tell me."

Ella took a deep breath. "I went to Grace's for dinner," she said.

"Whoa," Sydney said. She hadn't been in that house since Astrid died. She didn't want to. The idea of it gave her the creeps. Just like the photo-filled cabin.

"What was it like?" she asked. "Was it hard?"

Ella stared at her a moment before answering. "She screamed at me. She threw me out of the house."

"Grace?"

Ella nodded.

"But why?"

Ella looked away, her body shaking again. "Because I went into her room."

"A's?"

Ella didn't answer, she just cried harder.

"Oh God, El, I'm so sorry. That must have been awful."

"And I just wanted to see her, you know, I just wanted to be somewhere where she was, and so I went into the cabin, and then—and then—"

"I know," Sydney said. "I can see why that would have freaked you out. I'm an idiot for—"

But Ella looked up then, put her hand in front of Sydney's mouth, and she shook her head fast and strong.

"What?" Sydney asked, almost a whisper. It was so quiet between them for a moment that she could hear an owl in the distance. "What?"

"There's something else," Ella said, struggling to get the words out between gasps for breath.

"El," Sydney said. "You need to calm down."

Ella nodded, and she really did look shaken. Terrified, almost. She was taking this whole cabin thing *way* too seriously. It was creepy, yeah, but at the end of the day it was just a bunch of photos.

Sydney sighed, maybe a little too loudly. "What is it, Ella?" she asked. "Just tell me. What is it?"

Ella hesitated, and Sydney tried to act at least somewhat patient as she waited for her to speak. "Can we go inside?" she asked finally. "I just—I feel like I should lie down."

Sydney nodded. This was really getting theatrical, but she didn't want her to faint *again*. Especially not on her watch.

"Alright," she said. "Let's go."

They scrubbed the mud off Ella's legs and arms, and then they went to Sydney's room. Ella crawled onto the bed, stretching out over the covers.

"Are you feeling okay?" Sydney asked.

"No." She didn't even look at her—just stared at the ceiling fan. *Whir whir whir whir whir.*

"Can I get you some water or something?"

Ella shook her head.

Sydney sat down on the bed, carefully. She felt like any wrong move would break her friend, send her into another crying fit. She didn't want to hurt her anymore—she didn't want to hurt anyone. She didn't want anyone to hurt themselves.

"Here," Ella said, pushing her bag at Sydney.

"What?"

"Pull out my phone."

Sydney rolled her eyes. She hated drama. Especially the sober kind.

"Seriously, El, what is this about?"

"Just pull out my phone." Her voice was earnest.

Sydney did.

"Turn it on."

She sighed loudly and pushed the button, waiting for the familiar little trill, the colorful screen. "On," she said, her voice full of faux cheer.

Ella seemed to be almost holding her breath. She spit the words out fast: "Are there any calls?"

"No," Sydney said. "Not one. Are we going somewhere with this?"

Ella breathed a sigh that sounded like pure relief. "Okay," she said. "Just look at the recent calls."

Sydney shook her head. Ella couldn't just tell her whatever the hell was bothering her? They had to go through a song and dance?

But she forgot her annoyance in an instant—she felt a jolt, her heartbeat going double-time, as her eyes locked on the first name on the list.

CHAPTER ELEVEN

Even on Sydney's pretty, pulled-together, trying-to-stay-calm face, it looked like fear.

Ella watched her tuck the phone back in the bag, burying it as if that would make it go away. Maybe for Sydney it would.

Ella took a deep breath. A part of her felt better, now that someone at least knew. "Well?" she asked.

Sydney stared at her, like she was playing something out in her mind. Finally: "So this is why you're upset?"

"Wouldn't you be?" Ella snapped. "What? That's not enough for you?"

When Sydney spoke her voice was so soft and quiet that it only sounded patronizing. "El," she said.

"What?"

"You don't really think . . ."

"I don't really think what?" she asked, sitting up on the bed now. "What? What do you think?"

"I don't know," Sydney said. "It was obviously an accident."

"What do you mean?" Ella asked. She was up now, pacing back and forth, working it all out in her head.

"Like someone obviously called you by mistake."

Ella shook her head. "No," she said. "No. The phone was dead, Syd. Dead. Like it hadn't been used since—" she couldn't bring herself to say it. "Like it definitely hadn't been used in a long time."

"How do you know?"

"I told you," Ella snapped. "I went in her room. It was right there."

"You mean you went looking for the phone because of the call?" Sydney asked. "Why didn't you just ask Grace or Jake if they called you by accident? Then you wouldn't have to go snooping around her room and hunting down evidence."

Ella stared at her. Whatever Sydney had felt in that first instant—whatever fear or compassion or understanding she'd had—was gone as quickly as it had come. If this could be explained, then they didn't have to deal with it. If they didn't have to deal with it, then they didn't have to keep talking about Astrid. They could drink their way through the summer, worry about nothing more than bad hangovers. They could forget. It was clearly what Sydney wanted. And she'd do anything to get there. Ella wanted to tell her about the message, but she knew Sydney would just give a stupid explanation. It would be an "accident"—just like this.

"You don't get it," Ella said. "You don't get it at all."

She grabbed her bag and reached for the door.

"El," Sydney said, standing up and pretending to actually care.

"No," she said. "Just forget about it. I'll see you later."

And she walked out before Syd could object.

Ella didn't think she was going to be able to sleep.

After walking out on Sydney and walking home, she'd managed to evade her mom's questions about the dinner by saying that she had a stomach ache and just wanted to go to bed.

Her stomach felt fine. It was the rest of her that didn't.

Upstairs, she pulled out her computer immediately. She logged onto Facebook once more to check her messages—nothing.

Ben was online, too—he was always up until all hours of the night—he sent her a message.

Hey. You wanna talk?

Ella hesitated. He'd come over after she'd fainted, and he'd been usual kind Ben. He'd completely forgiven her anger from the night before. He'd even stopped her when she'd tried to explain herself. Things were good between them now. As good as they could be. She'd told him about the dreams. She'd told him that she was going to go to Grace's tonight. He probably just wanted to hear about it. He probably just wanted to be there for her. But she knew that Ben wouldn't understand what she was thinking right now. *She* didn't even understand what she was thinking right now.

Ella?

Still, talking to him would be better than sitting alone in her room and driving herself crazy.

Sure. Call me.

Her phone rang in a matter of seconds.

"Hey," she said.

"Hey."

Ella leaned back on her bed, staring at the ceiling. Maybe she could just talk to Ben all night and never sleep. She was afraid to.

"How was your night?" Ben sounded all genuine and actually concerned. "How was dinner?" She instantly regretted texting him earlier that she was going over there. But she took a deep breath. There was really no point in not telling him that, at least. "She threw me out of the house."

"She what?"

"Threw me out."

"Wait a second. Grace? Start from the beginning."

Ella rolled over. "There's really nothing to tell. I went into her room and she just, like, lost it."

"Wait, Grace's?"

"No," Ella said. "Astrid's."

"Ohhhh," he said, and she could hear that he was nodding. "Why?"

"What do you mean, why? I wanted to see it. I'm her friend."

"I know," he said. "Don't get upset. I'm just trying to figure it out."

"Figure what out?" she asked. "And I'm not getting upset. Why does everyone keep telling me to calm down?"

"I'm not telling you to calm down," Ben said, his voice just a tiny bit strained. "I'm just trying to figure out, I don't know, what happened."

"I'm *telling* you what happened," Ella said, making no attempt to hide her annoyance. "The door was closed, and I went in anyway, because I *wanted* to, and I was just looking. I wasn't going to mess anything up, and she just came in screaming at me, and so I left."

Ben was silent for a second.

"Okay," he said finally. "That makes sense."

"Wait, what?"

"It makes sense. I get it. It's natural for you to want to see. She shouldn't have done that to you."

"Thanks," she said.

"I'm really sorry you had to go through that."

Ella took a deep breath. "Ben, she was being so weird. You don't even know."

"What do you mean?"

"She was so mean to me. The things that she was saying, they were just, they just sounded so mean."

"She's grieving, El. Everyone does it differently."

"I know," Ella said. "I've just never seen her like this. It was . . . it was . . . scary."

"I'm sorry, baby. It will get better."

There he was again, trying to wrap it up, tie all the strings. But it was okay, because tonight, she didn't want to talk about it anymore. She didn't want to think about it anymore. She just wanted to be distracted. She just wanted to hear the sound of a warm voice. One that would be there for her. One that always had been before.

"So did you just go straight home?" he asked.

And she knew that she could have told him about the cabin, and she could have told him about the phone call. She could have told him about losing it at Sydney's but she didn't want to. Ben was even more practical than she was. He wouldn't understand. And she didn't want him thinking she'd lost it. She knew that Sydney was already beginning to. So she lied. She knew it was bad to lie to your boyfriend, but she did it anyway.

"Yeah," she said. "How was your day?"

And she lay there as he told her about hanging with his football buddies, messing around online, the funny commercial he'd seen on TV while watching baseball with his dad. And she let him talk until he couldn't talk anymore. Because she wanted to do anything but go to sleep.

Ella woke the next morning to seconds of peace. For a minute, she saw the sun shining through the windows, and she felt the breeze of the fan, cool on her skin, and she saw the phone, lying right next to her—she'd fallen asleep moments after saying good-night to Ben—and she forgot.

But it came back to her, like an actual stomach ache. The words she'd seen, Grace's screams, the way Sydney and Max had looked at her, like she'd gone nuts. The faces, all of Astrid's faces, watching her from the floor of the cabin.

And then she remembered her dream. She was back there, but the photos weren't on the floor. They were back on the wall again, staring her down. And the room was empty, but she heard the doorknob turn behind her, and she knew that when she turned around she'd see those eyes, she'd see those blacked-out eyes. She'd see her friend's hair. And she still wouldn't be able to do anything to help her.

Sydney called at ten, offered a half apology—"I should have been more understanding," *blah blah blah*—and asked her to go with her to the cabin to box up all the photos until they decided exactly what to do with them. They agreed to meet at noon. Ella didn't have work until later that afternoon—assuming she was still *allowed* to work for Grace—so they'd have time to get them together before another rainstorm could hit.

The ground had mostly dried from the night before, and it was easy to get to the clearing. Ella stopped once she got to the porch. She took a deep breath and looked at the dusty windows, peeling paint, and thin walls, even cracked in places. It seemed so different from the night before. It seemed so harmless. She stared at the names in front of her. Astrid. Ella. Sydney. So much of the place still looked just the same.

They'd been twelve when they'd found it. It was just Astrid and Ella, the summer after they'd first met, and it was a day like any other, the sun high in the sky and a brisk Appalachian breeze cool against their sweating skin. Astrid and Ella had been pushing the boundaries for awhile now. Each time they went deeper into the woods than they had before. There were boundaries, at least there were supposed to be, places where kids could play safely, where no one would get lost, where no one would come across an errant backpacker, hiking in from the trail. A kid, not one that they knew, someone older, someone who lived on the other side of the neighborhood, had wandered, gotten hurt, gotten stuck, and gotten lost. He was okay in the end, but it scared everyone.

They probably would have remained content with their play space, with the other neighborhood kids, if it hadn't been for him. But since the rules were made, since the boundaries were set, they needed to see more. And so they were wandering.

Astrid had long curly hair then and horribly thick glasses. It was before she'd gotten contacts, before everyone had started to see her beauty, before boys would stare at her and men would turn their heads so quickly in the street that Ella wondered if they'd get whiplash.

"Whoa," Astrid said when they reached the clearing. Whoa was right. A house. A place they hadn't known about. Right in their own backyard. Well, almost.

Astrid turned to her, her face alight, her eyes gleaming. "We should go inside." Astrid wasn't so afraid of things then. She was the brave one.

Even beneath their spindly, twelve-year-old bodies, the porch had creaked beneath them, like it wasn't a real house, like it was a playhouse, a pretend house out of a storybook.

Astrid and Ella had linked their hands together, had stood just where she and Sydney were standing now.

It had been dusty inside. Awfully dusty. Astrid unhooked her hand from Ella's. She ran her finger along the dirty wall, doodling squiggles, marking the space, even then, as hers.

"It's perfect," she said.

"Perfect for what?" Ella asked.

"Perfect for us. It'll be our clubhouse."

"We don't have a club," Ella said.

Astrid smiled. "We'll make one. We'll clean it up. We'll meet here. It will be our special, secret escape. We can't tell anyone else."

"Except Syddie," Ella said. Sydney was in their class in school that year. Sydney was their third musketeer.

"Obviously."

"And what'll we do here?" Ella asked.

Astrid shrugged. She skipped about the place, opened her arms wide, twirled around in the middle. Spun until she stopped, and her eyes tried to focus, and the dizziness stole her down, her body crumpling to the floor.

Ella was riddled with laughter. So was Astrid.

Ella started to spin, too. The dusty walls and cobwebs swept together, became one in her eyes; flashes of light from the window mixed with the ceiling and the floor and the red of Astrid's hair; Astrid giggled beneath her, and then Ella stopped, and the cabin swerved, taking her over until she fell, struck down by silliness and splayed out on the floor next to her friend.

When the laughter stopped and there was nothing left but the sounds of the birds outside and the slightest patter of the creek in the distance, Astrid turned to Ella. "We have to claim it," she said, jumping up onto her feet. "Come on."

The water in the creek felt clean, and they chucked their shoes aside and dipped their feet around, sloshing through the wetness, feeling the rocks beneath them. Ella leaned down to wash off the thick coat of dirt on her hands.

Astrid picked the rocks up to examine them, then quickly cast each one aside.

"What are you looking for?" Ella asked.

"It has to be sharp," she said. "For it to work."

"For what?" Ella asked.

Astrid ignored her question. She did that sometimes, when she was singularly focused. "Help me find one with an edge."

Ella began to pick them up herself, but they were river rocks. They were smooth and round. Perfect for skipping. She found a flat one, whipped her wrist back and cast it forward. It skipped one, two, three, four, five times, and then it sank into the water, leaving a trail of rippling circles behind it.

"Got it," Astrid said, jumping up. She held it out to Ella. "Just what we need."

Astrid took it to her wrist, scraping the rock against her skin. A scratched white line appeared, then just a trickle of red at the top, dark and rich against her pale white skin.

"Oops," Astrid said, blowing on the wound at her wrist. "Come on. It'll be awesome. I'll show you."

Now, Ella's eyes locked on Astrid's name, no different than it had been that day. It was this permanent, physical proof that she'd been here. It made everything all the more real.

"You okay?" Sydney asked, and Ella looked at Syd. "I know you're a little frazzled from last night."

Ella nodded. Sydney didn't get it, but at least she was trying. "Maybe you should go first."

Sydney walked right up and opened the door, but when she got inside, she stopped short.

"What," Ella asked, but she took a couple more steps, and then she saw. The walls, the once-ravaged walls, the walls were covered—imperfectly yes, but still covered—in photos, almost as if what had happened had never been. Astrid's faces. All around her. Staring her down. Just like the dream. Everything was just like the dream. Ella's heart began to race.

"Did you do this?" Sydney asked. "Did you do this last night?"

Ella shook her head. "No," she said. "No. It wasn't like this last night. I was here." She felt her breathing quicken.

"Stop," Sydney said, but even she looked freaked out. "Someone must have just put them back up I guess."

But Ella couldn't help it. She thought of the message, the call, the dreams.

"You still don't get it," Ella yelled. "You don't know what it was like to find her," she said. "She was right there." Ella pointed at a space just a foot or two away from them. "You never had to see her like that," Ella said, her voice cracking. "She was just lying right there." She felt her heart beating a million miles an hour. She wanted it all to stop. She wanted it all to go away. Forever.

She wanted to escape, and wondered if that was exactly what Astrid had wanted. She understood her friend and hated her for it at the same time.

"I know," Sydney said. Her hands were on her shoulders now. She was trying to calm her down. She hugged her. She didn't let go, wouldn't let go, as Ella felt herself begin to shake. "I wish I was there with you," she said. "I wish you hadn't had to find her. I wish you hadn't had to tell me."

Ella wriggled out of Sydney's grasp. "No you don't," she said. "You really don't."

Sydney was quiet.

"What is going on?" Ella asked, looking straight at Sydney. "What the hell is going on?"

Sydney didn't answer at first. She just sat down, setting the empty shoebox between them. Ella followed.

It was quiet between them for a moment, but Sydney broke the silence first. She always did. "Someone is playing a seriously sick joke on us."

"You think so?" Ella asked, her train of thought completely interrupted, thoughts of last night pressing at her from every angle. "What do you mean?"

"What else could have happened?" Sydney asked.

Ella didn't have an answer. She couldn't think of anyone who even knew about their spot. Ben, maybe Becky, some people at the café.

None of them could have done this. Why would they? None of it made sense. Unless . . .

"You don't think," Ella started, unable to say it, unable to wrap her mind around all that was running through it, unable to pause and think levelheadedly, because she couldn't pause here. All she felt were the chills and the wind and the image of Astrid, lying on the floor. She couldn't think clearly.

"I don't think what?" Sydney asked. Her eyes widened, and for a second, Ella thought that maybe they were on the same page. Maybe Sydney was thinking what she was.

But then Sydney got that look she got when she had an idea—the same one she got when she figured out the perfect new line for a song she was working on with Max. "It could have been anyone," Sydney said, her chin resting on her hands. "She's famous, and so are we. *This* is her consecrated ground."

"You mean because she—"

"Killed herself here?" Sydney interrupted. "Yes, that's exactly what I mean. It was in the paper. There are only so many abandoned cabins in the woods that you can get to from her house. It doesn't take a genius to figure out that it was here. Anyone could come here. Think of all the kids from the college. Any of them could have done it."

"But why?" Ella asked. "Why?"

"Who knows," Sydney said. "Drunk college students do stupid shit all the time."

Ella shook her head. Sydney's bullshit explanation was just that. Bullshit.

"So you're telling me that some stupid college guys just decided to come put up photos of a girl they didn't know right after I get this crazy phone call?"

"I told you, it was probably just—"

"An accident," Ella said. "I know, but what if it wasn't? I didn't tell you because I thought you'd think I was nuts, but it's not just the phone call," Ella stammered, trying to get it all out at once. "I posted on her wall—Astrid's—and I know it sounds crazy but I got a response."

"A response," Sydney said. Slowly. Incredulously. "I look at her page every day. I never saw that."

"It disappeared," Ella said. "Like minutes after I saw it."

Sydney raised her eyebrows. "El," she said. "What exactly are you saying?"

And she didn't want to say it out loud—she almost couldn't say it out loud—because Sydney really would think she was crazy—without a doubt, she would. It almost sounded like she already did.

But the photos stared back at her, taunting.

I miss you, too.

Those six little letters on her phone.

Astrid.

"What if it wasn't anyone else?" she asked.

"What do you mean?" Sydney asked.

Ella took a deep breath, and she still didn't know if she could say it, but the words were right there in her chest, ready to burst forth, and in an instant, they spilled out of her, and then she couldn't take them back.

"What if it was Astrid?"

CHAPTER TWELVE

Seconds felt like years as Ella waited for Sydney's response.

Sydney's eyes were wide and she was staring at Ella as if she were somebody else. "Maybe we should get out of here. This place is driving you crazy."

"Don't call me crazy," Ella snapped, but she didn't know what else to say. All of the worries and fears had turned from thought to reality in a split second.

Sydney stepped forward and it looked like she was going to reach out and touch her, comfort her. But she didn't.

"I'm sorry, I just think this is all really getting to you," Sydney said.

"Of course it's getting to me," Ella said. "Our best friend died. How is it not getting to you?"

Sydney's jaw dropped. She took a step back. "Are you saying that just because I don't believe all this Falling Rock ghost bullshit that I don't care?"

"I'm just saying that you're very calm and collected for someone whose best friend just died. I mean, you're going around like nothing's happened. Like it's just any other summer."

"You better stop right there, Ella," Sydney said. "Seriously."

But the words were coming out so fast that she didn't know how to stop them. She didn't want to stop them. They felt so good to say.

"Why do you want me to just *forget* about her?" she yelled. "Why?"

Sydney shook her head, stepping towards the door. "You have no idea what you're talking about," she said. "You have no idea what I'm going through."

And with that, she stormed out of the cabin, slamming the door shut behind her.

Ella was left alone, the words ringing in her ears. It was just her and the photos of Astrid—everywhere.

But she couldn't take them down. Not now. Someone had put them up. For some reason, someone had done it.

It wasn't up to her to take them down. It was up to her to find out what they meant.

∽∾

Ella walked straight from the cabin to Trail Mix. She didn't want to be late. She got to the café just as Becky was finishing up.

"Hey," she said, all shocked and somber, like, *You've missed a lot of work lately—are you sure you're okay?*

"Hey," Ella said, trying to sound as normal as ever.

Jake barely looked at her. She couldn't tell if he was intent on counting up the tip jar or just purposely trying to avoid her. She couldn't tell if she was mad at him from the night before or just mad because he wasn't saying hi. She didn't know if she really even wanted to talk to him or not.

Ella headed to the back room to get her apron. Claire turned around as soon as she walked in.

"You're here," she said, giving her a big hug. "I'm sorry about last night. I really am. Grace just gets a little . . . overwhelmed sometimes."

"Thanks," Ella said, and she felt her voice start to crack. "But she wasn't overwhelmed, she was furious," Ella said. "She was so mad at me. I didn't mean to do anything wrong. She should know that. I've never seen her like that."

Claire's mouth opened as if to say something else. Then she shut it again, quickly. Succinctly.

"You don't worry your pretty little head about Grace," she said, patting her on the shoulder. "I'm just glad you're here."

"But—" Ella started.

Claire's hand was on her shoulder, almost pushing her out. "Jake needs your help, sweetie. Go on."

Reluctantly, Ella turned and headed back to the front.

Becky was gone, and Jake was staring at her, an inquisitive look in his eyes.

"What?" she asked.

"Nothing," he said, throwing his hands in the air and turning back to the register without saying another word.

She grabbed a rag and started wiping down the tables. He was probably mad that A) she'd had the nerve to go into Astrid's room, and B) she'd come here and asked about Grace—he had pushed her out, after all—so she spent the next twenty minutes purposely avoiding him, making every chair and table spotless, brewing the pots, restocking the sugar containers. After what had happened with Sydney, she couldn't take any more confrontation. Not now.

But then he did the last thing she expected. He started whistling.

First, it was "I'm a Little Teapot," and then it was the *Star Wars* theme. Ella moved on to mopping the floor while he took the occasional customer. But when he hit the long note of a song he'd just done about ten times, she couldn't help herself.

"What in the world are you whistling?"

Jake raised his eyebrows, his mouth stilled a second, mid-whistle. He gave her a half-smile. A *don't be mad at me* smile. "Swing low."

"Swing low?" she asked.

"You know," he said. "Sweet chariot?"

Ella narrowed her eyes. "The church song?"

"What's wrong with that?" he asked, mock hurt spreading across his face. "We're in the *South*," he said. "Gotta get my gospel on."

Ella half-laughed, half-scoffed. "West Virginia's the South, too," she said, scrubbing the table harder.

"Not like this," he said.

She didn't respond.

"Okay, we also might sing it in my a capella group . . ."

"A capella?" She looked up.

"I know," he said, raising up his hand. "It sounds mad nerdy. Trust me, it's cool when I do it." Then he gave her this killer smile that was so goofy she couldn't do anything but laugh.

Claire shut the door to the back room, and Ella gave the place a quick glance—there were no customers to be seen. She realized that this was her chance.

"Last night," she said.

"I really wasn't trying to get rid of you," he said. "I was just trying to help."

"I know," she said, smiling again. "But I was just thinking about Grace and—"

But Jake just shook his head. "Let's not talk about it. It's a new day. We're past that."

"I know, but—"

"Ella, last night sucked. I shouldn't have asked you. It was my fault. Let's just enjoy today. Okay?"

"But Grace. Did she really think that I was trying to—"

Jake held up his hand. "Let's just put it behind us. *Please.*"

And his eyes looked so sad and pleading that she felt like she didn't have any other choice.

"Okay," she said reluctantly.

Jake smiled. "Thanks."

"It's okay," she said. She put the mop down and walked back behind the counter to heat up some milk. She was worn out from the night before—she was worn out from this conversation—and she wanted a chai.

Jake turned towards her, but she stayed focused on the machine. "Ella," he said, his voice soft now. Friendly. "I've actually been meaning to ask you something."

"What's that?" she asked, her ears perking up. Maybe he'd changed his mind. Maybe he did want to talk about last night.

"You know that band I mentioned, The Black Rabbits?" he asked. "You know the ones that sound like The China Dolls?"

"Oh," she said, "yeah." She tried to hide the disappointment in her voice. He definitely did *not* want to talk about last night. The milk started to bubble.

"Well it turns out they're playing in Pinbrook tonight, and I wondered if you wanted to go with me."

"What?" she asked, without turning around so he wouldn't see her surprise. She thought he might wax poetic about Indie music. She didn't think he was going to ask her to go somewhere *with him*.

"I think you'd like them," he said. "It could be cool."

Cool, she thought. *Cool.* He probably just wanted to do something nice after last night. It couldn't be anything more . . . She pushed the idea out of her head. It was a show. A harmless little show. In Pinbrook. It wasn't even that far away.

"And I know you have tomorrow off," he continued, "so you don't have to be worried about being out a little late."

The milk was really bubbling now, threatening to go over the rim.

Ella managed a laugh. "What, do you, like, memorize my schedule?" she asked, buying time. Ben had mentioned something about hanging out at one of the football player's houses, but she never really liked that scene anyway. She hadn't even *really* said she'd go. He'd just kind of offhand mentioned it. It's not like she was a required attendee.

"I like it when you're here," he said.

She felt herself blush, and she turned the steamer off. The milk was about to spill any second. He was standing right behind her, waiting for an answer. It was unnerving.

"Okay," she said finally, as she dipped her finger in, testing the milk. "I guess."

"Perfect," he said, and out of the corner of her eye, she saw him turn back towards the front. "The show's at nine and Google says its like an hour drive, so I'll come get you around eight?"

"Sounds good," she said and she wiped down the machine instead of turning to face him, because she knew if she did, he'd see a smile written all over her face.

And she didn't want him to see it. Not yet.

When Ella got home, she sent a quick text to Ben telling him she couldn't go. She said that she was going to a show, and thankfully, he didn't ask anything else. So what if he'd just assumed it was with Sydney? She hadn't said a word that wasn't true.

She still had a few hours before nine, so she headed up to her mom's studio. She wanted to feel the clay again—to work on something real, hell, maybe even make something this time—something she could touch, something she could use for the fair. She knew it had to be coming up soon—she needed to check the dates.

Plus, she knew if she didn't keep busy she'd just start to think—about how a dead phone could call her, how the photos got on the wall, how Grace seemed almost like a different person now, how much she'd hurt Sydney by what she'd said—and how even after all that, she hadn't gotten one step closer to understanding *why*.

Ella grabbed a mound of clay and threw it as hard as she could onto the wheel. She dipped her hands in water and she started to work, spinning the wheel fast while she carefully centered it. She didn't want to ruin this one.

She thought she'd make a simple bowl—she always made them for the girls on each of their birthdays, giving them beautiful edges and bright colors. Astrid had loved them. She'd place them around her room and fill each one with jewelry, coins, notes, and knick-knacks.

Ella was almost done when her she heard footsteps on the stairs. She saw her mother walk in as she finished the edge, slowly taking her foot from the wheel.

"Sorry," she said, backing up. "I didn't know you were working."

"It's okay," Ella said, taking her hands off the bowl. "I just finished."

Her mom smiled. "I just came to ask what you wanted for dinner. I didn't know you'd be at the wheel." She clasped her hands together. "I'm so glad to see you up here again."

Ella just shrugged and gave her mom a look like, *Don't get used to it. I'm not making any promises.* One little bowl would not put the world back together.

Her mom walked closer. "It looks good," she said. "It's almost a perfect form."

"Maybe I can sell it at the fair," Ella said.

But her mom leaned forward, narrowing her eyes. "El, you know that the fair's this weekend. It won't be ready."

"What?" Ella asked. She'd known that it was coming but had no idea that it was so soon. In the wake of everything, she'd completely lost track of time. She always made pots for the fair. The Falling Rock Fair was like *the* big deal of the season. Her mom had a booth. River Deep played. It had always been such fun. It was their thing.

Her mom must have seen how upset she was. "It's why I've been up here almost night and day, baby," she said.

"I know," Ella looked down at her hands. "I just thought there was still time. Why didn't you tell me?"

"You've had so much going on," her mom said. "I didn't want to add another thing for you to worry about. You can do some pieces next year."

But Ella stood up and just walked towards the sink. "It doesn't matter," she said, as she started washing her hands.

She could hear her mom walk towards her. "I know you're upset, dear, but—"

"I *said* it doesn't matter."

"Okay," her mom said. "I'll just be downstairs." And Ella heard her footsteps slowly echo down the stairs.

Ella turned on the water as high as she could and scrubbed her hands until they turned red. She wiped them off on the towel and then stomped back to the wheel. She couldn't believe she hadn't made anything for the fair. It would be the first time she'd ever missed it.

Ella walked back to the wheel and looked at the bowl— exquisitely centered, nicely formed—and she hated it. She hated how perfect it was, how it would need to dry and be glazed and be fired; she hated this summer, how it made no sense; she hated her mom for not reminding her about the fair, and Ben and Sydney for not being able to ease any of this pain; and a part of her, a tiny part of her, hated Astrid for leaving her in this messy broken scary terrible world. For leaving her all alone. For taking the easy way out.

And without thinking, Ella scooped up the bowl and threw it down on the ground as hard as she could, watching it splatter and break and ruin.

And then she knelt down slowly and began to clean up the mess. Because there was nothing else she could do.

CHAPTER THIRTEEN

Jake was driving really fast.

And he was talking even faster. "Now this," he said, "is my favorite track. Well, it's my favorite of their more synth-y stuff. The best of their acoustic is 'Blue Heart,' no question. You like it?"

Ella started to answer but before she could he was turning up the volume, leaning towards the speakers, as if he might miss some crucial part of the song if he didn't lean close enough. "Listen to this, right here," he said, turning it up again. "That beat," he said, his hands gripping the wheel so hard his knuckles turned white. "That beat is so sick. Listen, you hear that? That, *da* dum dum *da* dum dum da."

Ella nodded, half laughing. He'd been going on about the music since he picked her up at 8:20. He wasn't exactly the best with time.

"Seriously," he said. "Listen."

"Okay," she said. And she did. She closed her eyes, pushing it all away, her ruined pottery, the phone call, the cabin—all the questions she had about Grace. She let herself swim through the sound. She let it wash up around her and drown her. The music wooed her and enchanted her—just like it did him.

"I'm sorry," he said, leaning back again, turning the volume down a little, and she opened her eyes. He turned to her and smiled so he looked almost . . . bashful.

"Sorry, sometimes I get overly excited about things."

Ella laughed. "Don't be sorry," she said. "It's a good thing."

Music snobs were always passionate—and she liked that—but she wondered what it was that she got excited about. Was there even anything? Pottery? She liked it, liked the way the clay moved at her

143

command, the way she was absolutely in control. But not like this. Not in this all-consuming way that moved Jake so much that he actually had to interrupt himself. The one thing that had always been important to her—so important to her—was her friends, and she'd always prided herself on being a good one, but now she wasn't even sure about that. A good friend would have known what was going on with Astrid. A good friend would have *done something*.

"So have you heard much of their music?" Jake asked. He was zipping past a car on the freeway now, and she instinctively braced herself. Ben—her *boyfriend*—had a cool Jeep, but he never drove this fast.

Jake was waiting for an answer.

"The Black Rabbits?" she asked.

He nodded.

"Honestly, not really," she said, pushing hair out of her face. Ben also never drove with the windows down. Unless the AC was broken. And then he complained about how hot it was the whole time. Maybe she should have just told him that she was going with Jake. It wasn't like she was doing anything *wrong*.

"Well, you, my dear, are in for a treat. You're going to *love* them. They're like The China Dolls on crack. But like, *good* crack."

Ella laughed. She'd expected him to be a little disappointed in her musical knowledge. Sydney had acted flat-out astounded when Ella had said that she didn't know who Woodie Guthrie was. Like Ella had committed some crime against music or something. Jake didn't seem to care.

She liked that. She also liked how he'd called her dear.

Jake swerved around another car, and before she knew it they were on the exit ramp.

Pinbrook was what people called a highway town. It wouldn't have been much of anything except that it was so damn convenient to everything else. It had about two restaurants and a movie theatre, but the music venue, The Cat, was close enough to the college to get some good acts. Or so she heard. Sydney had gone to see some bluegrass band there a couple of times. Ella had never been.

The Cat was just a few blocks off the highway. They pulled into a gravel parking lot, and Jake turned off the car.

He flipped down the sun visor and pulled the tickets out.

"For you, my lady," he said, handing her one. "Nice shirt, by the way."

She looked down at her mom's old Grateful Dead t-shirt that she'd found in her bottom drawer. After her pottery disaster she figured she'd try to look nice for the show—or at least semi-hip. She'd finished it off with skinny jeans and her coolest sneakers. She wondered if he thought she was trying too hard. She wondered if he noticed the clay that was still caked beneath her nails.

"Thanks," she said. "And thanks for asking me."

"My pleasure," Jake said. "Thanks for coming with me."

She smiled. "I'm really glad that I did."

Outside The Cat, a gaggle of kids in plaid took drags from their cigarettes between glances at their iPhones. She and Jake walked through, and the scent of tobacco hit her strong—she hated cigarettes—she didn't understand why after everything that they knew now, medically speaking and all, someone would even start.

A girl with a nose pierced like a bull took her ticket and marked her hand, and they walked through the door, Jake leading the way.

Inside, the air was a little clearer, but the room was dark.

"I'm going to hit the restroom," Jake said. "Meet you back here?"

"Okay," she said, and he left her alone, with the hipsters and the punks and the scene kids who all looked so much like they belonged.

Sydney would have fit right in, but Ella, even in her vintage t-shirt and painted-on jeans, looked terribly out of place. These people were pierced about everywhere you could be—most of them had loads of tattoos—while she didn't even have her ears pierced (she avoided pain at all costs), and the closest she'd ever come to a tattoo was a butterfly number on her back that Astrid had done in henna one day down by the river. It had worn off in a week.

Ella leaned against the back wall, trying to become invisible. She pulled out her phone to pass the time—no new messages, new calls, nothing—but it only made her think of Astrid. So she put it back in her purse and tried to focus on this night. On going to a show. Having Fun. Being normal. The questions and the hurt would still be there tomorrow, waiting.

She wished she had a drink. Not for the alcohol, just to have something to do with her hands. Instead, she shoved them deep into her pockets (no easy feat in skinny jeans) and waited.

After what seemed like an eternity, Jake came back. "Sorry," he said. "Long line. You want a drink?"

Ella held up her X-marked hand. "I don't think we're allowed," she said.

Jake held up his with a smile. No Xs.

"Nail polish remover?" she asked.

He just looked at her like she was nuts. "Fake ID," he said—and then he threw up his hands. "I know, I know, not the most upstanding thing in the world. But you have to have one to go just about anywhere in Chicago."

"Why does everyone think I'm going to judge them?" she asked, realizing immediately just how judgy that made her sound.

But Jake was unfazed. "I don't think you're going to judge me," he said. "It just seems kind of like you like to play by the rules."

"What do you mean?" she asked.

Jake ticked off his fingers. "You looked extremely flustered when you were late to work, I've yet to see you take anything longer than your allotted fifteen-minute break." He paused for effect. "Plus, I could tell you were totally freaked out by my speeding."

Ella frowned, but she knew that he was right. The only truly daring thing she'd ever done—going into Astrid's room—had shaken her to the core.

He must have seen her disappointment even under the dingy lighting. "Hey," he said. "I'm just giving you a hard time." He smiled. "Seriously. It's not a bad thing. Rules are good. Rules give the world order. Some people jibe with that order, and some people don't as much. It's no big deal."

"Rules are for prudes, right?" she said, thinking of Sydney constantly dragging her into the beer line or Ben trying to get her to go to one of his macho drunken football parties. "For people who turn their homework in on-time and don't fall down at parties and have the same boyfriend all through high school." She stopped to take a breath.

"See, rules are good for something," he said, smiling, but it sounded less like a statement and more like a question.

"Yes," she said, shifting her weight from foot to foot, and shoving her hands deeper into her pockets. "In that way, I guess, yes."

Jake nodded, but he looked like he was thinking hard on something.

Finally, he broke the silence. "So did that long answer mean that you do or do not want a drink?"

Ella didn't hesitate this time. "I'll have whatever you have."

Jake smiled and quickly headed to the bar, while she watched a few skinny boys on stage pack up their equipment and make way for a new set of skinny boys setting up what must be The Black Rabbits' stuff.

And sure enough it was. A guy with a ridiculously long beard for his age pinned up a backdrop, a big bunny silhouette painted across it.

Jake was back in minutes.

He handed her a beer can, cold and dripping with sweat, like it had been pulled right off an iceberg. "We got here at the perfect time," he said, leaning closer to her for a minute. "Looks like they'll be on soon. You want to go up a little closer?" he asked.

"Sure," she said, and they walked forward, Jake leading, weaving through everyone until they were right at the front, a dusty stage before them. Ella could have reached out and set her beer on one of the amps.

They didn't say much after that. Between the people behind them and the guys on stage, testing the different sound levels or whatever it was that they tested (Sydney claimed it was like mega super important, but Ella had always wondered why it had to take *forever*), it was too loud to really say much.

So she sipped on her beer—it was bitter and watery—as her eyes darted from the stage to the crowd to the equipment to the eager look on Jake's face, taking it all in. It was strange, she realized, that this was really the first show she'd ever been to without Sydney in it. The first one she was going to just for the music. Not for support. Not because it was what a good friend would do.

How had she gone seventeen years without experiencing that? She took another sip, realizing that there was still so much for her to do. So much for her to see. And the thought hit her like a knife, tearing through her, sharp and jagged, because it was so horribly, undeniably true. There were so many things that Astrid would never do.

But she didn't have time to dwell. Jake turned to her as a group of boys with creative facial hair and neon t-shirts walked on stage. "Here we go," he said, leaning close—just for a second.

Up on stage, they didn't say anything. They didn't introduce themselves. There was just the screaming of the crowd around them, and then there was the sound.

It started with an electric guitar, a note, long, rugged, and loud. And then the keyboards. And a big black box that she was pretty sure was a synthesizer. And then their voices—all together.

Hey, you. Hey, you.
You don't know me. You don't know me.
Hey, you! Hey, you!
You don't know me now!

She turned to look at Jake, but he was in another world already, singing along with them, jumping up and down to the music.

So she turned her attention back to the stage, and the guitars were getting louder, more playful, and the guy on the keyboards was rocking out, and that beat, that bass, it was so undeniable, so intrusive, so *present*, unlike anything she'd ever heard before.

Like this was their moment, all of them, every person in this room, and these guys were just keeping time.

And before she knew it, she was jumping, too, and she could feel her beer spilling, splashing her in the face, and she didn't know who she was hitting or bumping into, but it didn't matter, did it? Because they were all there, bumping together, and there were lights, red and green and blue and yellow and pink—even pink—and she felt like she was in a movie, or another world, one she'd never known, one she'd never had admittance to, and here was Jake, his shoulder brushing against hers as he jumped along with her, giving her the ticket, welcoming her in, letting her be someone she wasn't. Letting her fool every single one of them.

Letting her become someone new.

And the guitar went faster, and it danced, and it jumped, too, and it wouldn't—couldn't—stop, and she thought it would go on forever, until it cried, wailed, stopped. *Shut up.*

You don't know me now!

The crowd burst into cheers and screams, and Jake leaned close, shouted in her ear:

"On crack, right?"

"Yes!" she screamed back.

And then the bass started thumping again.

They drove much of the way home in pleasant silence. She was too exhausted, too exhilarated to say much of anything. It had been *delightfully* too much for her. Too many lights. Too many sounds. Too many people with too many tattoos. In the best possible way.

She'd walked in scared, unsure, feeling out of place, feeling like Sydney was the music person, like she didn't have the right to have opinions of her own, to go to a show that wasn't Syddie's, and then she'd walked out feeling she was part of some movement that she couldn't put words to—that didn't need words.

Ella stole a quick glance at Jake. His eyes were focused on the dark road ahead. His strong hands grasped the wheel.

She owed it all to him.

Finally, they reached the exit that led to Falling Rock. Apart from a couple of bars, the place wasn't much for late nights. It looked like a ghost town as they drove down the main drag, peppered with occasional streetlights and trees but not much else. They passed Trail Mix—it was too dark to see inside—and Ella wondered what it would be in fifty years, if someone would turn it into a hair salon or a yoga studio. She wondered how long people would remember that it was Astrid's place.

She wondered what Astrid thought of it now.

After a few more blocks, Jake turned onto her street. It was a windy night, and she watched as the trees swayed around them.

He pulled into her drive and put his foot on the brake, but he didn't turn off the car. Ella heard the *vrum-vrum-vrum* of the motor, counting down the seconds they had left together.

Jake turned down the music—not like him—and turned to face her. "Thanks for coming with me," he said.

She smiled (why could she not stop smiling?) and she looked down at her purse. "Thanks for taking me," she said. "It was amazing."

Jake smiled, too. "I'm glad you liked it."

She opened her purse, fumbled with her wallet. "How much do I owe you?"

"Oh," Jake said, putting his hand on hers. "Don't worry about it."

"Oh," she snatched her hand away, and she knew that that made it more obvious than ever. "Are you sure?"

"Just get me a latte at the café next time."

"They're free for us," she said.

"Well, make one for me then."

Ella laughed, and as much as she just wanted to think about the music and the night and the way Jake's eyes crinkled a little when he smiled, she knew that if she didn't bring it up now, she never would. "I know your mom said it was okay for me to work today, but I don't know how much Grace really wants me there anymore. She was really upset last night."

Jake looked at his hands. The engine still ran. He didn't look at her when he spoke. "My mom will keep you on, don't worry," he said. "I'd miss you too much if she didn't."

The engine puttered on. She couldn't help but smile at the thought of him missing her, but still she wished he would say something else. She wished he'd talk about Grace.

Ella cleared her throat. "But Grace is still mad?" she asked.

Jake hesitated. "You probably should be getting inside," he said. "It's late."

"Okay," she said, but she didn't move. "Thanks again." She turned towards him then, looked him right in the eyes, hoping that he would change his mind. Hoping he would let her in.

But he didn't say another word. He just looked away, focused his eyes on his hands, the steering wheel, anything but her.

She didn't have a choice. She grabbed her purse and slowly opened the door. She was out of the car and her feet were on the concrete when he stopped her.

"Ella," he said.

"Yes," she turned back, catching her breath. And at that moment, she didn't even know what she wanted more—for him to say something about Grace or for him to just say something to *her*. She didn't even know what he could say. What words could accurately describe how she felt in this moment, with the good and the bad all tangled up together? *What did she feel?*

"You shouldn't worry about Grace," he said.

"Okay," she said, hesitantly, waiting for him to say more, wishing so much that he would. Wishing that she could know everything that he knew. Right now. Was that why she was so excited to be around him, or was it something else?

"I mean, you can't always take what she says—*what she does*—to heart."

"What do you mean?" she asked.

"It's not totally her fault."

Ella narrowed her eyes at him. "She threw me out of her house. I wasn't even trying to—"

"I know," he said with a sigh. "I'm just saying, don't take it personally. It's not about *you*."

Ella looked at him like she didn't know him, because for a second, she felt like she didn't. *It'll be okay*, she wanted to hear. *You guys will work it out. She'll let you back in. She'll be okay.* But not that she shouldn't care. How could she not?

"You know I practically grew up in that house. With her. She was like a second mother to me. How could I not take it to heart? I know I'm not one of you, but I feel things just like you guys do."

"Whoa," Jake said. "Calm down. I didn't mean it that way. I don't mean that you don't have a right to be upset. I just meant that—"

"You just meant *what?*"

"I just meant that sometimes Aunt Grace, well sometimes, she just doesn't know what she's saying."

"You keep on saying things but you aren't saying what you mean."

Jake looked ahead in front of him, as if reading the front of her house for answers. He glanced down at the clock. "Don't worry about it, okay? It's getting late," he repeated.

She was getting so close, and now he was cutting her out. Just like Grace had.

"How am I not supposed to worry about Grace? Why don't you just tell me what you're talking about? I have a right to know—I probably spent more time with her than you ever did."

He looked straight at her then. "No," he said. "You don't. I know you loved A, and I know you spent a lot of time at her house, but it's still *our* family, not yours. You really should just stay out of it."

Ella felt like she'd been hit with an anvil. What had happened? How had things gone so terribly wrong? This was Jake. Nice, sweet, near-perfect Jake. What had she done?

But his face stayed tight, not open like it usually was. His gaze was firm.

"Fine," she said. "Thanks for tonight."

And she slammed the car door shut and walked inside without looking back.

CHAPTER FOURTEEN

The next morning, Sydney's phone rang persistently, jolting her out of her sleep.

She picked it up and strained to focus at the name on the screen. *Ella*. Probably to give her another lecture about how she should care more. As if she didn't. It wasn't that easy to just burst into tears every other conversation. She almost wished it were.

She hit ignore and rolled over.

But in minutes it was ringing again. She looked at the clock. It was almost eleven. She probably should get up anyway. The fair was today, and she wanted to dye her hair, even though Astrid, the one who'd always done it before, wasn't here to help.

She let it ring through without hitting ignore and sat up in bed. She stared into the mirror over her dresser. Her roots were showing and she was tired of red, anyway. Even if it was a totally different, completely artificial, Red 40 kind of red, it still reminded her too much of Astrid.

She wanted a change.

Her phone started ringing again.

"You don't give up, do you?"

"I'm sorry," Ella said. She sounded tired. "Are you up?"

"Well, I am after you calling me three times."

"I'm sorry," she said again.

"Stop saying you're sorry," Sydney said. "Why did you call?"

There was silence on the other end and then a rush of words. "I didn't mean it, Syd, really. I don't think that you don't care. I was just freaked out and scared and you were calling me crazy, and I was just trying to defend myself, I was just trying to explain . . ."

"By implying that I don't care that Astrid died?"

"No," Ella said, and even through the phone, Sydney could hear the girl getting emotional. Here we go.

"I loved her, too," Sydney said. "I miss her every day. Every second. Maybe I don't cry as easy as you, and maybe I'm not scared and freaking out, but I still feel it. All the time."

"I know you do," Ella said. "I know."

"Do you?" Sydney asked. "Because you act like I just want to forget about her."

"I know," Ella said. "I'm sorry I said that. But it seems so easy for you."

"It's not."

"Okay."

There was silence. Staggered, dragged-out silence.

Sydney knew that neither of them wanted to talk about the one thing that must be on both of their minds. The words that Ella had spoken, the ones that started the whole fight. Could Ella really believe that? The freak-out about the phone call, the dreams, the obsession with the cabin staying just as is—it had all seemed at least semi-normal until now. But this was new—this was a whole other level.

Sydney's anger softened as she tried to put herself in Ella's place. As she tried to imagine being so torn-up, so distraught, that her mind could take something so far . . .

"I'm sorry," Ella said again.

Sydney took a deep breath. "Okay," she said. "It's fine. Let's just not talk about it. We both said a lot of things that we regret."

More of that brutal silence.

"Can I come over?" Ella asked.

Sydney shook her head. "I have to get ready for tonight. I have to dye my hair."

"I can help," Ella said. "I've done it on my mom before."

"This isn't highlights, El. It's a whole bleaching, dyeing thing."

"I can do it. It's all on the box, right?"

"Yeah," she said.

"Astrid always managed just fine."

And it was out there. Just like that.

"Admit it," Ella said. "You need me."

Sydney ran her fingers through her hair and flopped back down on the bed. There was no use fighting Ella when she wanted something, whether it was an A on her calculus assignment or a date with Ben. She always got it in the end. "Okay, okay," she said. "Fine. You win."

"I'll be over in twenty," Ella said. And she hung up the phone.

Sydney was installed in the upstairs bathroom, box opened, towels out, and tools spread around her, by the time Ella arrived.

That was how Astrid always did it. Neat and orderly.

"Hey," Ella said as she walked into the room. She set her bag on the counter and surveyed the plastic cap, the powdery dyes. "This looks doable."

She picked up the box, reading over the directions, eyebrows knit. "Purple Passion?" she asked, laughing—it was nice to see Ella laugh for a change—"Who names these things?"

"I like the name," Sydney said, looking at herself in the mirror, taking one last mental snapshot of the way she looked with bright red hair. "It suits me."

"Alright," Ella said. She clasped her hands together. "Let's do this. Head down."

Ella began to rinse her hair under the spigot, and it felt nice, relaxing. Like she could stay there forever.

Ella turned the water off and carefully lifted her head out from under the spigot. Sydney toweled off her hair while Ella began to mix the peroxide.

"So what did you do last night?" Ella asked.

"Nothing," she said. "Just practiced." In reality, she'd talked to Max on the phone for an hour about nothing in particular.

"That's cool," Ella said. She paused what she was doing. She so obviously had something to spill.

"Well go ahead," Sydney said. "What did you do? You want to tell me."

Ella rolled her eyes, but that didn't stop her.

"I went to a show."

"A what?" She whipped her head around to face Ella, splashing water all over the mirror.

"A show," Ella said, a mark of annoyance in her voice. "You know, where people go up on stage and play instruments."

"Very funny," Sydney said, wiping down the mirror. "But you never go to shows. Where was it?"

"Pinbrook."

"To see who?"

"The Black Rabbits."

Sydney narrowed her eyebrows at her friend. She didn't know that Ella had even *heard* of The Black Rabbits. "You went to see The Black Rabbits?" she asked. "With who?"

"With *whom*," Ella said, but as she said it, she blushed, and the beginnings of a smile crept up at the corners of her mouth. A smile that could only be about a . . .

"Oh my God," Sydney said, and it came to her so quick that she knew she had to be right. "You totally went with Jake."

Ella shrugged.

"So Ben was okay with it?" Sydney asked.

Ella put the mix down and put her arms on her hips. "It's not a crime to go to a show with a friend, you know."

"So you didn't tell him."

Ella sighed. "I told him I was going to a show. He didn't ask who I was going with."

Sydney shook her head in disbelief. In the midst of what seemed like a near mental breakdown, Ella was carrying on a flirtation with Jake. It was so un-Ella.

"And don't get too excited," Ella added. "He was an asshole at the end of it."

"What happened?" Sydney asked.

"I don't want to talk about it."

Sydney smiled because she knew that meant that Ella definitely *did* want to talk about it.

"He just started to tell me about Grace and then he stopped and he thought I was prying, and—"

"Were you prying?" Sydney asked.

"Of course I was prying," Ella said. "Would you expect anything less?"

Sydney couldn't help but laugh. Ella was always indignant when she thought she was in the right—which was very, very often.

And for a second, she sounded just a little bit more like herself.

An hour later, Sydney's hair was smeared with purpley goop and covered in a plastic cap.

"How much longer?" Sydney asked.

Ella looked down at her watch. "Five minutes."

"So you're definitely going to stay for the show tonight, right?" she asked, looking at Ella in the mirror. They were sitting on the edge of the bathtub, waiting.

"Of course," Ella said. "Why wouldn't I?"

"I don't know," Sydney looked down, but Ella lifted her chin back up.

"You don't want it to drip all down your face," she said.

"I thought maybe since you just went to a show last night—"

"Syd, I don't have like a music cap for the weekend."

Syd laughed and so did Ella. "Okay," she said. "So how many pots did you make this year?"

Ella looked down at her hands. "I didn't make any," she said. "I totally forgot until yesterday, and it was too late to dry, and I just—"

"You *forgot?*"

"I know," she said. "Trust me, I was upset about it."

"It's really starting to burn," Sydney said. "Can we rinse now, please?"

"Okay," Ella said, turning on the water.

"I thought you had like a date book that you wrote everything important down in."

"I do," Ella said. "I just haven't looked at it since . . ."

Sydney pulled the plastic cap off and leaned her head over the sink. She looked back at Ella. "You going to help me rinse this?" she asked, but Ella was staring straight ahead, as if in another world.

"Sydney, that's it!" she said.

"What? What's it? This really is burning."

"Sorry," she said, walking up to the sink and slowly pushing Sydney's head under the spigot with a touch too much force. She talked louder than the water.

"That's it," she said again. "The important place where you write things down. Astrid's journal. Maybe she left a note in there."

And just like that, things were so far from normal again. Like that, they were back where they had been, just yesterday. Sydney wanted to say something—she wanted to tell Ella that they couldn't know that for sure, and that even if they did, they couldn't very well get their hands on the journal—after the other night, Ella would probably not be invited back to Grace's anytime soon—much less read it. She wanted to beg her to forget about all this and to just enjoy the fair tonight. She wanted one night—just one night—where they didn't have to talk or think about Astrid.

But she couldn't. Ella would think that she didn't care about Astrid—or her.

And the thing of it was, she did care. So much. That's why it was so hard to see Ella like this, obsessed. Looking for answers, looking for a sign, when Sydney knew in her heart that anything they could find would only make them feel worse. What could be in a journal, in a note, but solid, undeniable proof that they'd failed her?

She felt the water run cool against her scalp, and as it rushed around her, she squeezed her eyes tighter. She felt Ella's fingers in her hair. "I'm telling you, Syd, she's trying to tell us something. When we were in that cabin, I just knew."

Ella dug her fingers deeper, washing off all the goop, unveiling something fresh and slick and beautiful, and Sydney thought of

Astrid's hands, softer, doing the same thing. The way when they were done she'd always say, in her old-timey voice, "Alright, Miss Collette, I think you're ready for your close-up." She thought of how, if she'd only tried to see Astrid, to *really* see her—instead of just the color of her stupid hair—how maybe none of this would have happened. But it had—*God,* it had—and now she just wanted to forget. She wanted Ella to give up this fixation, so they could just be normal again, so they could grieve together, move on together. But Ella was too caught up in the cabin and the journal and all of the things that would never, ever bring Astrid back.

And then the thought hit her like a brick—she could lose Ella, too. Maybe not physically, definitely not in the same way, but they could grow apart, they could lose touch, they could change.

They were so different, but Astrid had always been the one who held them together. With her gone, there was no guarantee their friendship wouldn't die, too.

That's when she felt it: tiny streams. Hot against the cool water rushing around her. Tears. The water keep running, until all of the goop was finally gone, and she knew that Ella wouldn't even see that she'd cried.

That night, Sydney tugged on her bow, letting it moan. *Wail.*

The crowd screamed and cheered along, going wild.

They were right on the edge of the woods, and Sydney's hair matched the sunset, which danced behind the clouds.

She finished the note as Max began to sing the last verse, and the crowd was singing, dancing, clapping on the off beats—they were finally starting to catch on, they were really getting a following—just like Astrid had always believed that they would.

Max stopped singing—there was only one note left—and Sydney dragged it out, feeling the momentum, the rush of it all. Letting her fiddle cry.

And she looked out at the crowd, and her eyes caught Ella's, right near the front, and for a second she saw her smile.

And then with a quick flick of her wrist the show was over.

"Thanks for coming," Max's voice rang out. "We're River Deep!"

Once their equipment was safely off stage, Sydney and Carter finished packing up while Max chatted it up with a giggling, longhaired fan-girl. He always said that in order to be successful, they needed to engage with the crowd. Give them a little something to love. Well, he certainly was giving *her* plenty. It was like watching a train wreck. Max went on about the power of the music while this wide-eyed freshman just drank it right up like cheap wine.

Sydney rolled her eyes, and Carter just shrugged, but she couldn't help feeling a weight in her gut like one of those river rocks. Not the kind that are good for skipping. The kind that just sink.

Shouldn't he be sharing this moment with them, with her? Shouldn't she be the one he was smiling at, going on about the music? She knew that he was just getting back at her for throwing him out the other night. But couldn't he just yell at her? Couldn't they talk about it?

"You were great," Carter said, smiling all wide. Like he did.

Sydney zipped up her case, wishing that it meant as much coming from him. "Thanks."

The two of them carted the last of the gear over to his mom's minivan, where a bright-eyed Mrs. Cheever was mirroring her son's goofy smile. She was their unofficial equipment manager.

"Y'all were fabulous," she said. "Just fabulous."

"Thanks mom," Carter said, wrapping an arm around his mother. He was almost twice her size.

"And you, Syddie. That voice. You're going far dear. Very far, I always say. Don't I, Bubs?"

Carter winced at the name, even though Sydney had heard his mom use it a million times. "You certainly do."

"Thanks," Sydney said, and Carter hugged his mom goodbye, and in a minute it was just the two of them, and they were quiet. Out of the corner of her eye, she could see Max, walking towards another stage, blond freshie in tow.

Sydney scanned the crowd for Ella. She'd said she'd meet her here after the show.

She looked at Carter. "You haven't seen Ben, have you?" she asked. Carter shook his head.

Sydney pulled out her phone to see if Ella had texted her. Nothing. She sent a quick text. *Where are you guys?*

"You want to wait?" Carter asked, as she threw her phone back in her purse. "I'm hungry."

"Hungry or hangry?" Sydney asked. He was so tall she had to look almost straight up to meet his eyes.

"Bordering on the latter," Carter said with his puppy dog face. "Barbecue?" There was a stand not too far away that had the best pulled pork sandwiches in the whole entire world.

Sydney looked back down at her phone. It had taken them almost an hour to get everything fully packed up. Ella should be here by now.

Carter leaned down towards her. "They'll find us," he said. "They probably just wanted to catch the next act or something."

"Okay," Sydney said, but she didn't quite believe it. Ella was one to stick to plans.

"Come on," Carter said. "Let's at least get something to eat."

They got their sandwiches and headed back to the main stage, just as Broken Brothers were beginning their set. The group was a Falling Rock institution, complete with long curling gray beards, potbellies, wifebeaters, and suspenders. Once, long ago, they'd had a little success in Nashville. Now they mainly performed on the street corners in the summer and dominated the local folk scene. Carter loved them. So did everyone. Sydney stared at the saxophone player, thinking of Astrid and her mysterious, never-talked-about dad. Was that why she'd always loved music so much? Did he play for her? Which songs? Why did she have all these questions now, when it was way too late?

"You okay?" Carter asked, and she nodded quickly. She didn't want to get upset right here, right now. She scanned the crowd again for Ella—nothing. She pulled out her phone and checked it for maybe the tenth time. No new messages.

"Aren't they awesome?" Carter asked.

"Uh huh," she said, but she was so damn distracted. By thoughts of Astrid, worries about Ella. Everyone. So she pulled out her flask and took a swig. She wanted to actually enjoy this. She *loved* this band. She didn't want to waste the whole night.

Ella was fine. She was probably *just fine*.

And there was nothing she could do about Astrid. It was something she had to accept—or forget. She chose forget.

She took another swig and then offered her flask to Carter, and he took it happily. Everything Carter did, he did happily. He took a drink, handed it back.

She didn't wait to take another. "One more?"

Carter gave her a look like he was considering signing her up for AA. "You okay?" he asked.

"Yeah," she lied. "I'm fine. Yes or no?" She pushed the flask back at him.

He shrugged. "What the hell? It's our night."

Our night. The words buzzed through her as he took the flask from her, their hands touching as he did. His fingers were warm like the whiskey going down her throat. They felt nice.

Broken Brothers kept going, and the music strummed all around them, and there were so many people now, and she and Carter finished the contents of her flask, and as the sky got darker, the crowd got thicker. The liquor made her feel cozy, lit a fire inside her chest—made everything light, just like she wanted. She stopped checking her phone, and she pushed away thoughts of Max and the blond girl, and before she knew it, her body was moving along with Carter's. They were swaying side to side, her shoulder grazing his arm. And she looked at him, and he looked down at her, and then the banjos strummed louder, sweat dripping off of the old men's faces, and for a second, she was happy again, and then Carter slipped his hand in hers, and it was just friends, really, it was just a friendly thing. It was just Carter showing he cared, having fun, and for a second he clasped her hand tighter, and she wondered if maybe she had always been wrong . . .

"Sydney!" She heard a voice behind her. Startled, she let go of Carter's hand and turned around.

It was Ben.

"Have you seen Ella?" he asked. His face looked tense, strained, like he was trying to push away thoughts that he didn't want to have.

Sydney shook her head. "I haven't seen her all night. I texted her but she didn't answer."

"I can't find her," Ben said. "After your set, we went to get food, and we were standing in line together, and then I turned around, and she just wasn't there."

"Maybe she went to the bathroom or something," she said.

Ben's face softened for a minute. "I looked all around. I couldn't find her. Maybe you could go in and check?"

"Sure," she said, even though her blood was already pumping faster.

"You need me to do anything, dude?" Carter asked.

But Sydney shook her head before Ben could answer. "I'm sure she's just in the bathroom," she tried to sound confident. "Don't worry about it."

And she grabbed Ben by the arm before Carter could protest. Having Carter with them would only make it worse. Then it would be a search party, and she was sure that Ella had just gotten distracted or gotten caught in the bathroom or that the barbecue didn't sit right with her or something. *Nothing's wrong.*

She and Ben pushed through the crowd and finally made it to the clearing. Behind them, people cheered as Broken Brothers finished a song.

"Did you call her?"

"Of course I called her," he said, and the strain was there again. "Straight to voicemail. Her phone's probably dead."

There was a set of skeevy public bathrooms near the river. "Be right back," she said to Ben, and Sydney pushed through the line of girls and didn't bother to stop and explain. She ignored the protests, walking inside. Water pooled on the bottom of the tile floor.

"Ella," she said loudly, walking down the aisle, looking under each stall for a pair of sandals she would recognize. A pair of sandals she'd known for years. "Ella?" she called again. Nothing. Suntanned girls came out of the stalls and pushed around her.

"Ella," she tried one more time. There was no reason to worry. There was really no reason to worry. They were being ridiculous. But she knew she hadn't thought that there was any reason to worry about Astrid either. And now she was dead.

Sydney walked outside, and Ben's face fell when he saw her.

She shook her head, without bothering to explain. "Come on," she said. "We'll check everywhere. Don't worry," she said. And she said it so convincingly that she almost believed it herself.

The craft stalls and tables were deserted. The vendors had long stopped selling. Most of the tables were turned over, in the process of being packed up and carted away. A few stray artists were still putting up their stuff. Still, they walked the length of it, calling Ella's name. Nothing.

There were three stages, and they pushed through the crowds of each one. They didn't bother to find Carter again. Sydney's heart beat faster with every face she saw that wasn't Ella's. Nothing was happening, she told herself. Nothing bad was happening. But that was the thing. That was the shittiest part of it. That feeling she'd had once, that feeling of safety, that feeling that bad shit happened to other people, not to you, that was gone. That had left quickly with Astrid. Bad things did happen. Bad things happened every day. There was no reassuring yourself that everything would be okay. Because if Sydney had learned anything this summer, it was that it sure as hell wouldn't.

The food was set up near the edge of the woods. It was after they'd retraced their steps multiple times that they saw it—an opening, a clear one, a path, into the thick woods—and she knew beyond a doubt that Ben was thinking the same thing that she was.

He was the one to speak first: "Does that lead to your cabin?" he asked.

Yes, she knew. Yes, of course. Because they'd taken that same path a million times to get to the river. To tube and sun and talk about things that now seemed so meaningless, so trivial. Because she knew that Ella had been obsessed with that damn cabin since those photos had appeared. Because she'd been obsessed with anything Astrid might have left behind since she'd gone and left them.

"Yes," she said, her voice surprisingly calm. And she walked forward, away from the lights and the music and the sounds and the smells of the fair.

Straight into the thick and heavy darkness where she knew Ella would be.

CHAPTER FIFTEEN

Ella hadn't intended to leave. But she'd definitely seen red.

Ben had been in line, ordering more sweet tea, and someone stepped on the back of her heel, and when she turned to cast an annoyed glance, she forgot about the redneck behind her. That was when she saw the red, glistening in the light of the moon and the stage and the corndog machine.

She turned back to Ben, but he was already up at the front, paying, and then the red was gone, disappearing into the woods, and she knew that she didn't have a whole lot of time, and before she could even remember making a decision, she was pushing through the crowds and drowning out the music and focusing all her senses on that one point in front of her.

She knew that Ben would freak, and Sydney would definitely think she'd lost it. She would have texted, but her phone was dead. She felt a chill as soon as she stepped into the woods. There were no lights now—she didn't have her flashlight. She didn't have anything. But up ahead, she heard the light rustle of leaves. She knew that someone was out there.

Her heart pounded as she pushed through the brush and tried to stay on the path. She didn't go this way as often, and never in the dark. The sounds of the woods were amplified now that she was away from everyone else—the flutter of wings, the clicking of cicadas was so loud, she felt like it would overtake her.

She stopped to see if she could still hear the rustling. It was silent up ahead. What if she really had lost it?

But in moments she heard loud thuds. Ella broke into a run, pushing leaves out of her face, moving only by the light of the moon.

"Stop," she screamed. "Wait!"

Branches scraped against her, and the goosebumps prickled on her arms, on the back of her neck, even on her calves, as she ran as fast as she could.

The crackling thuds turned softer, reaching the clearing. Ella quickened her pace, and she was almost there—God help her, she was almost there—she was terrified, but she couldn't stop—and she could see the faint light of the clearing and that flash of red, but before she could get out, her toe caught on one of the roots—and she wailed in pain as her knee hit hard, sharp rock.

She heard the rustling again. Running. Leaving. Why oh why was she always leaving?

Ella ignored the pain, grabbing a branch, and she was almost up, almost ready to keep running, keep chasing until she got an answer, but then the branch gave way, and she lost her balance, tripping forward, into the clearing, and for an instant she saw the cabin—its door wide open, beckoning—until her foot caught another root and she was stumbling again, her body twisting as she fell, her head hitting the ground with a thud.

And in an instant, everything went black.

She didn't know how long she was out, but when she woke up, she was on the ground, staring up at the stars. Right away she remembered why she was here.

She pulled herself up to a sitting position and carefully drew her knee towards her chest. Pain shot through her body and from the eerie light above she could see that her shin was covered in blood. Her head ached.

Slowly, carefully, she stood up. She knew she should turn around right then and head back to the fairgrounds to find Ben and Sydney. But she didn't know what time it was. She didn't even know if they'd still be there.

Her whole body ached now, and she needed to sit down. Just for a minute. Just to get herself together.

She walked slowly towards the cabin, each step sending knifelike pain through her leg. She reached the porch and pulled the door open. She walked in, dragging it shut behind her.

Ella ambled her way over to the cabinet—she could at least light some candles and figure out what to do next. Chills ran up and down her spine as she inched forward, one hand on the wall, darkness surrounding her completely. The smoothness of the photos of Astrid guided her way.

There was a smell. One she couldn't place, but one she knew that she knew.

And then she wasn't touching the photos anymore. She felt it, the cabinet, their cabinet, the rough-hewn wood and the crack down the middle. She found the handle and pulled, and she felt a pain, a dull, solid pain in her toe as something landed on her foot. She knelt down, slowly, hanging on to the handle so she wouldn't fall, and she found something smooth, round and cylindrical, then skinny at the top. She held it up to her nose and sniffed. An empty wine bottle.

Ella put the bottle down, and felt her way to the candles. She fiddled with the matches, and then she struck one, and all of a sudden there was light before her. She lit the candles as quickly as she could and then shook out the fire of the match.

Lifting one of the candles up, she turned around, gasping as she realized where that smell had come from. There were flowers everywhere. Some in pots, some strewn about the perimeter of the room. White flowers. Pink flowers. Frilly, ugly, and cheap. The perfect flowers for a girl who always pulled for the underdog—who preferred stale, candy-dish candy to chocolate; bad horror movies to anything with an actual plot.

The flowers that everyone kind of hated. Well, almost everyone.

They were carnations. Astrid's favorite.

CHAPTER SIXTEEN

The door of the cabin was open when they got to the clearing.

Lights flickered from inside.

Sydney ran in as fast as she could and screamed when she saw Ella, lying there, curled up on the ground, surrounded by a circle of candles that made her skin look pale and ghoulish. But that wasn't the worst part. It was the flowers. All around her. Everywhere.

Astrid's flowers. The ones she always said never got their due. The ones she thought were so pretty even though no one else ever did. Carnations.

In a flash, Ben was behind her, pushing her out of the way. He knelt down next to Ella, knocking the candles over. Wax spilled across the floor.

Ella's eyes flickered open. She looked startled, as if coming out of a dream.

"Hey," she said. "Hey." She started to sit up.

Ben had his arm around her, but his voice was stern. Angry. "Are you okay? Why did you just leave me like that? We were worried sick."

"I'm fine," Ella said, looking at Sydney now, too. "I'm fine."

But Sydney shook her head. This was bad. This was really bad. She'd known Ella was upset, she'd known that she was having a hard time dealing with everything, but this? She'd turned this cabin into a tomb, with flowers and candles and her lying right there in the middle. It was sick.

"What are you doing?" she asked. "Why the flowers?"

"What do you mean?" Ella asked. "I didn't put them here."

Ben looked at Sydney then, his eyes questioning. Scared.

"How did they get here then?"

"I don't know," Ella said. She stood up now, with Ben's help. "They were here when I got here."

"And the candles?" Sydney asked. "They were just sitting here, too?"

"No," Ella said, like it was the most obvious thing in the world. "I got them from the cabinet, and I lit them."

Sydney looked at Ben, trying to get a read on what he thought.

"What?" Ella asked. "Why are you guys looking at each other like that? You think I did all this? You think I put all this here?"

Ben stared at Sydney for a moment longer before turning back to Ella. He was questioning her, just like she was. It was written all over his face. Ben had never been a good poker player—he wore his emotions like his state championship ring—out in the open, for everyone to see.

"No," Ben said finally, and his voice was soft and trying to be comforting but it came off as patronizing. Sydney knew that Ella would hate that. "No we don't. But you've been gone for almost two hours. What have you been doing?"

Ella looked at Sydney then, her eyes imploring her to believe her, to stand up for her, to explain to Ben all of the other kooky stuff that had been going on. But she couldn't. Maybe if this was the only thing, maybe it would have been easier to take. But the flowers, the phone call, this new claim of a *message*, and now the obsession with the journal—none of it made sense. What if this was just Ella's twisted way of dealing with Astrid?

Sydney looked down. At her feet and the cracks in the wood floor beneath them.

What if this, the flowers, the photos—all of it—had been Ella the whole time?

She looked back up and Ella was still looking at her, but differently this time. Defeated. She turned back to Ben.

"I'm sorry," she said. "I didn't mean to run off. I thought I saw something in the woods, and I was only going to be gone a minute, and—"

"What?" Sydney asked. "What did you think you saw?"

Ella looked at Sydney, then back at Ben. "It doesn't matter," she said. "I thought I saw someone I knew."

Jesus, Sydney thought. *Good God almighty she's losing it.*

"And then I fell, and I came here to rest—"

"You fell?" Ben asked, his voice rising to panic.

"Yeah," she said. "Trust me. I'm okay."

"Did you hit your head?" Ben asked.

"Yes, but—"

"Geez, Ella, you could have a concussion."

"I don't have a concussion," she yelled. "I'm *fine*."

"Fine," Ben said, throwing his hands up and taking a step back. "You don't want me to help. I get it. But maybe instead of just disappearing you could have actually told me where you were going or why you were leaving and not have left us freaking out—"

"I'm sorry," Ella yelled again. "Okay? I'm sorry. I can't change it now."

Ben looked at Sydney, obviously asking for some help.

But she didn't know what to say, what she could say, that would convince Ella that they couldn't go on like this. So she knelt down, grabbing a bunch of the flowers, then another. It was the only thing she could even think to do.

"What are you doing?" Ella snapped. She ran up to her. "What do you think you're doing?"

Sydney didn't answer. She just kept picking up more flowers. This had to stop.

Ella grabbed her arm, jerking her around. "Stop it," she said. "Stop it."

"Why do you care?" Sydney was yelling now, too. She knew she shouldn't, but she couldn't help it. "Why does it matter? You said you didn't put them here."

"But someone did."

"Who, Ella? Who?"

But Ella didn't answer. She grabbed at the flowers in her hands, clawing at them, trying to get them back. Petals fell to the floor.

It was too much. The wild look in Ella's eyes, the candles, the darkness, the smell of those flowers. It was suffocating her. It was swallowing her whole.

And in a flash, she let go. The stems and petals fell to the ground between them.

"Fine," she yelled. "If this is what you want, have it. It's yours."

And she ran out the door before they could stop her. She pushed into the woods and moved as fast as she could, not caring about the brush and the branches at her ankles. Not caring about the scratches she felt with each new step. Not bothering to watch out for thorns or burrs or the tricky areas.

She didn't care if she hurt herself. She just ran.

Broken Brothers were packing up, and the crowd was beginning to disperse when Sydney got back.

She stopped to catch her breath, and she heard her name.

"Sydney," Carter said, emerging from the dwindling crowd. "What happened to you? Are you alright?" He looked down at her legs, his eyes narrowing.

She followed his gaze. They were covered with scratches from her quick escape, and a thin line of blood ran down her right shin. She looked at Carter, and his eyes were so open and caring and . . . *good* . . . that in a second she knew she could trust him. She knew that, in some way, he'd understand. He always did.

"No," she said. "I'm not alright." And the story, the night, came rushing out of her—the way they'd found Ella in the cabin, the flowers, their fight. How she knew that she'd lost Astrid, but she was afraid of losing Ella, too.

When she was done, Carter gave her a hug, a strong one, the kind that she needed, the kind that she never got from Max, who'd kiss her and touch her but never just hold her with nothing else involved. His skinny arms surrounded her, and she could feel his muscles tense, like he was putting everything into this one simple hug.

Her cheek pressed against his chest, and after a minute, she felt his hand in her hair, stroking it softly with his fingers, his fingertips just barely grazing her neck, and then he squeezed and pulled her tighter, and she wanted to dissolve into him, to be absolved by him, to lose herself in this one embrace, this one moment, this solidness, this buoy in the jagged sea that was her summer.

And when he pulled back, he wore a smile, like, *I'm still here. I'm still holding you.* But instead, he said, "Come on. Let's get you home."

Everyone was in bed by the time they got to her house. The two of them tread quietly—her mom would freak out if they woke Darcy—and Sydney headed to the bathroom and fumbled around until she found the first aid kit, tucked in a cabinet behind George's economy-sized fish oil caplets and Darcy's old Pull-Ups.

Sydney grabbed two beers from the fridge—she didn't care if they noticed tomorrow—not tonight, not now—and she flipped on the porch light and headed outside.

She sat down on the swing, and Carter took the beers and uncapped them on the buckle of his belt. She smiled up at him as he handed her one. That was her Carter, her favorite enigma; one minute he was going on about relationship advice, and the next he was doing party tricks like he was training to be a frat boy.

He took a big sip, and his mouth instantly scrunched up. "What the hell is this?" he asked.

"IPA," she said. "It's good." That was the one thing that she had to hand to George. His all-natural snobbery had exposed her to a lot of good beer. Even if it was only by sneaking one or two at a time.

"Sure doesn't taste like Natty," he said.

"You mean it doesn't taste like watered-down piss?" she asked, taking a sip and savoring the bitter hoppiness, the weight and presence of it. "No, it doesn't."

Carter shrugged. "I guess booze is booze."

Then he kneeled down so he was right in front of her, almost like he was going to propose or something, but he just set his beer down and opened the first aid kit.

"Now," he said. "About those legs."

They didn't need words now, not anymore. There was already the humidity, the moisture all around them, rich and thick, filling the space. And the sound of crickets and the hoot of an owl, coming from the woods. And the smell, the smell of honeysuckle. The sweet smell of honeysuckle reminding her that it was summer, after all; that there were good things in the world. That everything didn't smell like old cabin and burning candles and saccharine carnations.

Carter wet a cotton ball with hydrogen peroxide and ran it over her legs. It stung softly, fine little scratches of pain, but it wasn't so bad. He worked slowly, cleaning up the blood, now dried, along her legs. He was good at this, and it was incredibly soothing. And despite the heat, she got chills at his touch. Little pinpricks. Goose pimples. Like her legs knew it more than she did, that there was something new here. Unexpected.

He dabbed on some Neosporin and bandaged her cuts, and then they drank, and they talked, and they laughed even. About the worst song she ever wrote. The girl Carter had had a crush on last year, Lisa Long, who was just as irritating and annoying as her name promised she would be.

"Her hair's platinum," Sydney said.

"You're one to talk. You dye your hair like once a month."

"Oh, you know you love it," Sydney said with a smile. "Come on, it's my signature. Plus, it's not frosted like I'm trying to get on *Girls Gone Wild.*"

Carter smiled. "Yeah," he said. "I actually don't know why I even went for her. She's not really my type."

"Oh, you mean bleach-blond, tall, skinny, and perfect looking isn't your type?" Sydney asked, raising an eyebrow.

"You just said you hated her hair," Carter said. "Now you think she's perfect looking?"

"I don't," Sydney said, taking another sip of beer. "But I know that everyone else does."

Carter chuckled at that, but his laugh dipped down a notch. "Trust me," he said. "She's not my type."

Sydney felt her face get hot, felt a blush starting to form, but she wasn't exactly sure why. Their two beers turned to four, which, in turn, became six. There was no way that George wouldn't notice now. When the last beers were drained, they stood up, and Carter stumbled, and so did she. She grabbed onto his shoulder for support.

"I'm not sure if I should drive home," he said.

Sydney hiccupped. "You want to walk?"

Carter tripped over the door frame as he stepped inside. "I'm not sure I should walk either."

Sydney looked at the clock. It was two A.M. She couldn't very well throw the boy out on the street.

"You're not just pretending so you can get in my pants, are you?" she asked, between hiccups.

Carter held up his hand. "No," he said. "Scout's honor. I can sleep on your floor."

"Okay," she whispered. "But you're going to have to sneak out tomorrow."

"No problem," he said.

"Come on."

They tiptoed up the stairs, carrying the six-pack of empty bottles with them. When they got to her room, she shoved the evidence in the back of her closet and sunk into her bed, kicking off her shoes and tossing a pillow and a blanket over to Carter.

"You need anything else?" she whispered.

Carter shook his head. "Just sleep." He stretched out on the floor. The blanket was way too small for his body, and he looked like some kind of a giant in a nursery school.

Sydney stared at the ceiling and pulled the sheets up over her. A few moments later, she kicked them off, letting the fan blow against her body. Sleep, she thought. Pure, easy sleep. Wouldn't that be nice? No dead friends. No cabin. No flowers. No freshman groupie. No worries about the future. Just pure and unadulterated rest. When was the last time she'd had it? When she was a child? When she was drunk? After she and Max hooked up, before she snuck out of his room and headed home in time for the whole-grain family morning routine?

Sydney turned on her side.

"Carter," she said.

"Yeaahh," he mumbled, his words a slur.

"Are you awake?"

A pause.

"Carter? Are you awake?"

"Uhhh huhhhh."

Her mind was fuzzy from the beer, but she needed to ask, before she lost her nerve. "Do you think," and her voice started to crack, and she saw Astrid's face, at the party, at the cabin, in this very room—ready, almost ready to say something, begging for help even though she'd never really asked for it, begging to be asked—but she kept going. "Do you think that if maybe I had been a better friend Astrid wouldn't have done what she did?"

"Ah, Syddie," Carter said, and he sat up, and their faces were so close. "No, I don't. I really don't."

She took a deep breath. "I do."

His eyes glistened in the light of the window, and they could have kissed right then, right there and then, and it would have been easy, and every question that they'd had about each other would have been answered, at least a little bit, right in that moment. But that's not what she wanted. Not right now. Maybe not ever.

"Come here," she said.

"Up there?"

Sydney nodded, even though it was too dark for him to see.

"Come lie with me," she said. "Nothing else, okay? Just that."

"Sure," he said, and he stood up. He set the pillow next to hers and crawled in. He was so big and gangly that his feet hung right off the edge. And without asking, like it was the most natural thing in the world, he turned on his side and draped his arm across her. And she turned, cuddling against him, feeling the weight, the strength of him behind her. And he squeezed her tighter, and she shut her eyes, letting sleep steal her away.

CHAPTER SEVENTEEN

Ella winced as a dull burst of pain shot through her leg. She was on her way to Trail Mix, and it was hot. Her palms were sweating, and she pushed the hair out of her face. Her phone buzzed, and she pulled it out of her purse. Ben.

"Hey, I can't talk long," she said, without waiting for him to speak. "I'm on my way to work."

"I just called to see how you were. I know things were rough for you last night."

Ella paused. She wished she could just take it for what it was, Ben checking up on her—he was so damn sweet—but thinking about everything made her sad. After Sydney had stormed out, she let him lead her slowly back to his car, her arm draped around his shoulder the whole time. He made her sit with him for an hour, making sure she was okay to go to sleep. They talked about everything and nothing, he apologized for yelling, and he said that he understood, that she could always talk to him, and then he took her home, and he kissed her long and sweet like they used to, and she felt his arms tighten around her, and she knew that he should be all that she wanted, that he should be the one she could turn to. But as she pulled her lips from his, she couldn't help but think of the way he'd looked at Sydney in the cabin, like he almost didn't believe her, and she knew in her heart that he just didn't understand. He couldn't.

"I'm okay," she said.

"You sure?"

"No."

Ben was silent on the other line, working out something to say to that.

"You want to hang out tonight?"

Ella paused—she was free, technically speaking—but the idea of hanging out with Ben made her feel tired and worn out. She knew she should appreciate what he was trying to do for her, that she should go to him, let him help her. Problem was, it wouldn't help. She knew it wouldn't. What she needed right now was not going to come from Ben.

"I think I just want to take it easy," she said. "I'm not really up for anything."

The disappointment was thick in his voice. "I love you, El. I'm just trying to help."

The tears stung her eyes, but she held them back. "I know. Tomorrow," she said. "Let's do something tomorrow."

Ben's voice perked up a little. "Pat's having a party. You wanna go?"

Pat McAllister was their kicker and one of Ben's best friends—he was actually nice but it was always all good-old-boys and cheerleaders at those parties. She was totally not in the mood to go. But she knew she owed it to Ben.

"Sure," she said. "Let's do it."

"Alright babe," Ben said, his voice a little lighter. "Get to work."

"Okay," she said. "Talk to you later."

And she could hear him say "I love you" again as she hung up the phone.

Ella opened the door to Trail Mix to see Jake at the front, wiping down a table. He looked up as the door clanged behind her.

"Hey," he said, a smile wide across his face. "I'm glad you're here."

And the sight of Jake, smiling at her, made her feel so happy, so relieved, that she forgot to be mad about their argument from the other night. It was just good to see him. So good.

"Hey," she said. She headed behind the counter to set her stuff down and grab an apron. Becky was at the machine, cheerily making a latte. She waved.

"I was thinking you could take register," he said, looking right at her. "Or would you rather brew? Either's fine. Becky's on the machine."

"I can do the register," she said. "Thanks."

"No problem," Jake said with a smile. "Whatever you want."

The next four hours flew by—there was a line of customers almost to the door the entire time. She stayed on the register, Becky made the drinks, and Jake bounced back and forth between the back room and the front. There was so much she wanted to tell him. And they hadn't had a single minute together.

They finally hit a lull when her shift ended, but by then, Jake was in the back room with his mom, door closed.

Ella hovered at the counter, taking extra long to divide up the tips, hoping Jake would come out of the back before she left—after what had happened when she'd walked in on Claire and Grace, she was scared to just walk right in.

But in minutes her replacement came—a new girl from the college —and she had no choice but to go.

So reluctantly she took her share of tips, tucked her apron in one of the cabinets, said goodbye to Becky, and left.

She was nearly off the premises when she heard her name called from behind.

Her heart nearly jumped out of her chest.

It was Jake.

"Hey," she said. "Did I forget something?"

He shifted his weight from one lanky leg to the other. "I didn't get to talk to you at all in there. I wanted to say bye."

She had to stop herself from grinning, right there in front of him.

"Well, bye," she said. And then she did let herself smile.

Jake laughed. "Bye."

She wished that she could just tell him everything, right then. But she could see more customers going into the café. She knew that he had to go back.

She adjusted the bag on her shoulder. "I'll see you later," she said, and she turned around and started to walk away.

"Wait," he said, bounding over to keep up with her. "How are you getting home?"

"I'm walking," she said. "It's not that far."

He put his hand on her shoulder, his fingers on the place where her bare skin met her tank top. "Let me drive you home."

His hand seemed to hold her in place. "Don't you have to work?" she asked, a part of her praying he'd say no.

"It'll take five minutes," he said. "It's the least I can do." He didn't wait for her to say yes. "Just give me one second," he said, backing away, releasing her, taking his electric touch with him. He ran back to the café like he'd been given new life. She saw him mutter a quick explanation to the new girl and was right back out.

"Come on," he said, a smile on his face, and she followed him to his car.

She wanted to tell him about last night, but she didn't know quite how to start, so they drove to her house almost in silence. Jake kept taking quick breaths, opening his mouth like he was on the verge of talking, and then shutting it again. It was weird that Astrid's death had brought this strange cheery goofy new person into her life. It was weird that even though they'd known each other only a few weeks, she knew that she cared about him.

It was weird how much knowing that made her miss Astrid even more.

Finally, they reached her driveway. "Thanks," she said.

"I'm sorry," he said. "I'm sorry I said all those things the other night. I didn't mean it."

"You probably did a little bit," she said, but she said it without anger.

He took a deep breath. "Okay," he said. "I did. My family, we just don't talk about stuff like that. You know, all that old-school, 'don't air your dirty laundry' business."

"I know," she said. "It's okay."

But she didn't want to get out, because she couldn't get the thoughts of last night out of her head. She knew that if she didn't tell him now, that she never would. She wondered if he'd believe her? She wondered if he'd think she was crazy, too?

She took a deep breath. Part of her trusted him. Part of her knew it would be okay.

"There was something I wanted to tell you," she said. "Something happened last night."

He looked at her differently then, his eyes narrowed. "Is everything okay?" he asked.

"Yes," she said. "I mean no. I don't know. I was at the fair, and then I thought I saw something—and anyway, it doesn't matter—but I went into the woods, to the cabin where . . ." her voice trailed off. "Do you know that cabin?"

Jake shook his head.

Ella's eyes widened. She'd just assumed that he'd known the whole story.

"Grace never told you about the cabin in the woods near her house?"

"No," he said. "Why?"

And for a brief moment, she considered telling him everything—all of it. How she'd found Astrid there, how this place, this horrible, wonderful place was just steps from Astrid's house, from where he was staying now. She wanted to tell him about the message, about the dreams, the photos—about every worry and thought and fear.

But she couldn't. She wasn't sure if she should.

Was there a reason that Grace had told him something else? Was there something that she didn't know?

"What about this cabin?" he asked, waiting for her to speak.

But Ella shook her head. "It's not really important," she said.

Jake's eyes were wide now, too. Concerned. "Are you sure?"

"Yeah," she said. "I don't know. The point is that Sydney and Ben, they just think I'm crazy for thinking about her all the time. For needing to know why she left. But I just feel like if I did, then maybe all the rest of it would make sense."

He looked right at her then. "I don't think I have the answer to that, Ella."

"I know," she said.

Jake paused. He took a deep breath. "I wish I did. I wish there was something I could do to make it better for you."

And in a second, Ella had an idea. One that she knew she shouldn't voice. One that she certainly shouldn't suggest. But it was there, and she couldn't ignore it, and if she went through with it, if she convinced him, then maybe she would find something that would make it all make sense. Maybe she could convince Sydney and Ben to actually believe her. Maybe she'd understand why Grace hadn't told him the truth.

It was now or never.

"There might be something you can do," she said, finally.

Jake perked up, and even though his mouth didn't follow, his eyes smiled.

"What is it?" he asked. "Anything."

"I'm afraid you'll get mad," she said.

"Just say it."

Ella took a deep breath. She thought about the journal that was sitting right there on the dresser, that she could read if she only could get in there again. The journal that could have the answer that she needed.

She spit it out before she lost her nerve. "I want to see her room again, and I know Grace won't allow it, and I know it's not my place, and I know—"

Jake started shaking his head.

"Don't be mad," she said. "Don't be mad at me for asking. Please."

He kept shaking. "No," he said.

"I know. It's too much."

"No, not no. Not like that. I'm shaking my head because I can't believe I'm about to say yes."

"Wait, what?"

"I'll help you."

"Really?" she asked, relief flooding through her, and promise and possibility and excitement. She was getting closer. In some strange and stupid way she was getting closer to what she needed.

Jake nodded slowly. "Though Grace will kill me if she finds out."

"I won't tell her," Ella said before he could change his mind. "I promise."

"I know."

"How are we going to do it?"

Jake laughed for a minute. "God, we sound like a pair of bad thieves." He turned back to face her. "I'm off tomorrow—can you come then? Grace always goes out for a few hours in the morning."

Ella nodded eagerly. "Yes. Of course. Yes."

"Okay," he said.

"Thank you so much, Jake," she said. "I can't believe you're doing this for me."

Jake shrugged. "You deserve it."

And she felt just the slightest bit lighter, because she knew that he was right.

Ella walked briskly the next morning. It was a lovely day out. Too lovely. She wasn't tired—she felt energized. She'd dreamed that she and Astrid were together in her house, in her room, the things Astrid had cherished spread out around them, the books and the makeup and the clothes and the pictures. Astrid opened her mouth. She moved her lips like she was speaking but no words came out. "Louder," Ella said. "I can't hear you." But Astrid just kept moving her lips. Like she wanted to say something to her. Like she couldn't.

Soon the house was right in front of her. It was still Astrid's house. It always would be. She thought of the first time she'd been here. How Grace had opened the door for her and ushered her into the messy place. How it was fall and they ate tomato soup and grilled cheese while planning out their Halloween costumes.

How Grace had seemed so carefree. She hadn't made them clean up their dishes. She let them rip pages out of all her magazines. They'd looked in her bedroom where there was writing all over the walls. Not all of it made sense, but it was cool. Here was a house where you could write on the walls! Ella had stayed over, and Grace had let them stay up as late as they wanted. She played loud music long into the night. They'd had the house to themselves the next morning. Astrid said that any day she wasn't working her mom would always sleep in really late, whereas Ella's mom was always hassling her to be up by eight—even on a Saturday. But Grace wasn't like that. With Grace, there were no rules.

Ella had never stopped to think whether Astrid had liked it that way. She'd never stopped to think what it was like when she wasn't over. What it was like for Astrid then. She'd never stopped to think about what the writing on the wall actually meant.

Ella hovered on the sidewalk near the mailbox, hesitating to walk right up to the door. She felt like she was breaking some rule. Grace had invited her in once, and now she was taking advantage of that. But so many things had changed since then. Things didn't make sense anymore. It wasn't as simple as tomato soup.

She took out her phone and texted Jake: *I'm here. All good?*

He responded almost immediately: *Yeah. She's out.*

Ella slipped her phone back inside her pocket and walked carefully towards the door. Jake opened it up before she could even knock.

He didn't smile like he normally did. Maybe he was back to protect-the-family Jake. Maybe he thought that this was somehow wrong. And in a way it did feel wrong, sneaking around because the mother of your dead best friend would be mad if she knew what was actually going on. But Ella didn't care, and apparently Jake didn't either. He opened the door wide, and she carefully walked in.

It was weird being in the house with just Jake. In a way, she'd even call it exciting.

"How's your day?" he asked, standing in the hallway, obviously attempting to talk about anything other than the one person who'd brought them together. Who'd brought them here.

Ella smiled. "It kind of just started."

Jake laughed. "Yeah, I guess it did." He walked towards the kitchen, and she followed him in. It was the natural thing to do.

"Do you want, like, a drink or anything? Some water?" he asked.

Ella shook her head, and the two of them leaned against the countertops, facing each other. She shoved her hands in her pockets, and Jake stared at the ceiling. Why was this so hard? Why couldn't she just go straight to the room she wanted, to the place that maybe, just maybe, had an answer for her? She knew why. Because she wasn't supposed to be here. This wasn't her family. This wasn't her problem. This was his territory, and even though she was in the door, she felt like he was defending it, like he was walking the line between wanting to help her and keeping up the family status quo.

So she looked at him and said it with her eyes. *Please.*

And even though he'd already said it was okay, he seemed to make a choice, to cross a line, right there in that moment. "I guess you just want to see her room," he said. Ella nodded.

"Come on."

They walked down the hall as if walking on a tightrope. Carefully.

Astrid's door was shut tight. Like, *Keep out. You know you're not supposed to be here.*

"Jake," Ella said, putting her hand on his arm, and he felt so warm and safe, she wished that she could touch more of him. She wished that she could touch all of him. She wished that she was allowed.

Jake turned to her.

"Thank you for doing this," she said. "I know what a big deal it is."

Jake nodded, and their eyes stayed locked. And they were so close, so painfully, excitedly close, that it felt like it would be wrong to pull away.

But Jake broke their gaze, placing his hand on the doorknob, turning it slowly. He walked in before her, and she followed quickly behind. It was the same as it had been before. Everything frozen in time, as if Astrid had never left.

Had she?

They stood there in the middle of the room, and for once she didn't want Jake near her. She didn't want Sydney, and she didn't want Ben. She just wanted to be alone. She knew that she *had* to be here alone.

"Is it okay if I just sit here for awhile?"

Jake nodded. "I'm just going to watch TV," he said, but before he left, he looked right at her. "Just try to keep things as they are," he said. "I have a feeling Aunt Grace would notice."

"Of course," Ella said, even though she had no intention of following that rule. Jake pulled the door behind him, leaving it open just a crack.

As soon as he was gone, she walked straight to the dresser. She wanted to see it. She wanted to read it. She wanted to take it, damn it.

But she stopped short.

The necklace. Astrid's necklace. The one she always wore. Every day. The one that she had died in.

It was hanging right there, right on Astrid's jewelry tree. How had she not seen it before? And in an instant she realized what had bothered her so much at the wake—why she had looked so not like Astrid. It wasn't just the makeup. It wasn't just the dress. It was that she had never before seen Astrid without her necklace.

And in that moment, she realized that the necklace wasn't buried with her like it should have been. Here it was, hanging with her other chains and lockets.

Why had this silly key been so important to her? Why hadn't Grace let her wear it in her death? Ella had asked her once why she always wore it. Astrid simply told her it was the key to one of the drawers in the desk in her house—that she'd put it on long ago and liked it so much that she'd never taken it off.

That had been answer enough for Ella then. Now, it wasn't.

She picked the necklace up, running her fingers along the slim, silky red ribbon that acted as the chain. She held the metal key in her hand—it was lighter than it looked. She squeezed tight, feeling the swirls at the top, the divots at the bottom, and she opened her hand back up.

But in the hall, she heard footsteps, and she realized that Jake wasn't going to let her just hang out in here forever. She carefully put the key back in its place—she could think about that later—she needed to get the journal before she worried about anything else.

Ella ran her eyes along the top of Astrid's dresser.

But the journal wasn't there.

Ella heard more footsteps, and she didn't stop to think. Grace had hidden it somewhere. She knew that she had. She opened the top drawer.

She flipped through, nothing but t-shirts and tank tops. One from the fair. Another for River Deep that the two of them had handmade with those felt letters you get at the craft store. She pushed the drawer shut, moved on to the next one, whipping it open.

There were dresses, lots of dresses. Beautiful ones that Ella had borrowed, cotton and silk and polka-dotted and striped. Ella flipped through every one, each bringing to mind a memory, a dance, a party, a day in the woods. And in an instant her finger felt something smooth. She quickly pushed the clothes aside and there it was. A thick, beat-up, leather-bound notebook. The one that Astrid was always scrawling in. The one Ella had seen so many times—in classes, when they were at the lake, on a long car ride—the one that seemed to steal their friend sometimes. The one that took her to another world, took her inside her Astrid head, shut them out.

Ella took the notebook out of the drawer with shaking hands. A part of her almost hated it. Maybe if Astrid hadn't been so devoted to it, to this thing, this inanimate, falling-apart thing, then maybe she would have told them something. Maybe they would have been able to actually help her. Maybe they wouldn't be in this mess.

Maybe Ella wouldn't be sneaking in rooms, weighing the importance of skeleton keys. Maybe she'd be spending one last high-school summer with her best friend. Maybe she wouldn't be left chasing after a ghost.

Ella's heart raced as she stared at the book.

"You okay in there?" she heard Jake through the door, and she jumped, dropping the journal on the floor.

"Fine," she said, and without hesitating, she slid the drawer shut, picked the journal up, and tucked it safely in her purse.

CHAPTER EIGHTEEN

Sydney woke up missing Carter.

She didn't expect it—it surprised her, really. It's just that the morning before had been so nice. She liked waking up with his arm still snugly tucked around her. Slowly dragging herself out of bed and looking at him as if they had a secret. Their awkward high-five good-bye because what else could she really do? Softly opening the window and watching his lanky body climb down the tree.

She liked the way a day later her bed still smelled a little bit like boy.

Sydney reached her arms above her and stretched her legs across the bed. There was so much space without him in it.

She knew that she didn't like him like she did Max—her heart didn't quicken when she looked at his face—he wasn't nearly as beautiful—he wasn't nearly as smooth. Instead, she liked his gangliness, his silliness, the way he could hold her and make it all better, even if just for a second. She liked the fact that he was Carter.

Sydney rolled over and grabbed her phone off the nightstand. It was noon already. She almost wanted to send him a message. They hadn't spoken since he'd left yesterday morning, and they'd see each other again at practice tonight—she wanted to make sure they were still on cool, friendly terms. No matter what may or may not be going on, she wasn't ready to process it. Not yet. But what would she say?

Thanks for staying over—you were decidedly not creepy about it.

I don't think I like you, but I don't think I don't like you either. What do you think?

I might have been just leading you on to get back at Max—let's not take it too seriously.

Promise me this won't ruin our friendship.

Maybe we should just pretend we didn't cuddle?

Do you need any more socks?

But it didn't matter, because her phone rang then. It was Ella.

She held the phone in her hand, deciding whether to answer. They hadn't talked since she'd stormed out. She didn't know what to say, how to say it. Part of her felt that Ella wouldn't even listen to a word she had to say—and certainly not to reason. But the other part of her—the *I want to be a good friend* part—knew that Ella needed her now more than ever.

She clicked answer. "Hey."

"I'm glad you answered." Relief flooded her voice.

"Is everything okay?" Sydney asked. "I meant to call yesterday . . ." her voice trailed off.

"It's okay," Ella said quickly, almost dismissively. "I have something to show you. Can I come over?"

"Uhh, sure," Sydney said reluctantly. She was afraid to deny Ella anything right now. Anything that could help her even a little bit. "Just give me like an hour to shower and stuff. I'm still in bed."

"I'm outside your house," Ella said.

"What?"

"I came straight here. I need to come up."

"You said everything was alright."

"It is," Ella said. "I just have something to show you. Trust me, I've seen you without makeup before."

Sydney couldn't help but laugh. "Okay," she said. "Come on."

Almost instantly, she heard the doorbell ring and her mom's footsteps. Ella wasn't kidding when she'd said she was right here. She was up the stairs and in Sydney's room in seconds.

"Geez," Sydney said, pushing back the covers and hopping out of bed. "You don't waste any time." She pulled on a pair of pants while Ella caught her breath. "Okay, okay," she said, flopping back down on the bed. "What is it?"

Ella threw her bag down and pulled out a leather-bound book. It looked familiar. It looked like . . .

Ella tossed it over.

"Whoa," Sydney said. Her hands began to shake as she realized what it was. "Is this—"

"It's Astrid's," Ella said, her voice shaking as much as Sydney's hands.

Instinctively, Sydney threw it back on the bed. It was her friend's. It was probably one of the last things that she had laid her hands on. It was her personal property, her deepest darkest secrets. It was everything Sydney hadn't asked her, everything she'd been dying to tell. Everything she'd died without telling. Sydney felt scared and dirty and curious all at once.

"How did you get this?" she asked.

Ella paused—it looked like she was weighing whether to tell her the truth or not. "I took it from her room," she said finally.

Sydney shook her head. "How did you even—"

"I needed to read it," Ella said, and in that moment she seemed so genuine, so real, that Sydney almost believed that it was that simple. But then she thought of the cabin and those horrible flowers and every theory and story and she knew that this was just another step down a dangerous path.

"But how?" Sydney asked.

"Jake let me in," Ella said, calmly. "I found it, and I just came here."

"I should have known," Sydney said, and she felt sick all of a sudden. Somewhere along the line, things had gotten way out of hand. Playing around the cabin was one thing, but sneaking into a dead friend's house was another. "El, this is going too far."

Ella sighed. "Since when are you the voice of reason?"

"Since you seemed to have lost yours," Sydney said.

"That's not fair," Ella snapped. "You've never cared about the rules."

Sydney shook her head. "I'm not breaking into people's houses, Ella."

"I didn't break in. Jake let me."

"Okay," she said. "And he let you just take her journal?"

Ella rolled her eyes, as if it were the most obvious thing in the world. "Of course he didn't. I stuffed it in my bag and came straight here."

Sydney looked down at the journal, scooting back on the bed, further away from it. "Ella," she said. "Why did you bring this to me?"

Ella flopped back on the bed, and her eyes crinkled up and Sydney thought that she might cry. But then she took three deep breaths and she closed her eyes and she spoke. Her voice was soft. "I couldn't read it," she said. "I thought about it, but I couldn't. Not alone."

Sydney stared back down at the journal, thinking of everything it could hold. "Ella," she said. "I don't think I can, either."

Ella sat up straight then, her eyes wide again. "Please," Ella said. "I just can't. Please."

Slowly, Sydney picked it up, feeling the width, the weight, of it in her hands. She was terrified, she wanted to make it disappear—to burn it, mail it, put it in some safe deposit box and swallow the key—but yet she couldn't help wanting to know what was inside.

"Please," Ella said. "She was our friend."

Sydney hesitated. "It doesn't belong to us."

Ella's eyes got wide and her voice got louder. "It doesn't belong to *Grace* either."

"We don't even know if she read it."

"She did," Ella said. "Trust me. I just know. Why shouldn't *we*?"

Sydney took a breath. She knew that in some weird way, Ella was right. If anyone should read it, it was them. "Okay," she said slowly, her hands beginning to shake. Maybe, just maybe, it wouldn't condemn her. Maybe even if it did, it would feel better than this—this heavy, abstract guilt.

"Okay."

She flipped it open. "Property of Astrid" stared back at her. Sydney felt the knots tighten in her stomach.

"No," Ella said. "Don't start there."

"What do you mean?" Sydney asked.

"It won't be there," Ella said, her voice raising. "Turn to the back."

She stood up, began to pace back and forth.

"What do you—"

"Just turn to the back," Ella said, her eyes wild, her breathing growing quicker. "If she wrote anything, any note or anything, it would be in the back." Her voice trembled. "Whatever she wrote last."

"Okay," Sydney said. "Just calm down, please. I can't do this if you don't calm down."

"I can't calm down," and her voice was almost scary now, and Sydney couldn't tell if El was about to scream or cry but Sydney looked in her eyes and she felt like if she didn't do it now, Ella would truly be lost.

She turned the book over quickly. Opened it. Stared at the page.

Ella looked away. "Just read it," she said, almost as if she were in pain. "Please just read it."

Sydney's eyes scanned the page, and she felt instant relief. She didn't know how to tell Ella that there was no answer—that this wasn't what she wanted. It wasn't their reason. Their goodbye. It was dated the night of their graduation, a few weeks before Astrid killed herself. But she cleared her voice and read anyway, trying to stay steady. Trying to stay calm.

We graduated tonight. We put on our caps and gowns and we walked along to the silly music. Everyone pretended like we were starting some great chapter, but I knew that we weren't. Ella will leave in a few months, even Sydney won't stick around, but I'll be stuck here, and things will be just like they are. I wish that my dad could have been here to see me. Maybe that would have made it better, more bearable. But I know I'll never seem him again. Never—

Sydney threw the book down. "I can't do this," she said, because it was all rushing at her—sucking her back, like the stupid spinning rides at the state fair that always gave her a headache. She remembered the night well—how could she forget it? Astrid had come over before the ceremony to get ready. She'd never been all that into makeup but towards the end of the year she'd seemed to lose all interest whatsoever—it seemed so obvious now, it seemed so much like they should have seen it coming, but at the time it had just seemed like makeup, like the best thing she could do was doll her friend up for their graduation photos—and she knew now that she should have done more, she should have done so much more.

But she hadn't. She'd helped Astrid get ready, lining her eyes with heavy liner and curling her eyelashes, coating her lids with sparkle shadow. The skin around her eyes was puffy. "Are you alright?" Sydney had asked. "It's just allergies," Astrid said. But of course it wasn't allergies. Why in the world had she let herself believe her? Why had she thought she'd had all the time in the world to help her friend?

Ella picked up the book and kept reading, even though Sydney didn't want to hear it anymore. God, she didn't want to hear it at all.

—There's no new chapter for me. Even if I'd applied anywhere, I know that it wouldn't make a difference. There's no other way to look at it, I'm stuck.

Ella shook her head in disbelief. "What does she mean she didn't apply anywhere?" Ella asked, her voice rising to a panic. "She told me she was wait-listed."

"That can't be right," Sydney said, trying to sound convincing. She'd known that Astrid kept things to herself—but that she'd deliberately misled them?—even after everything, it was hard to believe.

How well had they really known her?

Ella read it aloud again. Then she looked straight at Sydney.

"She lied to me."

Sydney struggled to find words that would make Ella feel better. "Maybe that's not what she meant."

"What else could she mean?"

"I don't know," Sydney said. "Nothing."

But then Ella's eyes were wild again. "Maybe there's something else in here," she said, flipping the pages back, scanning each one. "Maybe there's some kind of explanation. Maybe something happened. Maybe she couldn't apply for some reason. Maybe she wasn't really lying."

Ella scanned the book, and Sydney wanted to hug her and hold her and find a way to somehow make this all better. But she couldn't—Ella was on a mission—a mission to find out anything—a mission to memorialize their friend, to practically re-create Astrid's death. But didn't she get it? The more they found out, the worse it got. The more they knew, the further they were from moving on. From finding some kind of normalcy. From enjoying their lives, for God's sake. Why couldn't Ella just let it go? Push it away? It made her angry, and she no longer wanted to hug her, she wanted to shake her, to scream at her. *Give it up. There's nothing we can do. She's gone. Stop trying to bring her back.*

Ella's face fell, and she stopped flipping through the pages. "It's just more of the same," she said. "Graduation. School. She doesn't explain why she lied. She doesn't even say goodbye."

"Of course she doesn't," Sydney yelled. "What, did you think she was going to leave a tidy little note in her diary? If we wanted to know, we should have asked. We should have asked her before it was too late."

"But," Ella said, "but we didn't know."

"We should have," Sydney said. "What is all this going to do now? It's too late. It won't bring her back. It won't change anything!"

Ella shut the book and stood up quickly. "Something is going on," Ella said. "Look at the cabin. Look at the things that have happened to me. Look at what I've seen."

Sydney shook her head. "We can't have this conversation if you're not even going to be logical."

Ella raised her voice then, too. "When have you ever been logical? How many times have I urged you to apply to a good school or to end things with Max or to finally just forgive your mother for the fact that she's happy? But no, it's always about some feeling you have. Now I have a feeling and you're ignoring it. I guess I'm not allowed to go by my gut like you are."

"You're talking about things that are crazy," Sydney yelled. "You're talking about things that are impossible."

Ella shook her head, her eyes darting about the room. "You'll never understand if you don't want to," she said. "You'll never—" but then she stopped because her eyes locked on Sydney's nightstand,

and in an instant, her voice took on a new tone. The hopelessness was gone. Replaced by something else. "What's that?"

"What?" Sydney asked, but as she turned to follow Ella's gaze, she knew. Her friend's eyes were frozen on her aunt's book. That damn book. Boy, was this not good for her cause.

Ella pointed at the bewitching offender.

"Nothing," Sydney said. And she flipped it over, as if to negate its very existence. Which didn't help. At all.

Ella quickly grabbed it. Her voice was calmer now. She had purpose. "The other history . . ."

Sydney interrupted her. "My aunt gave it to me. She just pushed it onto me like all her mumbo jumbo."

"I know what it is," Ella said. "But I didn't know you were *reading* it."

"No," Sydney said. "I was just looking through. Just to see what all the fuss was about. Since everyone in this town seems so totally caught up—"

But in moments, Ella's whole demeanor had changed. "You totally were reading it. Like . . . like a tiny part of you believes me."

"No," Sydney said, trying to keep her voice firm. Or at least as firm as possible under the circumstances. She had been caught red-handed. Why, oh, why hadn't she at least put a cover around the thing? "No, I don't."

"Oh, but you do," Ella said. "Just a little. Or you wonder." She had a smile on her face for the first time in maybe . . . forever. A real one. Not the cloying type that she favored when she was trying to make a point. "Do you think that everyone in this whole book is crazy?"

"Umm, it is possible," Sydney said, sarcastically, but Ella just ignored her.

"And you think your aunt is crazy, too?"

"Again," Sydney said. "Totally within the realm of reason."

"And me?" Ella asked, her lips almost forming a pout.

And that was the thing. That was what got Sydney—every time she thought about the flowers and the candles and all that Ella seemed to believe—that had kept her reading the stupid book when she knew that she shouldn't. Ella was a bunch of things—bossy, proper, indignant—but crazy had never been one of them. She was the one who reasoned, who made the right choices, who ran through all the consequences before taking a single step. And here she was just begging Sydney to break every rule of logic, to believe that their dead friend was trying to talk to them, almost like they were twelve-year-olds sitting around a campfire.

She couldn't do it, but she couldn't very well condemn her friend to insanity either. There had to be an explanation.

"I don't know," Sydney said. "No, I don't think so. I *can't* think so, but Ella, listen to yourself. It doesn't make sense. Listen to what you're saying, to what you're asking me to believe."

But that was enough.

"I'll prove it to you," she said. "I'll show you. You'll feel it. I know you will. You loved her too much not to. Don't you get it?" she asked, her eyes wide. "We're the only ones who can. We're the only ones who knew her, who loved her well enough. We're the ones that she's reaching out to. No one else. Just us."

"But you *can't* prove it," Sydney said. "There's no way."

But Ella was flipping through the book quickly. "I know it's in here somewhere."

"How do you know?" Sydney asked.

"My mom has a copy," she said. "Your aunt gave it to us ages ago."

Sydney couldn't help rolling her eyes.

Finally, Ella stopped. "This is it," she said. "The last chapter, 'Communicating with the Dead.'"

"Oh, God," Sydney said. "You're not serious."

"We could go to the cabin," Ella said. "Tonight. We'll sleep there. Just like old times."

"We could never get through a single night there," Sydney said. "We were always running scared back to Astrid's house within an hour."

"All the more reason to finally do it," Ella said, her eyes still alight.

But Sydney just shook her head. "I have band practice."

"We can meet up after," Ella said.

"Come on. Just say that you'll give it a chance. Just say you'll try it."

Sydney hesitated, looking at her friend. She wanted to cross her arms and say no. She wanted to say absolutely not. She wanted to grab Ella and shake her and make her believe that whatever was going on, it wasn't going to bring them any closer to healing.

And she opened her mouth to do it. Even though she didn't believe what Ella was saying, the thought of going back there made her feel ill. She wanted to be far away from it all.

But Ella's eyes were so sad and so hopeful and so passionate and so *angry* at the same time that she was afraid to say no. As much as she hated the idea, she hated the thought even more of Ella doing it alone. She remembered Ella's words that night at Johnny's. *You have to be there for me. It's your job. You're the only best friend I have left.* She knew that Ella needed her now more than ever.

And the thought pressed down on her from all sides, squeezing her, crushing her—what would have happened if she had done more for Astrid? Had been there for her when she needed her? How much differently could things have turned out?

Where would they be now if she'd only bothered to open her eyes—to ask?

Sydney took a deep breath. "Okay," she said. "But this is it—this doesn't mean I'm going to play detective with you or read her diary or sneak into her house or look on Facebook for messages that don't exist."

"Okay," Ella said. "But you'll do this with me. Tonight?"

Sydney let out a defeated sigh. "Yes," she said. "We get done around nine."

Ella's smile broke across her face again, lit it up like sunshine. Haunted, deranged sunshine. "Can I borrow this?" she asked, holding up Aunt Audie's book. "I don't want to have to dig up our copy."

Sydney nodded.

"Great. Meet you at the cabin, then," Ella said with authority.

"Meet you at the cabin."

CHAPTER NINETEEN

Ella headed straight to the cabin as soon as she left Sydney's house. She wanted to read through the rest of the journal before tonight, and their old haunt seemed like as good a place as any.

Ben called her on the way, but she quickly hit ignore. She didn't want to talk to him right now. She didn't want to talk to anyone right now. She had too much on her mind—too much to figure out—too much to prove.

When she got to Astrid's house, she hurried through the side of the yard. The dewy grass wet the edges of her sandals, and she couldn't help feeling like she was being watched. She stopped, looking back at the house, but the shades were all drawn.

She took a deep breath. She knew that she needed to stay calm, now more than ever. She could feel that she was getting so close.

The clearing was bright and sunny. Carefully, she opened the door and held her breath, unsure of what she'd see on the other side. She stepped in, but things were just as they had been the other night. Flowers. Candles. No sign of a difference. She let herself breathe.

The room smelled faintly of coconuts. *Had it been like that before?* But she wouldn't let herself be scared—she spread out the blanket, took out the journal, and sat down.

The "Property of Astrid" page sent a jolt through her, but Ella quickly flipped past it. They'd already read part of it—she might as well do the whole thing. But she stopped—thinking of her friend, scribbling in this thing over and over, always shutting it tight when she was done—Astrid hadn't shared this with her. Was it really okay for her to just jump right in like she would a paperback novel?

But Astrid hadn't shared anything with her. And now she was gone. If she knew more, maybe she could have done something. If it hadn't been for all her damn secrets, she might be alive today.

Ella took a deep breath and turned the page. It started when they were sixteen, in just eleventh grade. The beginning was fairly mundane —even normal. The pages were filled with Astrid's tight handwriting, sometimes so tight that the lines were filled double. It was almost as if Astrid had set out to make this one book last her whole life. Ella felt a pang of sadness as she realized that it had worked.

She found the usual journal scribblings. Did this today. So and so broke up with so and so. A boy smiled at me in class. I dropped my pencil and he picked it up. I wish he liked me. Ella couldn't help but smile as she remembered every crush her friend had had that year—they'd all called it the year of the boy. Sydney had long discovered and, according to her, mastered, the art of the French kiss; Ella had had quasi-boyfriends, the ones that hold your hand between classes and kiss you behind the soda machines in the lunchroom, on and off since fourth grade, but Astrid hadn't even given boys so much as a look until that year. The pages were full of them. Johnny, the Emo Boy in her art class; Thomas, the wavy-haired Music Whiz who wasn't quite popular but was still friends with their entire class; Matt, the too-cute-to-be-a-Math Geek; the list went on.

There were so many boys. Probably not a single one of them knew that the quiet, reserved girl was filling her diary pages with detailed descriptions of the shapes of their earlobes. But she and Sydney had still pressed her for the details on every crush, no matter how fleeting and short-lived. She and Sydney had been the ones Astrid let in.

As Ella read on, the pages became less about boys and more about the things they did. Sydney got a car. They had more mobility —more fun. Astrid described in detail the first time they'd gone to the rock quarry, the way the water felt on her skin, even though she only ever dipped her toes in. She talked about clothes and the new dresses she got. She talked about how stupid Sydney could look sometimes when she was drunk.

It was as if nothing ever went wrong. Astrid never talked about missing her father. She never even mentioned her mother. She never mentioned any of the bad things that happened between them—when Sydney had accused Ella of being jealous of Max, when Ella had decided for a week or two to sit at a different lunch table with some of the other football players' girlfriends (she still felt bad about that). None of that was there as she turned the pages. There was a description of her newest purchase from the thrift store, down to the last polka dot, but that was all. There was nothing to tell Ella why she'd gone and left them. There was nothing to give any indication that she'd had so much of a reason to leave. But still, there was a wrongness to it. Ella could see it in the strain of the almost-touching letters, in the way she pressed down her pen so hard. Reading it now, it seemed almost fake. All the bad stuff forgotten—all the good stuff in brilliant detail. It was like a Technicolor picture—so bright and vibrant and amazing—but the colors were off.

Was Astrid still okay then? Or was it all just another lie?

The light through the window dimmed, and Ella's eyes were beginning to feel strained. She set the journal down and walked to the window.

Her breath caught in her chest, because in the corner of the woods she saw red hair. A flash of cornflower.

She froze, her heart racing now, and then she bolted for the door, ran to the edge of the woods. When she got there, she stopped. Listening.

Nothing there. No one. Not a single patter. Not a step. The woods would make noise if someone ran through them. Especially right in the middle of the day. When there were no owls or cicadas. When the only noise was that of the running brook in the distance.

She was just about to turn back to the cabin when she saw it. There on a twig, dancing in the breeze.

A tiny piece—maybe a centimeter thick, a few inches long.

A tiny piece of fabric.

Of cornflower blue chiffon.

Ella ran back to the cabin, stuffing the journal and Sydney's book into her bag as quickly as she could.

She had to get out of here—she could calm herself down, get everything ready, come back tonight. It would be okay, she told herself. It would all be okay.

But she couldn't stay here. Not now.

She ran to the edge of the clearing, not bothering to shut the cabin door behind her—she was a few steps into the woods when, on impulse, she turned back, knelt down, and snatched the blue silk from the branch.

This is real, she told herself. This is proof.

She clenched it in her fist and she ran—through the woods and past Astrid's house as quickly as she could. It wasn't until she was down the road, several streets away, that she let herself catch her breath.

She slowed to a walk as she approached her street.

The sun hadn't yet set, but the street lamps were already beginning to glow as an old man stood in his driveway, hosing off the dirt and the clay—everything appeared so normal, so lazy, just like any summer day—and as her breathing calmed, she opened her hand.

And that's when she stopped short. Right there in front of the old man's driveway.

The sheer blue fabric was gone.

Ella doubled back, but it was no use—she couldn't find it anywhere. She got all the way back to Astrid's house, but she didn't go any further—she couldn't take anymore—not until tonight.

So she headed home and ate something and showered and tried to clear her head. She told herself that she'd had it, that she'd held it in her hands. She thought of the vision—of the red hair in the woods—and she tried to piece together what exactly was real and what exactly was not.

When she was clean and calm, she went to her room, flopped on her bed, and opened Sydney's book, flipping quickly through the pages until she reached the chapter that she wanted. When she found it, she scanned her eyes across it, skimming the history of séances and mediums, the benefits of communicating with those who have gone, until she found it, set apart—*Conducting Your Own Séance.*

She'd only gotten to the second step when she noticed the phrase "At least three people are needed." And then she remembered. Even during their silly faux séances together they'd always followed that rule. There'd never been any reason not to.

There'd always been three of them.

Ella shut the book. Who could she ask? There was Ben—he'd probably agree, just to placate her, but she knew he'd be judging her the whole time.

And in an instant she knew—who knew Astrid well enough, who had helped her the most of anyone so far, who she hoped, at least, she could trust.

Jake answered on the third ring.

"Hey," she said, and she didn't wait for an answer. "I need your help. Can you meet me tonight?"

CHAPTER TWENTY

It was the first time Sydney had wished that band practice would run over.

But it wrapped anyway. As it always did. There was no escaping the sleepover-slash-séance from hell.

When she'd gotten there, Carter had greeted her with this ridiculously big smile. Like, *Hey, we shared a bed! I'm going to sit here and just grin about it.* She'd given him a terse "hey" and had been trying to avoid the disappointed look on his face all night. She had too much to deal with regarding Ella. She didn't need any more emotion right now.

Now he was taking extra long to pack up his mandolin, while Max bounced around surprisingly chipper. Maybe he had gotten laid the other night.

"What are you kids up to tonight?" Max asked, as he ran a hand through his perfect hair.

Carter looked up at her like someone who'd just had their Wii stolen. Like, *I don't know, what are we doing?*

Ugh.

"I'm booked for a séance," Sydney said confidently.

"A what?" Max asked. Even Carter's eyes opened wide, his sad-puppy look momentarily replaced by curiosity.

"You heard me," she said. "It's sort of a sleepover, too."

"What are you talking about?" Carter asked. He seemed to have officially lost his hurt—for the moment, at least. Max looked at her, agape.

"Yeah, you're not actually having a séance?" Max asked.

"Oh, I am," she said, her eyes growing wide. "Not like I want to. Ella's gone apeshit, and I have to do that good best friend stuff, you know. Apparently we're supposed to meet Astrid in a cabin, or something."

Carter looked a little incredulous, but Max just laughed. She instantly felt bad—right in her gut. She was supposed to help Ella tonight—not make fun of her behind her back. She didn't mean to portray Ella this way, like someone to be laughed at. She didn't think she was. And yet, when she said it out loud, it just sounded so nuts. It was almost a relief to laugh about it for a minute.

"I gotta see this," Max said.

"Well, bring some booze, because I'm going to need *something* to get through it."

"Uhh, done," Max said, slamming his case shut. "I got a new fake, and I've been dying to try it out."

"Wait, you're serious?" Sydney asked. She hadn't been. She was so averse to the idea, she couldn't imagine that anyone would actually want to join in.

"Why not?" Max asked. "It sounds like fun."

Fun. Sydney was pretty sure that that wasn't the point. And yet, she'd been dreading this all through practice. Would it really be that bad to have another person to get her through it? They could drink and loosen up and maybe Ella could even see how silly it all was. Maybe Ella just needed an outside perspective to show her just how far off course they'd gotten. No matter what happened, she'd still be there for Ella. She'd still be supporting her. That's what was important —that's what she'd asked for.

"I'm coming, too," Carter said. "Sounds cool."

The two of them stood there looking at her, waiting for an answer.

What the hell, she thought. She didn't have the energy to fight it.

"Your ID better work," she said to Max. "Because we're going to need a lot of booze."

CHAPTER TWENTY-ONE

Ella waited for Jake at the edge of Astrid's yard, near the woods.

He was supposed to meet her right at nine, but it was almost nine-fifteen. She shivered. The night was cool now, breezy. She almost wished she'd brought a jacket. But it would be warmer in the woods, where the wind couldn't get them.

Finally, she saw the back door of the house open, his dark hair shining ever-so-slightly in the moonlight.

He walked briskly towards her. "Sorry I'm late," he said.

"It's okay," she said, but as she did, a light caught her eye. Astrid's room. And for a second, she saw Grace, peering out. They were so far back that surely she couldn't see them. Could she?

"You okay?" Jake asked, but the light was off now, and it wasn't worth the worry. She had enough to worry about already—the flowers, the fabric—all of it weighed on her, sent shocks through her body—but at the same time it gave her some glimmer of hope, proof that she wasn't losing it, that there were things she had to uncover, that she was really getting somewhere. That she only needed to know more.

"Did you bring what I asked you to?" she asked, and Jake nodded.

"I've gotta say I've never stolen food for a girl before."

"Thanks," she said. "We didn't have any bread in our house." And she tried to focus on the here and now, to forget about Grace's eyes, staring out at them from that window, about the chiffon, silky smooth in her hands—then gone, like it had never even been there in the first place.

"No worries," Jake said. "But are you going to tell me what's going on? I never took you for the late-night picnic type."

"Just follow me," she said. "I'll explain when we get there."

"Okay," he said. "But Ella, what's that for?" He looked at her hand where she held a hula-hoop. She'd felt ridiculous carrying it over here, and now she felt even sillier, but the book had said that a circle was needed. This was the only circle she had.

"I told you I'll explain everything," she said. "Just come on."

Ella turned her flashlight on and pushed through the first bit of brush. She moved faster once she found the makeshift path. She walked with purpose, because she knew that she still had so much to do. Asking Jake here meant telling Jake, letting him know the truth, that this was the place that Astrid had killed herself, instead of whatever Grace had told him. She hadn't had the strength for it the other day—she hadn't known if she should—but now that she needed him, she didn't have a choice.

"Whoa," he said. "Slow down." And as he said it, he grabbed her hand, as if it were the most natural thing in the world. She whipped her head back at him. That wasn't supposed to happen.

She shook her hand free, but it burned where he'd touched it.

"Sorry," he said, his voice almost embarrassed. "I just don't have a light—I don't want to lose you."

"Grab my backpack then," she said.

"I'm sorry," he said. "I didn't mean anything—"

"Don't worry about it," she interrupted him. Her head was clear now—and she wanted it to stay that way—free of distractions. She was ready for whatever was coming, and she was ultra-alert. She could hear every sound. Every crack of a twig beneath her feet, the quiet crooning of running water in the distance, the sound of Jake breathing, in and out, in and out.

She felt different, too—walking through these woods that had practically raised her, had raised the three of them—but with some-one completely new—she'd been right, she didn't need a jacket in here. The warm air hugged her, while the trees whispered to her that she was doing the right thing.

Soon they reached the clearing. She shone the flashlight in front of her, and the cabin stood there, almost swayed, basking in the light, waiting for her. For both of them.

"Whoa," Jake said. "What's this?"

"Come on," she said. "Let's go inside."

He followed her across the porch and through the door. Once she was inside, she pulled out the blanket and the candles from the armoire. She put the hula hoop in the middle, the candles inside.

Jake opened his backpack and handed her the loaf of bread.

"So are you going to tell me what all this is for?" he asked.

She shone the light on his face, and he squinted, shook his head. She aimed it lower, by his torso, so she could still see his face, but it looked so strange now, almost like everything was haunted.

"I know it sounds crazy, but I feel like she's trying to tell me something." She pulled out the book and flipped to the séance page. "I thought that, I don't know, maybe we could contact her somehow, maybe we could get some answers. I don't know. It can't hurt to try."

Jake narrowed his eyes at her, which made him look even more gaunt.

"You think I'm crazy?" she asked. "I know everyone does."

"I think you're hurting," he said. "I think you're trying to understand. I don't think it's crazy," he said. "Trust me. I know crazy. You're not it."

She wanted to ask him what he meant by that, but she didn't have a chance.

"The thing I don't understand is, why here?"

She took a deep breath. "That's what I wanted to tell you, and I'm sorry I didn't yesterday. You know the cabin I told you about?"

"I assumed this was it."

"Yeah," she said. Breathing in. Breathing out. "This was our place," she said. "We spent all our time here. With Astrid."

Jake nodded, but his face remained unassuming—naïve.

She was going to have to just come right out and say it. And so Ella clicked her flashlight off, because she couldn't look at his face when she did. Maybe she shouldn't have brought him here. Maybe he'd think it was just cruel.

They stood there, alone, in the dark. Even the bugs outside were silent, as if giving them this moment.

"It's not just our silly little clubhouse," she said. "It's where . . ."

He let her words hang in the air, but he didn't say anything.

"Where she . . ."

"Where she *what*?" But in an instant, his voice changed. "Oh."

She clicked the flashlight back on, but his face didn't look angry. Just sad.

"I'm sorry," she said. "I wanted to tell you the other day, but I just couldn't. I don't know why Grace didn't just tell you—"

Jake shook his head.

"Grace doesn't tell me shit," he said.

"Whoa."

"I'm sorry," he said. "I know I shouldn't say it, but she kept everything from us. She hides so much. We didn't even know that Astrid was having problems, and when your daughter's having issues, and you know that . . ." now his was the voice that was trailing off.

"Know what?" she asked. "Know *what*?" She felt like she was almost begging. She felt like she'd get down on her knees and beg if she had to.

"Let's just say that Grace was probably the least surprised at what happened with Astrid."

Ella shook her head. How could her own mother not be surprised? And if she hadn't been, then why wouldn't she have helped her? It didn't make sense. It didn't make any sense.

"But why?" Ella asked, her breathing getting heavier. "Why wouldn't she be surprised?"

Jake kept shaking his head. "No," he said, taking a step back from her. "I didn't mean it like that. I just mean that Grace has dealt with some hard things, okay?"

Ella's eyes narrowed. She felt that she was getting close. Close to something.

"You mean when Astrid's dad died?"

But now Jake was the one whose brows knitted up, confused. "What did you say?"

"When her dad died," she said again. "Is that what you mean? The hard thing?"

"Who told you that?" he asked. "Who told you that he died?"

Ella shrugged. "Astrid. Grace. Everyone."

Jake just shook his head.

"What is it?" she asked. "What is it that you're not telling me?"

Jake took a deep breath, like he was making a decision. Let her in or let her out.

"Ella," he said, and his eyes looked sad, so sad, like he was losing Astrid all over again. "Astrid's dad didn't die. He left."

Ella shook her head. She felt like her world was coming undone. Alive? He couldn't be alive. Astrid had said it plenty of times. To her. To Sydney. To anyone who asked. *My dad died when I was eight. I don't want to talk about it.*

"But Astrid always said . . ."

Jake spit the words out. "Astrid always said what Grace wanted her to."

"It doesn't make sense," she almost screamed. "You said it, too, when she lost her dad . . ."

"Yeah, she lost him," and now Jake was the one who was yelling. "The bastard just left them, just because things were getting hard. She *lost* her dad. But he didn't die."

Ella shook her head. She didn't believe it. She couldn't believe it. It wasn't just that Astrid had covered up her moods, that she'd told her she'd applied to State when she hadn't—it went way deeper than that. Her friend had been lying to her about her family—about her very own father. The entire time she'd known her.

"Ella, he's alive. I saw him at the wake."

Ella's jaw dropped as it all came together. The man in the suit, crying over Astrid's casket. The way Grace had pushed him away.

But she didn't have time to ask Jake anything more. She heard a noise behind her and turned around to see Sydney at the door.

CHAPTER TWENTY-TWO

"Hey," Ella said, trying desperately to pull it together as Sydney walked in.

Sydney gave her a quick wave. "I hope I'm not interrupting anything," she said, staring right at the two of them. Ella instinctively took a step away from Jake, but she didn't have time to answer before Max breezed in like he owned the place, Carter in tow.

"Oh, sweet, there's, like, candles and everything," Max said. "I should have brought my Ouija board." He set a case of Natty Ice on top of the blanket.

"You guys want a beer?" Sydney asked.

Ella shook her head vehemently. She was already reeling from what Jake had just told her. She didn't need this. Not now. "You can't drink at a séance," she stammered, trying to get out her words without completely losing it—she all of a sudden felt like if she made one wrong move, she'd burst into tears.

"Who says?" Max asked.

She just stared at him, then back to Sydney. "It goes without saying."

"Take a deep breath, and calm down," Sydney said, grabbing one for herself. "Who says spirits don't drink? Come on. Let's sit."

But Ella shook her head. "No," she said. She looked to Jake but he just shrugged—he looked preoccupied. And after everything that had happened, he had a reason to be. So she grabbed Sydney's arm before she could take a seat and dragged her out the door.

"Why did you bring Max?" she asked as soon as they were safely outside.

"Why did you bring Jake?"

"Because we need three people," she said. "It said so in your aunt's book."

"Whoa," Sydney said, her eyes getting so big that Ella could see every stroke of liner. "You really are serious about this."

"Of course I'm serious," Ella found herself snapping. Anger made it easier to hold back the tears. "I thought you were, too."

"I'm only doing it for you," Sydney said, as if that were an excuse.

Ella shook her head as she felt her face get hotter. "If you're going to do it for me, do it for me. Don't just ruin it because you didn't want to do it in the first place. Don't make a joke of this," she said. "Please."

Sydney waited a minute before speaking, and Ella watched her go over it all in her head. Weighing whether to keep fighting or just give in. Sydney had always been an easy one to read.

Finally, her face softened, and she uncrossed her arms and let them hang at her sides. "I'm sorry," she said. "I really am. I just—the whole thing creeps me out and I thought if I brought them, I don't know, it might be easier."

Ella narrowed her eyes at her friend. "But you don't even believe me—why would it creep you out?"

"It just does, okay?" Sydney said. "Listen—I'll make sure they—I mean, Max—behaves. Okay?"

Ella hesitated. Part of her wanted to demand that Max leave—she hated the idea of going back in there and doing it all in front of him. But Sydney was here and she was ready. And Ella didn't know if she'd get another chance to show her. To prove to her what was going on. Whatever it was.

If she asked Max to leave, she didn't know if Sydney would leave with him.

"Alright," she said. "But if he starts doing anything—"

"I'll make him leave," Sydney said. "Promise."

They walked back in together and sat down next to each other, forming a circle, Jake sitting so close that if she turned at all, their knees would touch.

"So what now?" Max asked, opening his beer with an impossible-to-ignore click. "What's all that?" he gestured at the bread and candles in the middle of the hula hoop.

"The bread is for nourishment," Ella said, as calmly and seriously as possible. "It's supposed to attract the spirits."

Max stifled a laugh, but Sydney gave him a shove, coming through, at least. "Shut up," she said.

"Okay okay," Max said, lifting up his hands in mock innocence.

"We'll be good," Carter said, shooting Max a look. "Scout's honor."

Ella cleared her throat. "Jake, you want to take the bread out of the bag and put it on this?" She pulled out a small plate—she'd made it a couple of years ago, and it was one of her favorites, glazed in varying shades of pale blue.

There were already a few candles lit, but she ceremoniously lit three more—she wanted the circle to feel complete.

"What can I do to help?" Sydney asked.

"Just arrange them around the plate."

Sydney grabbed a couple and set them down carefully. They were mismatched, warm and colorful. They smelled like middle school—Vanilla Delight, Lavender Romance—and for a second, Ella was back at her old 8th-grade locker, spraying herself down with some flowery number, Astrid standing next to her, asking to try it—

"What next?" Sydney asked, jolting herself away from the hallway full of kids, from Astrid's face, eager to wear the new scent.

"Okay," Ella said, staring at the people around her: Jake, deep in thought, probably about his family, about how much Grace had kept from all of them; Carter, watching Sydney watch Max; Max, sipping on his beer. They were so far from middle school now. They were so far from even a month ago.

Ella flipped to the first page of the chapter. "It says we should all hold hands."

Max laughed—outright this time.

"Will you stop it?" Sydney asked.

He just laughed harder then. "I'll pass," he said. "We're not in preschool."

"It's so the circle stays unbroken," Ella said, trying not to scream. "You have to."

Sydney grabbed Max's hand, but he pushed it away.

"Hey," Carter said. "Don't be a dick."

"Don't call me a dick," Max said.

"Then don't be one," Carter snapped back.

"Fine," he said, shaking his head and holding out his hands, which Carter and Sydney quickly took. "We should have just gone to Pat's party," he said under his breath.

And that's when it hit her—Pat's party. "Shit," Ella said, louder than she intended. *Ben.* She'd told Ben that she'd go with him. She'd already blown him off once last night. She grabbed her purse and pulled out her phone. She had three missed calls already—she'd turned it on silent for the séance—all from Ben.

"What is it?" Sydney asked.

Ella stared at her phone, deciding. She should stop what they were doing, call Ben, explain that she wasn't coming—or at best, that she'd be late—that's what a good girlfriend would do. That's what a good *friend* would do.

That's what she should do.

But she didn't.

"Nothing," she said. She put her phone back inside her purse and reached for Jake and Sydney's hands. Jake gave her an encouraging squeeze.

"Alright," she said. "Let's go."

She glanced at the book, pushing thoughts of Ben aside. "I'll try and summon her, and we'll see what happens."

Sydney turned to her, her face almost understanding. "You ready?"

Ella nodded. "Everyone, close your eyes. We have to keep our hands locked or the circle will break. Okay, repeat after me," she said.

"We are seeking Astrid. Come, Astrid, and communicate with us."

There was a pause—an agonizing pause—and she wondered if they were all going to burst out laughing at her in a second—even Jake—but then she heard Sydney and Jake join in, and eventually Carter and Max.

"We are seeking Astrid. Come, Astrid, and communicate with us."

Silence, except for a snicker or two from Max. Ella shut her eyes tight, waiting.

Even though her hands were shaking and her mouth felt dry, nothing happened.

After a minute, Sydney leaned towards her. "What are we supposed to do now?"

"I don't know," she said. "Wait, I guess." She took another peek back at the book. *Repeat as necessary.*

"Okay," she said. "Let's say it again. Ready?"

She waited a second, and then she started them off: "We are seeking Astrid. Come, Astrid, and communicate with us."

Silence.

"Uhh, nothing's happening," Max said.

"Shut up," Sydney snapped. "Anything, Ella?"

Ella opened her eyes and looked about the room. God, she wanted something to happen so badly. One tiny thing to show Sydney that she wasn't crazy. To prevent Jake from thinking the same thing. To make Max feel like the asshole that he truly and sincerely was.

But there was nothing.

"Let's say it one more time," she said.

"We are seeking Astrid. Come, Astrid, and communicate with us."

It was silent for a moment, and Ella almost let go.

But then the wind came in fast, rushing around them, shaking the cabin, raising goose pimples on her skin.

In moments, the wind had stopped and silence followed. Ella opened her eyes to see that everyone else had their eyes open, too.

"Don't move," she said, looking straight at Max—then around the circle. "I think I hear something."

"Me too," Sydney said, and for a second, she almost looked scared.

There was a rustling, a definite rustling. Like someone was moving through the woods.

And then in seconds the sound got louder and was followed by a solid thump at the door. A loud one. One that even Sydney couldn't ignore.

"What the hell was that?" Sydney asked, her voice bathed in surprise and fear.

Even Max and Carter were squirming, but Ella didn't want to lose this—not yet. "Keep your hands together," she yelled. "We can't break the circle."

Jake squeezed her hand tighter as the thumps circled the room, on the door, on the walls. Following them. Behind Sydney. Behind Jake. Behind Carter. Behind her.

They were taunting her. They were taunting all of them.

Thump.

Thump.

Thump.

THUMP.

This is what she wanted, she reminded herself. This is what she begged for. But now that it was here, she didn't know if she wanted it anymore. It was too real, now. Impossible to ignore.

"Screw the circle," Max said loudly, unclasping his hands. "Someone is messing with us. We should go see who the hell it is."

The thumps stopped abruptly, and there was nothing but the wind through the leaves and the clicking cicadas and the up-and-down heaving of every one of their chests.

"Why don't you do it if you're so worried about it?" Carter snapped at Max.

"Why don't you?" Max yelled back.

"Because you're the one who's scared."

Ella jumped up before she could lose her nerve. "I'll look." She rushed to the door, whipping it open, because he might be there, she had to be there—Ella couldn't keep chasing and chasing and getting nowhere—but just like this afternoon, there was no one.

Even the branches were still. Keeping secrets.

But she thought of the silk and she thought of the flowers and she thought of the coconut smell, still in this room.

And she knew it as sure as she knew her own birthday.

Maybe she wasn't here now. Maybe she hadn't left a trace.

But she definitely had been.

CHAPTER TWENTY-THREE

Sydney rushed them out of the cabin as quickly as she could. Even though Ella said she hadn't seen anything, they were all pretty freaked.

Once they were out of the woods, they made the impulse decision to actually go to Pat's party—everyone was in agreement that drinks were badly needed—and even Ella seemed eager to go.

So they piled into Carter's car—Jake sat up front, and Sydney squeezed into the middle between Max and Ella. Max looked pseudo-terrified—he definitely wasn't cracking jokes anymore. Carter had his hands tight on the steering wheel and the music turned loud. Jake kept stealing glances in the side mirror—probably to look at Ella, to see how she was. Sydney just looked straight ahead as she tried to figure it all out.

What exactly had happened to them?

Carter hit a speed bump and she went flying into the ceiling, banging her head. Ella turned immediately, while Max just continued to stare out the window. "Are you okay?" she asked.

"Yeah," Sydney said, rubbing the top of her head. Yet another reason why she needed a drink. A strong one. She looked at Ella. She was the only one of them who seemed okay. Amazingly so. "I'm sorry I didn't believe you," Sydney said.

Ella's eyes widened, and she looked almost . . . happy. "You do now?"

Sydney hesitated. Stuff was happening in the cabin. There was no denying it now. But what Ella wanted to believe . . . well that's just what Ella wanted. There had to be an answer, an explanation, that would make it all make sense.

"I don't know what to believe, El," she said finally. "I really don't."

In minutes, they were in front of Pat's house. Sydney had been here once before for some kind of cookout. Cars lined the street, turned every which way, promising them that the party would be big.

The boys got out of the car, but Ella stayed put. "What?" Sydney asked.

"Stay here a second," she said, her eyes super serious. "I need to talk to you."

Out of the corner of her eye, Sydney saw Jake look right at Ella as she said it—then quickly look away.

"We'll be there in a sec," she said, and the boys walked away, leaving them alone.

"What is it?" Sydney asked. "Are you okay? I know what happened back there was really freaky—trust me, I get it—"

"It's not that," Ella said.

"What then?" How could anything be more serious or pressing than what had happened tonight?

Ella looked at her straight-on. "You have to tell me the truth, okay?"

Sydney nodded. "Of course."

Ella paused before she spit the words out.

"Did you know that Astrid's dad is alive?"

Sydney froze.

Her eyes darted around the car—an old soda cup, dirty socks, Ella's face so serious that she couldn't be making it up—and her heart felt like it might jump out of her chest.

"What?" she asked.

"Her dad's alive," Ella said in earnest. "We've seen him."

And Sydney was shaking her head now because she couldn't believe it. The saxophone player. The one who'd been ga-ga for Grace. He was dead. Car accident. Audie had told her. George, too. It couldn't be.

"No," she said. "Audie told me he died in a car accident."

"Yeah, that's what everyone said. It's not true."

"No," Sydney said. "No. It has to be. Audie said."

"Did she go to the funeral? Because Jake says he's alive."

"No," she said. "It was somewhere far away." She realized how futile it sounded as she said it. "She couldn't go."

Ella just stared at her. She waited a minute before speaking. "He didn't die," she said slowly. Surely. "He left them."

"I don't understand," Sydney stammered. "Audie said that they were in love. Audie said that he was nice. She said—"

"I don't care what Audie said," Ella's voice was firm. "Why were you asking her about him anyway?"

"I don't know," Sydney said. "He came up, and then she was just saying all these things, and he sounded so nice, and—and—"

"Why didn't you tell me any of this?"

"You were preoccupied." Ella rolled her eyes at that, but Sydney didn't care. She didn't have time to worry about her being mad—she was too busy trying to put it together. Trying to understand. She knew Astrid was reserved, she knew she didn't like to talk about the bad things, but her dad—she had a dad—living and breathing—and she'd told them he died?

"Wait?" she said. "Wait, what? You say we saw him?"

Ella nodded. "Remember the man in the suit who was crying?"

"What are you talking about?"

"At the funeral."

Sydney racked her brain—she remembered the casket and the way Grace had looked and the way Ella had seemed like she was going to fall apart any second if she didn't hug her, hold her together.

And then she saw him. The man, crying. Crying for his daughter.

And the tears came to her now, so hard and fast that she didn't even feel them coming until her face was wet, and Ella was the one holding her together now, as her body shook so hard that they rocked Carter's shitty old car.

Astrid's dad was alive. And she'd never told them the truth.

And in a flash Sydney knew it, and it was so real, it hurt, sending a new round of sobs right through her.

They hadn't really known their friend.

They hadn't known her at all.

CHAPTER TWENTY-FOUR

Ella managed to clean Sydney up before they left the car and headed into the party. She hadn't checked her phone again. She didn't want to. She didn't want to go at all, really, but she knew that it would be better to at least make an appearance. Plus, she couldn't leave Sydney now. Not until she'd at least calmed down.

It wasn't hard to find Max, Carter, or Jake. They were congregated around the cooler, on an enormous porch that opened up to a view of the mountains that was unreal.

Carter grabbed them beers, and Ella watched as Sydney opened hers quick. She took a gulp—a long one—swallowed, waited a minute. Took another.

"Careful," Ella said, but she opened hers as well, taking a sip as she scanned the yard for Ben. She didn't see him.

Jake grabbed another beer for himself and walked over to where she stood. "Hey," he said. "You guys alright?" He looked from her back to Sydney.

Ella nodded. He narrowed his eyes then and lowered his voice so it was almost a whisper. He leaned in close. "Did you tell her?"

But she didn't have time to answer.

"There you are," she heard Ben's voice behind her. Loud.

She turned around. "Hey," she said, putting on her best fake smile. "I've been looking for you."

"I've been calling you all night," he said. "*Allll* night."

"I know," she said. "I completely forgot, and my phone was off."

"*Why?*"

"For the séance," Max piped in.

She turned to him and gave him a look—not that he cared.

227

"Excuse me, what?" Ben asked, his voice getting louder. "Like to talk to dead people?"

He stared at her, his face red with anger. Or alcohol. Or both. She could tell that he was drunk—and it wasn't like Ben to get drunk.

"I'm really sorry," Ella said. "I should have called you."

"Yeah, you should have called me," Ben snapped.

"Whoa, dude," Jake said, stepping forward. "She said she was sorry."

"Shut up," Ben said, without even looking at Jake. Out of the corner of her eye, she saw Sydney, Max, and Carter slowly step away, giving them space. She wished she could just walk away with them.

"Did he go, too?" Ben asked.

She didn't answer, but that was answer enough. "I see," he said, nodding his head up and down. He threw his arm around her, giving her shoulder a squeeze. His beer can was icy against her skin, and he was holding her too tight. "So you're telling me that you blew me off so you could do something that I wasn't even told about with Indie Boy? Am I missing something?"

"Dude," Jake said, stepping even closer. "It's no big deal."

"*Dude,*" Ben said before looking back to Ella, and back at Jake again. "I wasn't talking to you."

"Hey," Jake said. "No need to freak out."

"No need to freak out? Says the guy spending all his time with my girlfriend?"

"All we did was go to a show together. No big deal."

Shit. Shit. Shit. Shit. Shit. Shit. Shit. Shit. Shit.

Ben turned back to her, his jaw agape. For a second he didn't look like angry Ben, like drunk Ben, like super-annoying, insecure Ben. He just looked like Ben. And he looked like he'd been betrayed.

"What is he talking about?" he asked, as if the whole macho thing had been an act until now. As if he'd really trusted her and was just giving Jake a hard time because he'd had one too many beers. The corners of his eyes turned down slightly, and she knew that she'd hurt him. It made her feel selfish. All hollow inside. "I thought you went with Sydney."

"I never said that," she said weakly, her voice shaky and soft.

"You never said that?" he yelled. His eyes were still sad but there was something else in them now. Fire. "You sure as hell implied it." He took another big sip of beer.

"Hey," Jake said, putting his hand on Ben's shoulder. *Wrong move.* "We can work all this out when we're all a little calmer."

"Get your hands off me," Ben said, giving him a shove. "And stay away from my girlfriend."

"You don't own her," Jake said, giving him a shove back. "If she wants to hang out with me, she can."

"Come on, guys," she said, but they weren't looking at her. "Don't do this."

But Ben wasn't one to be pushed. Especially not in this state. She tried to grab his t-shirt, but he shrugged her off, and before she could do anything else, he was pushing back, tackling Jake to the ground. Girls around her screamed and almost on cue, people crowded around as Ben and Jake's bodies fell to the grass.

"Fight," an annoying, greasy freshman yelled.

The fight-obsessed losers pushed in front of her, but she wiggled through in time to see Ben throw the first punch. Blood dripped down Jake's nose, but even though he was so much skinnier than Ben, he rolled away from him and lashed back, pushing him to the ground, his hand connecting with Ben's eye.

"Stop it," she pushed herself through and grabbed Jake's shirt, digging her fingers into his shoulder. "Stop it," she screamed, but he ignored her, shaking her off. They continued to go at it, and she looked up to see Sydney ushering Max and Carter towards the action. In a matter of seconds, they had pulled the two apart, Max holding Jake back, Carter offering a hand to Ben.

"Jesus," Ben said, still on the ground. Dirt and blood covered his face.

Jake spit in his direction, his saliva tinged with red. "You know, if you weren't such a controlling dick maybe she'd want to spend more time with you."

Ben jumped up at that, but before he could get anywhere, Ella stepped in the middle of them.

"Stop," she screamed. "Stop it!"

They calmed down, as if only now remembering why they were fighting in the first place. Her.

She turned to Ben. "You're drunk, okay? We'll talk about everything in the morning when it's clearer and you can realize what an ass you've been." Ben shrugged as he wiped some of the dirt from his face.

Then she turned to Jake who looked almost decidedly smug. "I don't need you to defend me," she said. "And I don't need you to mediate my relationship. And I definitely don't need you to judge who and who is not controlling me," she snapped. "I'm in control of me. No one else." And before he could protest, she pushed through the sweaty bodies around her, getting away as quickly as she could.

Sydney was right there, waiting for her, but Ella just shook her head. Between the journal and the cabin and the news about Astrid's dad and the breakdown in the car and now this, she didn't have any energy anymore. She didn't have the energy to be sad. She didn't have the energy to talk about it. She didn't have the energy to accept Syddie's help. She didn't have the energy to try and forgive Jake or Ben.

"Please," she said. "I just need to be alone."

"How are you going to get home?" Sydney asked, but Ella just kept walking.

"Ella," she said, grabbing onto her arm. "You can't walk, not this late at night . . . hold on one sec," Sydney said, as she disappeared back into the crowd.

Ella let out a sigh. All she wanted to do was go home and go to bed and forget about everyone, everyone in the whole world. Forget about the night. The whole year. Forget about Astrid. Forget they had ever been friends.

Sydney popped up a minute later, dragging Carter with her. "He can drive you," she said. "He hasn't had anything to drink yet."

"You don't have to."

"It's no big deal," Carter said. "I can come back as soon as I drop you off. I'm sorry shit hit the fan tonight."

"It's okay," Ella said. "Let's just go."

And Sydney gave her a hug—tight—and Carter led the way out, and she followed as quickly as she could because she didn't want anyone else to try and stop her.

It wasn't until she was home, until she was in bed, almost reaching sleep, that she heard the ding of her phone. She reached for it reluctantly—she didn't want to talk to anyone, not Ben or Jake or Sydney—she was prepared to be annoyed.

She had a new text.

She clicked.

And she felt her breath catch in her throat, because it was what she'd asked for, what they'd joined together to beg for tonight. It was the proof that she wanted and needed and feared at the same time. But having it didn't make her feel good—it only made her feel sick.

A text. A text from Astrid.

It's all my fault.

CHAPTER TWENTY-FIVE

"Well, *I* need another drink," Max said, once Carter was gone and the crowd had cleared. "Mine got spilled by your friend's asshole boyfriend."

"He's not an asshole," Sydney said, watching as Ben's football buddies surrounded him on the lawn. She didn't know what had happened to Jake, and she didn't care. She'd thought that his flirtation with Ella was cute, funny—something to tease her about—but now she just felt bad for Ben. Even if he had been an asshole.

"Whatever," Max said. "You want one?"

"Sure." Sydney followed him to the coolers.

In the distance, one of the football players pushed a blond-haired girl who looked to be about a size 2 into the pool. Sydney rolled her eyes, but Max looked like he enjoyed it. "We just had to come to a football party, didn't we?" she snapped.

"Well, we're here now," he said. "How about something a little stronger?" She followed his gaze. On the porch, there was a bowl of red punch with no ice cubes that looked brutally dangerous.

"Perfect," she said.

Max went straight to it and filled a plastic cup for him and another for her. He took a big gulp and his Adam's apple went *glug-glug-glug-glug-glug*. Sydney stared at the fuchsia stuff in her cup, and for a second, she wondered if this was how alcoholics got their start, if they all had a friend who died or some other stupid thing that they wanted to forget.

"I should drink less," she said. "When things get better."

Max just laughed. "As long as you don't start tonight."

Sydney nodded without looking up. She took a big sip, and the sound of it—the familiar slurp, the echo in her ears as it rushed down her throat—drowned out the thumping bass and the sounds of fake girls giggling by the pool. It sounded like the beginning of forgetting. It sounded like something good.

And she took another sip and promised herself that it wouldn't always be like this.

However long later, the world was beginning to spin.

Sydney was sitting on a dusty floor in a room of Pat Whoever's huge house drinking beer and playing Circle of Death, Max on one side, Carter on the other—he'd come back to the party at some point, and after a few cups of punch seemed just about as drunk as they were.

It was Max's turn, and he slowly turned over a King.

"Aha," Sydney said, focusing very hard on the King's stern face. "You get to make a rule."

Max stroked his chin slowly, and then his eyes lit up. "I've got one," he said. "When I say so, you have to do whatever I say."

"That's not a rule," Carter said, but his words were already beginning to slur. "That's bulllllshit."

"I'm the King!" Max yelled. "I can do it if I want." He burst into laughter.

"That's not a ruuullle," Carter said again, but Sydney could see that his eyes were drooping. He set his beer down and leaned back on his elbows and scooted towards the couch. He'd be out in seconds.

She pulled herself up, knocking her cup over, but it didn't really matter because it was empty, and she scanned the room until she found what she needed.

Bingo!

She grabbed a big fluffy pillow and stumbled over to Carter. He was lying on the floor, and she tucked it under his head. "There."

She sat back down and Max was staring at her.

"How about my rule?"

"Huh?" she asked.

"You have to do what I say."

"And what's that?" she asked. The room was definitely spinning now. Carter was beginning to snore.

"When I ask, you have to kiss me."

Sydney shook her head, leaning back, far away from him. Far, far away from him. That's not what he was supposed to say. She didn't want to kiss Max anyway. He wasn't the one she wanted anymore.

But Max took it as an invitation. He leaned forward again, put his hand on her cheek, guiding her back. "Come on, Syddie," he said.

And he didn't ask, not really. And she tried to focus, to squint away all the blurriness, as he brushed his thumb along her mouth, parting her lips, and pressed his to hers.

Her head was saying, *no no no*, but her mouth wasn't. It was opening, letting him in, because it made her feel so comforted, so wanted—and most of all, it let her forget—but then she opened her eyes for a split second, and in the midst of the spins, she saw Carter's face, looking back at her, more awake than he'd been before.

And she remembered why she'd wanted to say no, and she pulled back, pushing Max away with both hands. She glanced at Carter again. He was flipped over, feigning sleep. Or maybe he was asleep. Maybe he didn't care as much as she thought he did. Maybe he didn't want what she wanted.

It didn't matter. "I can't do this," Sydney stammered. "I can't."

"What?" Max asked, the comforting tone instantly gone from his voice. "What's wrong?"

"I can't do this anymore," she said, shaking her head. And she crawled over to the couch and pulled herself onto it and wished that none of it had ever happened. She wished she could change so much.

And she heard Max get up and she heard him call her a cock-tease, but she didn't care. She just kept her eyes shut tight and kept on wishing that this night had never happened until her tiredness took over and the spinning finally stopped.

She woke up to a pounding headache and a ceiling she didn't recognize.

"Ughhh," she heard below her, and she turned to see Carter, and for a second, she wondered if something had happened between them . . . but then she saw the tipped-over cans of beer and the cards scattered on the floor, and it hit her, worse than a headache. The séance, the thumping, the fight, the truth about Astrid's dad, the punch, the beer, the kiss . . . but it was more than that, it was Carter. Carter had seen them kiss . . . Carter must think . . .

"Ughhhhh," he said again.

"Are you okay?" Sydney asked.

He nodded, slowly pulling himself up to a sitting position so his face was right near hers. She sat up, too, and her new angle gave her a view of the room. They were in some type of home office. Cans were everywhere, and an empty bottle of Jack was turned on its side, as if even it were hungover.

Why oh why had she said yes to that punch?

Why had she let Max kiss her in front of Carter?

Hell, why had she let him kiss her at all?

The thought made her hurt now, deep in her chest. She took a deep breath. Through the doorway, she could see more people, still passed out. She wished that she were still asleep.

"Last night was . . ."

"Stupid," Carter said. It wasn't like him to interrupt her. It wasn't like him to interrupt anyone.

"Yes," she said. "Stupid."

Carter's hair was rumpled, and his face was pale, and he looked like he just needed a hug and a shower and a good painkiller.

She could at least give him that.

"I have Advil in my purse if you want it," she said.

But Carter shook his head. She'd forgotten. Guys were always too tough for painkillers. Just complain and bear it. Even nice guys like Carter.

"I'm sorry about—"

But Carter held up his hand. So close that it almost touched her lips. He moved it back a couple of inches, and her heart beat fast again.

"You don't have to apologize," he said.

And he looked so sweet and understanding and so . . . so Carter, that she couldn't help it. She leaned closer.

"Don't be mad at me," she said. "Please don't be mad at me."

She put her hand on his cheek—she could give him what he'd always wanted—right here, right now. She closed her eyes and met his lips, and it surprised her, took her breath away, because it was everything she wanted, too, all that she needed wrapped into one touch, one moment, one other world far away from this one. Where you closed your eyes and found happiness. Where you found escape.

But it was just a moment.

Carter pushed her away with both hands.

Her mouth hung partway open, and she stared at him, but his eyes weren't Carter-tender now. His eyes were hot with fire and anger. She didn't know if she'd ever really even seen it in him before.

"You made out with Max just last night," he said.

Sydney shook her head. She tried to lean closer, but he pulled back and jumped up. "I guess I'm just next in line?" In the hall, she could hear people starting to move around.

"No," Sydney said, standing up now, too. She shook her head. "No. Not at all. I thought you wanted me to."

Carter shook his head. He was so much taller, so much bigger than her. He looked down at her like she didn't deserve to breathe the air so high up where he was.

"You know you can't just toy around with people," he said. "Just because you're upset. Just because you're drunk. I'm sick of it," he said.

"No," she said, her voice cracking now. "No."

"I hope you find what you're looking for," Carter said. And he walked out of the room, slamming the door shut behind him. She didn't have the heart to follow him. She knew that he wouldn't listen to her anyway. She'd screwed this one up. She'd royally screwed it up.

Instead, she waited until she was sure he had gone, and she grabbed her purse and opened the door and walked slowly out into the main room. Some people were still on couches, others just starting to get up. One girl stared at her like she'd heard the whole thing.

But Sydney just kept her head down and walked out of the wretched place.

She'd lost way too much by now to care.

∽∾

When she got home she didn't go inside. She just got in her car and drove.

It wasn't long before she reached Audie's. She parked, walked through the shop without saying a word to her uncle, and pushed through the beads before anyone could object. "Audie," she called. "Audie, are you there?"

Her aunt appeared in seconds. "Sydney," she said. "My goodness in heaven, are you okay?"

She caught a glimpse of herself in the mirror—her hair was all over the place, her mouth sported a ring of red from that God-awful punch. The area around her eyes was black-tinged, raccoon-like. She didn't care.

"I need to talk," she said. "Can we sit down?"

"Did something happen? Are you alright?"

"I'm okay," she said. "I mean, I'm not. But I'm not hurt or anything. Don't worry."

Audie nodded and quickly led her into the living room. It was covered in floral chintz, knit afghans, and vibrant hues. She sat down, and Audie perched next to her so that their knees were barely touching. She looked worried, and as Sydney realized what she was about to tell her, she almost felt bad for dragging her into this mess.

"What is it?" Audie asked quietly. "You can tell me."

Sydney took a deep breath. She had to say it. It would make it real.

LEAH KONEN

"Astrid's dad isn't dead."

The gasp was audible. Audie just stared. She didn't protest. She didn't object.

"Wait, you believe me?"

Audie shook her head, closing her eyes. Then she opened them up quickly, pulling herself together. She placed one hand carefully on each knee. She seemed to remember all of a sudden that she was the adult in this situation.

"I'm so sorry that you—that she—I mean," Audie paused for breath. "I don't know what to say."

"But you believe me. I expected you to say that it wasn't possible. Just the other week you said that—"

"I know," Audie said with force, before collecting herself. "I'm sorry. I know what I said, and believe me, it's what I thought. I mean, it's what I had to think."

"Don't you even want to know how I found out?" She'd expected Audie to tell her she was crazy, not to just accept this impossible news at face value. She'd expected Audie to undo it, to prove her wrong.

"Yes," she said. "I do."

The words seemed to pour out of her. "It was Astrid's cousin, Jake. He told Ella, and she is, like, one hundred percent convinced, but she's also convinced that Astrid's living with us in ghost form, and she's also practically in love with this guy, so I don't know what to think. And I don't know why you're not telling me I'm wrong," she said, her voice shaking now, getting louder. *Tell me I'm wrong,* she thought. *Please. Tell me I'm wrong.*

Audie didn't answer right away. When she did, her face was scrunched up. Tight. "It's not easy. Trust me, I didn't think it was possible either. I really didn't. All these years I never really thought."

"But you're saying you considered? Why would you even think anything like that?"

Audie sighed. "I feel awful burdening you with this," she said. "When you've already gone through so much."

"Just tell me," Sydney said. "I need to know."

"Alright, alright," she said. "You're practically an adult yourself now." She took a deep breath. "There was talk," she said. "Ever since it happened. Falling Rock isn't that big, and you know how things get around."

Sydney nodded. "Okay."

"Some people thought it was weird, the whole string of events. He just disappeared, really—they had the funeral out of town, all that—and then I guess, I don't know, someone said something at one of the pubs off the trail that he used to go to. That he heard from him or something. He was a bad drunk, though—I didn't believe him. It was all hearsay. I mean, it was always easier to believe that than the fact that Grace would actually concoct a story so . . ."

"Awful."

Audie nodded.

"Jake said he was at the funeral," Sydney said. "And you didn't see him?"

"It's been almost a decade," she said. "And why would I be looking?"

Why indeed. For all Audie knew he was dead and gone. Why would she be searching for a dead person? And for a millisecond, the thought crossed her mind—Grace had orchestrated it for her husband—what was to stop her from faking the death of her daughter as well? What if everything that Ella had seen, everything she thought . . .

But then she remembered the wake, Astrid's cakey foundation and her lifeless face, and she knew it couldn't be. Astrid was gone. Astrid wasn't coming back.

Sydney looked at her aunt. "What should I do?"

Audie sighed. "What can you do?"

"Tell someone," she stammered. "Tell everyone."

"For what?" Audie asked. "To hurt Grace, to get back at her? She just lost her daughter. And no matter what she called it, she lost Robert, too. What good would it do?"

"The *truth* would be out there. Doesn't that count for something?"

"The truth is different for different people," Audie said, and it was so like Audie to say something understanding like that, she almost wanted to scream.

"But shouldn't everyone know?"

"The people who need to know, know," Audie said, discreetly brushing away a tear as she did. When she spoke again she sounded almost offended. "If Robert had wanted to stay, to be part of this world, he would have. Now he'll just be remembered as the good guy who died and not the man who left his wife and daughter."

But Sydney knew it wasn't that simple. Maybe he didn't care, maybe it made it easier for Grace. Maybe it eased the embarrassment, the shame. But she knew without a doubt that it wasn't better for Astrid. How could anyone come through that unbroken?

Sydney took a deep breath. "I just don't get it. I thought you said they were in love. And then he just left her. Like that."

Audie shook her head. "Don't let anyone tell you love is easy, Syddie. Don't let anyone ever tell you that. Because it's not."

And she thought of Astrid, of Ella, of Carter—even Max. And she knew more than anything that her aunt was right—that it wasn't.

But she couldn't help it—she wanted it to be, so bad. She wanted love to mean something. She wanted it to make sense.

Because if it had to be like this—if everyone you ever loved would break you, undo you, leave you, whether to another state or to another world—she couldn't take it.

She'd rather be alone forever than have to live with that.

CHAPTER TWENTY-SIX

Ella called in sick to work the next morning.

She'd tried to call her friend countless times, hands shaking, pulse racing, but nothing. The phone was dead. Dead as it ever had been.

She knew she wasn't sick. She wasn't even hung over—she hadn't been at the party long enough for that. But she was exhausted. Emotionally. Physically. Mentally.

More than that, she was scared.

Everything about last night was too much. Ben had apologized profusely over text. Maybe he was too embarrassed to pick up the phone. Maybe he'd known deep down that it would all go over better without actual communication. She'd texted back, said it was okay, more to get him to stop than anything else, because it wasn't, it totally wasn't—he knew it as well as she did—and he'd said that he wanted to talk. She hadn't yet responded to that. She knew that once they did she'd have a pretty sad case; she'd gone to the show without telling him, she'd invited Jake to the cabin instead of him, and even now, even though she hated how he'd said those things to Ben, even though she had a million other things on her mind, she couldn't help biting her lip as she thought of Jake, to keep from smiling. She hadn't had those bite-your-lip feelings since she first started dating Ben.

She shouldn't have those bite-your-lip feelings about anyone else besides Ben.

She hadn't talked to Jake, and she didn't want to—she had more important things to worry about. Something was definitely going on, there was no denying it now, and she knew that A's journal was in her bag, waiting for her. She knew that there was still so much more to find out. She couldn't waste any time.

The sun shone through her window, and Ella knew that on another day in another summer, she and Sydney and Astrid would have all been outside. They'd have walked to town to buy magazines and gum or practiced climbing Sydney's stupid tree.

Ella didn't get dressed yet—she didn't feel like it—the more she tried to understand Astrid, the less she did. The more she found out, the less she seemed to have known about her friend. But she had to keep trying. So she picked up the journal and turned to where she'd left off.

At first it was more of the same—detailed accounts of their days, the time Sydney had gotten lost on the way to Walmart and taken them on an ultimately fun scenic trip, the day that Ella and Ben had had their one-year anniversary, how the girls had helped her find the perfect outfit to wear to The Cheesecake Factory in the next town over. As she flipped through, she realized how strange it was that Astrid wrote so much about them, but so little about herself.

But as Ella kept reading, getting into their senior year, the journal started to change. It started to sound less like the Astrid she'd known. More like an Astrid who could be capable of something so horrible, so unthinkable. Of an Astrid who would eventually take her own life.

Some days there were just a few words. *Doing good today.* Some days just one. *Angry.* Some days there were drawings instead, not art-class drawings, with the sketchy pencil marks and the subtle shading. These drawings were hard and rough, so much so that sometimes they broke through the paper. They were big shapes. Long faces. Ella didn't know what to think except that they looked like what it felt to be scared.

And they definitely scared her.

And the stories, when they were there, they stopped being about school so much, about friends and crushes and lists of boys that Astrid had thought were kissable; they turned vague, cryptic. All pronouns and emotions. About *her* moods. *Her* looks. *Her* clothes. Whether *she* was happy or sad—*she wouldn't get out of bed all day*—pretty or slumming around—*she put her pearls back on, she hasn't done that since he left*—really there or in some other world—*she screamed at me when I left the house, she tried to pull me back inside*—

The *she* had to be Grace, but it was like reading about a whole other woman. One that Ella had never known. One that Astrid could hardly predict.

One that she seemed almost obsessed with.

Jake's words rung in her head. "Astrid's dad is alive . . . Grace was probably the least surprised of anyone." It still didn't all make sense. What exactly had happened?

And then Ella found a page with just a couple of sentences.

Went to Ella's today. I couldn't help it. I probably shouldn't have done that. She won't like it.

Ella stared at the page. It was dated a couple of months before Astrid died. April. Rainy April. Sad April. And in moments, she remembered. It came to her as if in a flash. Why had she not thought of it before?

On that day in April, Astrid had walked over, unannounced, the rain making her red hair deeper, darker, curled into wet ringlets. Astrid never wore much makeup, so her face just looked wet, like a child who'd been crying.

"Oh my God," Ella had said as she opened the front door. "Are you okay?"

Astrid shook her head and walked inside. Ella got a towel, and they walked up the stairs to her room. Astrid sat on the edge of the bed and shook. At first Ella thought it was from being wet, but it wasn't.

"What happened?" she asked.

Astrid spoke in bursts. "I just . . . all of a sudden . . ." she gasped. "She just screamed at me . . . she wouldn't stop."

Ella hugged her friend, her t-shirt getting wet. She didn't know if it was from the rain or Astrid's tears.

"Who screamed at you?" Ella asked. "What happened?"

But Astrid shook her head. "I wanted to talk about something, and she wouldn't let me. I wanted to tell you something, but I can't."

"Who did this?" Ella asked, pushing the wet hair off of Astrid's forehead. "You can tell me anything," she said.

"Not this," Astrid said. "Not this." More sobs rocked her.

"Shhh," Ella said, taking her friend in her arms. "I don't want to pressure you, but I'm always here when you want to talk, A. I'm always here to listen."

Astrid looked up at Ella, almost as if she were a different species, as if they were so different that Ella could never, ever understand. But then she nodded, as if trying to convince herself that what Ella said could be true.

"It'll be okay," Ella repeated, wrapping her arms around Astrid tighter, trying to calm her shaking body. "I'm here."

"I'm just afraid," Astrid said with a gasp, but she cut herself off.

Ella pulled back, rubbed her hand along Astrid's shoulder.

"Afraid of what?" Ella asked, but her friend just shook her head, the sobs shaking her again, the tears coming down in a rush.

And she never told Ella what it was that she was afraid of. She never told her what it was that she wanted so badly to say.

And worse than that, Ella hadn't pressed her. Ella hadn't asked. She hadn't even known it was Grace. The guilt hit her in the stomach like a punch. Why had she just let it go?

Ella felt her face grow hot, and a tear trickled down her cheek, but she just wiped it away. She was too tired for a breakdown. Instead she took a deep breath, and she kept flipping the pages, and it was just more drawings, more words here and there, and then there it was, that last page. So insufficient. Such a non-goodbye. Ella turned the page wishing that there were more. She ran her hands over it, but there was no more writing, just the back of the last page. Blank. Lined.

Empty.

But as Ella pulled her hand back she felt a sharp pain and then . . . blood. There was blood on her finger. She'd gotten a paper cut.

And she looked closer, and she couldn't believe that she and Sydney hadn't seen it before.

Tiny slivers, right along the spine.

There had been pages. *Astrid's* pages.

They'd been cut out of the journal.

Her friend's final words had been literally cut off.

Ella put her finger in her mouth, sucking on the salty drop of blood, as her heart quickened and her brain began to race.

Ella knew what she had to do. There was no time to waste.

Ella was out of breath by the time she got to Sydney's house. She'd run the whole way. Sydney's mom opened the door and looked at her with narrowed eyes.

"Hello, Mrs. Collette," she tried to say politely, between gasps for air.

"Hey dear," she said. "Are you okay?"

Ella nodded quickly. "Is Sydney here?"

She stepped back, making way. "She's in her room, but if she's not up yet, you're going to have to deal with her crankiness. Not me."

"Thanks," Ella said, running up the stairs.

She knocked on Sydney's door—two quick raps—before whipping it open.

Sydney groaned from the bed and flipped over.

"Hey," Ella said, walking over to her. "Hey. It's Ella." She shook her shoulder, maybe not so gently.

Sydney flipped back over and her eyes fluttered open. "Whoa," she said, sitting up quickly. "Whoa."

"It's okay," Ella said. "It's just me."

"What are you doing here?" Sydney asked. "Ugh. Can you pull that shade down?"

Ella walked over to the window and snapped it down. Sydney was still in her clothes from the night before. "What's wrong with you?" she asked. "It's almost one."

Sydney let out another groan. "I had a rough morning, okay?"

"I take it you guys kept drinking after I left?" Ella asked.

"It's not just that," Sydney said, and Ella knew there was a story there but she didn't have time for it right now. "Listen," she said, pulling the journal out of her purse, her hands already beginning to quiver in anticipation.

But Sydney interrupted her, holding up her hand. "Wait, what happened with you? Have you talked to Ben yet? Or Jake?"

Ella shook her head. "I don't want to talk about that right now."

"I'm sure that Ben was just drunk, and he's really such a good guy and—"

"I said, I don't want to talk about that right now."

"I know, but—"

"Sydney," Ella snapped. "Listen to me. There's something I have to tell you."

"Oh God," Sydney said—and she really did look upset. "What now? What else can there be?"

"Look at this," she said, pushing the journal in front of Sydney.

Sydney immediately shook her head vigorously. "No more story-time for me, thanks. Once was enough."

"Just look," Ella said, flipping the back cover open. "Feel that."

"Feel what?"

"Right here." Ella took Sydney's finger and ran it along the inside of the spine.

"Whoa," she said. "It's sharp."

"Exactly," Ella said. "The pages have been cut out."

Sydney looked up at her, and for a moment it looked like she was considering something, like she was weighing a choice. Like even she was interested—even she wanted to know—even *she* was shocked.

But the look left and her face went flat. She shrugged. "This doesn't mean anything," she said.

Ella couldn't help it. She snapped. "How does a mother slicing pages out of her daughter's diary not mean anything?"

Sydney just shrugged. She looked defeated. "How is that any worse than pretending your husband's dead?"

"Don't you think that's why I want to see them?" Ella asked. "They could explain what really happened."

Sydney just shook her head. "What are you even telling me this for? I'm presuming you want me to help you do some crazy thing."

"We need to get them back."

"*We* don't need to do anything," Sydney said.

"What do you want me to do? Just pretend I didn't see them? Just pretend they didn't exist?"

"Yes," Sydney yelled. "Yes! That's exactly what I want you to do."

Ella shook her head. She'd come too far now. She'd been through too much. She wasn't going to stop now. She was so close. "No," she said. "No. I can't."

Sydney sighed. "How would you even go about getting them?"

"I'll ask Jake. I'll look for them."

"You're going to tear up a house you were kicked out of for snooping to find a few sheets of paper?"

"What else am I going to do?"

"Give up!" Sydney said. "They could be anywhere. She could have burned them for all we know."

"No," Ella said. "You didn't see her room. Not a thing was touched. Not a single thing except the journal. She hid them. She didn't burn them. She wouldn't destroy anything of Astrid's. I know it. She wouldn't."

But Sydney just shook her head. Her eyes looked sad. Almost like she was going to cry. "And what then?" she asked. "When will it be enough? What else are we going to find? That she had a secret grandmother? That Astrid wasn't her real name? That she didn't speak a word of truth to us the entire time we knew her? It won't bring her back," Sydney yelled. "It'll just make us feel even more like shit."

"But we might know—"

"We might know what?" Sydney practically screamed. "What? Tell me what could we possibly know that would make anything any better? Tell me how anything we've learned so far has made it anything but worse."

"Sydney," Ella said, but her friend ignored her.

"No," and she did scream that time. "Don't you get it? I'm hurting, too. I may not be seeing ghosts and dreaming about Astrid every night, but I need you. I need you to be here with me. Do you know that it's a month tomorrow? *A month.* A month you've been playing this stupid game, and for nothing. I, for one, feel just as shitty as ever. It's selfish. You're doing this for you, don't you get it? Not for me. Not for Jake. Not for Grace. And sure as hell not for her."

Ella's eyes opened wide. She absolutely could not believe what Sydney had just said. "Selfish? You're the one getting drunk every night and hooking up with Max and leading Carter on just because you feel like it, and I'm the one thinking about Astrid. I'm the one trying to make sense of it all. You're calling *me* selfish?"

"You don't know shit about Max or Carter. And you can't talk, miss I'm-in-love-with-my-dead-friend's-cousin."

"Oh yeah? Well, at least I'm trying to get to know her family. At least I'm trying to figure out more about her."

"I knew plenty about her when she was alive!" Sydney screamed. "I don't want to know any more. I don't want to think about her anymore. Every time I do, I feel sick. I'm done," Sydney threw her hands up in the air. "Done."

Ella just shook her head. "You don't really mean that."

But Sydney was nodding. "I'm not doing it anymore. I can't do it anymore. I'm not listening to your bullshit theories or reading my aunt's book or hosting séances or stealing fucking journals. I'm moving on, okay? That's what people do. You should try it sometime. But oh wait, you can't. You're too fucking scared so you're stuck playing ghost hunter."

But Ella shook her head. She started to pull out her phone. If Sydney could only see it, she would get it. She would finally understand. "Let me just show you one thing," she said.

"No," Sydney said. "You've shown me enough."

"But—"

"I said *no,*" she said, her voice getting even louder. "Just get out. I'm done with this." And Sydney grabbed the journal, pushing it at Ella, practically shoving her out the door.

And it was then that she realized that it was no use. Sydney wouldn't understand. Sydney didn't even *want* to understand.

"You're wrong," Ella snapped. "You have no idea how wrong you are." And then she rushed out as quickly as she could, practically falling down the stairs, and was out the door before Sydney's mom could ask what all the yelling was about.

She ran her hand along the journal as she walked down the street. It was the only thing she could count on now.

CHAPTER TWENTY-SEVEN

Sydney burst into sobs as soon as Ella left.

She shouldn't have yelled at her. She shouldn't have pushed her away. She knew Ella needed her more than ever. But she already knew too much. She didn't want to see those pages. She didn't need to see those pages.

She'd lived them. She didn't need a reminder.

She'd gone over to Astrid's just a couple of days before she died, 49 hours, to be exact. She'd counted. Multiple times.

Astrid had said she wasn't feeling well, and Sydney wanted to see her. No one had answered the door, but it was unlocked, so Sydney let herself in. It was that kind of house. One without too many rules.

She knocked softly on Astrid's door, and when she heard her voice say, "What is it?" she slowly opened the door.

"Oh," Astrid said. "It's you."

Sydney took that as invitation enough to come in. "I wanted to see how you are," she said. "You said you were sick."

"I didn't tell you to come over," Astrid said, her mouth a thin, straight line.

"I'm sorry," Sydney said. She stared at her friend. She did look sick. Or maybe not even sick. Empty would be a better word. She was pale as a sheet, and she had deep circles under her eyes, like she'd forgotten how to sleep. Her bony legs weren't shaved, and they poked out of the sheets. She looked skinnier than ever.

"I just wanted to make sure you're okay," Sydney said.

Astrid just shrugged. "What's the point? You can't do anything to make it better."

"Do you have a cold or something?" Sydney asked, her eyes locked on her friend. "I brought some cough drops."

Astrid laughed, and her laugh was hoarse, almost as if she'd been to a concert, had spent the whole night screaming.

"I don't need cough drops."

Sydney sat down on the edge of the bed, but Astrid scooted back, like she was toxic or something. "What's wrong, A?"

Astrid stared at her straight, without blinking. "Nothing's wrong," she said, her voice almost childlike. "Why would anything be wrong?"

"You're freaking me out," Sydney said.

"Then leave."

"I just wanted to—"

"I don't care what you wanted," Astrid yelled, her voice definitely hoarse now. "You can't help, okay? Just leave me alone."

"Astrid," Sydney said, putting a hand on her shoulder, but she shook her away.

"Don't touch me," she said.

So Sydney stood up then, backing out of the room. "I can't be here for you if you won't let me," she said, as she made her way to the door.

Astrid was silent then, and Sydney turned back. For a second she almost looked like herself, weighing, waiting, wondering if she should open up to Sydney right then and there. If she should finally let her in. But in an instant that look was gone.

"I know," Astrid snapped. "That's why I'm telling you to leave."

And she shouldn't have let it get to her, she should have known that A needed help, that she was hardly even in control, that nothing she said in desperation should be taken at face value. But Sydney couldn't help it. She felt nothing but anger. Anger and a deep desire to get out. If her friend didn't want her help, she sure as hell wasn't going to get it.

"I'll call you later," Sydney said, heading out of the door.

"Don't," Astrid said, but Sydney just kept walking. She couldn't take any more. Astrid was a different person. With empty eyes. An emotionless voice. She was almost like a ghost.

Grace stopped her in the hallway. "What are you doing here?" she snapped. Her eyes were fiery. "Astrid's sick."

"I—no one answered, so I just came in. I wanted to make sure she's okay."

"She needs her rest," Grace said.

"Okay, I'm leaving," she said. "Sorry."

"It's fine," Grace said, but she didn't sound like it was fine. At all. "Just leave," she said. "Just let her rest. She doesn't need you."

Sydney wanted to yell at Grace then, she wanted to tell her that she did need her, maybe more than ever. But she couldn't. Grace was the adult. Grace was the mom. She'd trusted her, in spite of herself. Even though she shouldn't have.

Let her rest, Sydney thought. Let her rest forever.

Sydney stared up at the ceiling, trying to keep up with her racing mind. Why hadn't she pushed back? Why hadn't she shaken Astrid? Why hadn't she made her tell her what was wrong? Why hadn't she hugged her, told her she would always be there for her, even if she'd fought and screamed and tried to push her away? If she had tried, would Astrid have let herself be held, shaken with long overdue tears, finally told her what was really going on? Why the hell had she left?

But Astrid had sent a text to her that night, apologizing, saying that the cold medicine made her cranky. And when she'd suggested that they all meet at the cabin the next night, before a big party one of the seniors was throwing, how was Sydney to know that it would be the last time that they'd all be together? How was Sydney to know that there wouldn't be any more time to be a good friend?

She wanted to keep crying, but now she was all out of tears. It was too early to start drinking, and lately it wasn't making her feel better anyway. She wanted to rip the guilt right out of her stomach, but she knew that it didn't work that way.

Out of the corner of the room, her fiddle caught her eye. The one thing that wouldn't leave her—that wouldn't kill itself or yell at her or leave her with this palpable, horrible guilt.

Sydney sighed, pushing herself up to a sitting position, slowly standing up and grabbing the fiddle and bow. She sat back down, running her hands along the smooth, strong wood. And then she wedged it under her chin and pulled the bow across the strings softly, until the rich sound filled her ears and for a second, she felt peace.

It had actually been a really long time since Sydney had written a new song. One with chords, a melody, the whole works.

She and Max used to write all of their songs together. Then, after they broke up, things changed. She'd come up with a riff here, write a verse there—sometimes, if she was feeling particularly hung up on Max, or maybe if they'd recently hooked up, she'd make a try at writing one with him. It never worked as well as it had in the beginning.

Practice was at Carter's tonight. She hoped beyond hope that she'd have a chance to apologize for the night before—to explain.

Max and Carter were waiting for her when she got to the garage.

"You're late," Max said.

"So sue me," she said back.

Carter just looked down at his feet. Which was even more awkward and obvious given how tall he was.

"Hey," she said, smiling straight at him. And he looked up, and she swore that a tiny, mini part of him smiled back—a little bit. Or maybe that was just Carter. But he just went back to messing with his mandolin. It was his trick when he didn't want to deal with what was going on around him.

"You need to start getting serious about the band, Sydney," Max said.

Carter kept tuning.

"Are you for real?" she asked. "You're always late or drunk or hooking up with someone in the crowd."

"And you're always late and drunk and hooking up with the whole band."

Sydney whipped her head around to face Carter, as she felt her face go red. "You told him?" she asked.

Carter shrugged.

Sydney turned back to Max. "What does it matter to you? Like you actually care."

"I don't," he said. "I just don't think that you should be talking about me hooking up with fans," he said, "when you act like a groupie for your own band."

Sydney rolled her eyes. "Yeah right. You're just mad because you want to know that I'm still hung up on you so you can feel better about yourself and how lonely you are."

Max raised his voice then. "I don't *want* to know you're still hung up on me," he said. "I *do* know. And you pull poor Carter into the mix to make yourself feel better about it."

Sydney's jaw dropped. Even Carter stared at Max in shock.

Everything she'd ever loved about him—his hair, his smile, the way he had of looking her straight in the eye—seemed false now, like without it all, he'd be nothing, no one. Just another lead singer trying to get laid.

Max wasn't worth tears. Astrid was worth tears. Ella was worth tears. Carter was, too. Hell, even Ben was. Max wasn't worth a single drop of salty water from her eyes. He wasn't worth all of the ones she'd already spilled, all of the mornings after with headaches and regrets. He wasn't worth any of that. And she wasn't going to give him any more. Ever.

Her words came out in a yell. "I'm not hung up on you," she said. "And my feelings for Carter have *nothing* to do with you. But you know what, you win, okay? You win. Because you toyed with me enough to make me ruin it with him."

Max looked over to Carter. Then back to Sydney. "Oh what, so you like skinny momma's boys now?"

She briefly looked over to Carter, but then looked away because she couldn't stand to see the hurt, the embarrassment on his face.

"Fuck you, Max," she said.

"Fuck you guys," he said. And he grabbed his case and stalked off to his car.

Sydney watched him slam the door and pull away. Only then did she look back at Carter. "I'm sorry," she said. "I'm sorry you had to be part of that. It's our bullshit, not yours."

"You don't have to be sorry," he said.

"He's just such a dick," she said. "He always ruins everything. And what he said about you—"

"Sydney," he said, lifting up his hands as if she were about to attack him or something. "I don't want to talk about it."

"I'm sorry," she said.

"You don't have to say you're *sorry*."

"I'm sorry," she said again. "Shit. I just was hoping that this would go different. I just don't know why he has to be like that. I wrote a new song," she said. "And I wanted to show you guys, and I wanted to apologize, and now Max is gone and you're just mad."

She wanted him so badly to want to hear her song. She wanted him to sit there and listen or maybe say something about the fact that she'd just said that she liked him or maybe just smile at her like he used to when Max was a dick, to crack a joke and hug her and make everything feel better. She wanted him to forgive her.

But he just stood there. Because they were in this strange new world now. Where they were all a bunch of broken pieces that she was trying so desperately to fit together.

"Listen," he said, finally. "Max left. Maybe you should just go home, too."

She felt like someone had punched her in the stomach. But she deserved that, didn't she? He'd probably felt the same way about her more than once. She'd made her messy bed. Now she had to lie in it.

"Okay," she said. "I'll see you . . ."

"Later," he said.

"Okay. Later."

And she grabbed her stuff and walked away.

⧡

When she was back home, she pulled out the sheet of paper and took her fiddle out of its case.

She read the words of the song—her song—running her finger over the lines of the chorus that had come to her in a rush that morning. The one she'd written to make her feel better. The one that she didn't believe yet, but she wanted to, and that was the point.

No matter if you're here or no matter if you're gone
Believe me, dear, it won't be long
'Til we smile at the way we feel you near
And rejoice the fact that we're still here

She sung them softly, and it felt good to feel the words coming out of her mouth, emanating from her lungs. It felt good to feel.

And even though she felt like shit, even though she'd messed things up with Carter, even though even Ella wasn't talking to her now, even though the news about Astrid tore her, ripped her apart, maybe it wasn't so bad that she had no one to listen.

Maybe this one was just for her.

Her and Astrid.

CHAPTER TWENTY-EIGHT

It was a little after six when Ella saw Jake bobbing up the steps of the park near Trail Mix.

She'd called him at the coffee shop just an hour before, asking him to meet her—now as he approached, she felt like one of those people who arranged clandestine meetings in public places. She hadn't wanted to ask him to her house—her mom kept asking her what was going on with Ben (it was like some kind of mom sixth sense) and she knew that Jake coming over would only inspire more questions. Going to Astrid's house was obviously out of the question—at least if Grace knew about it—so she'd chosen here. It was a place that she and Astrid used to go to sometimes, after their shift ended. They never said too much. Just sat and looked out at the town—the world. It was beautiful here. A Blue Ridge wonder.

Ella noticed that Jake was holding two cups as he approached her. He handed one to her. "Thanks," she said, and she lifted it up to her nose. "Chai."

"Your favorite, right?"

Ella nodded. "How did you know?"

"I've seen you make it for yourself more than once," he said. And she smiled. For once she felt calm and peaceful, in control. She knew it probably wouldn't last, but it felt good anyway.

Jake sat down next to her. "Wow," he said, looking out at the sight before them. "I can't believe this is so close and I've never been."

"There's a lot of things in this town that you have to know to look for."

Ella took a sip, and the hot milk burned the tip of her tongue. She blew on it through the tiny sipping hole, and it made a whistling sound.

"I'm glad you called me," Jake said. "You're not sick, are you?"

"No," she said, without looking at him. "I'm not."

"I understand."

"I don't know that you do."

He turned to her then. "I know I was an ass last night," he said. "I know that Ben is good to you and that he was just drunk, and I know I shouldn't have goaded him. I know I only made it worse."

From her vantage point, Ella could see almost every shop in town. The restaurant where she and Ben had had their first date. The bakery that made the best sourdough. The thrift store where she and Sydney had bought their graduation dresses. It all seemed so meaningless now, compared to this. "I don't want to talk about Ben," she said.

Jake turned to her then. "You don't? I thought you were mad."

"I am," she said, without facing him. "Or I was. I'm not anymore. Don't worry."

"Are you sure?" he asked.

"I have more important things on my mind."

Jake nodded, and he didn't press her further. She loved that about him. He was so easygoing sometimes. He made it so easy to be herself.

Ella took another sip of chai and then set it down on the bench next to her. "I need your help," she said.

"My help?" He turned back to her, and in an instant, she thought that his eyes understood.

"Yeah."

"You don't want to go back in the house, do you?"

Ella nodded. "I need to."

Jake shook his head. "Is that why you're friends with me? Am I just a ticket so you can come in and out as you please? So you can learn more about us?"

"No," she said calmly. "Not at all."

"Then tell me what all this is about. Is it because of what I said about her dad?" he asked. "Because it wasn't that far from the truth. He was as good as dead, the way he treated them, and—"

"No," Ella said. "It's not that."

"Then what is it? Tell me."

And Ella wanted to. She wanted to tell him the whole thing. But she was afraid that if she did, he'd say no. There was something about their family that made them feel compelled to hide things for each other. That made them bend the truth. That made them keep secrets at any cost. Sometimes she thought he was different, but then in a flash, she didn't. She knew what side he'd take. There was no reason for him not to. It was all he knew.

"I can't," Ella said.

Jake rolled his eyes. "How do you expect me to help you if you won't even tell me what's going on?"

Ella looked down at her hands, and then back up into his eyes. "You haven't always been honest with me," she said. "I know you know things that you want to tell me. I know that you won't." Jake looked away from her but she kept going. "And I'm not asking you to tell me, okay? I promise I'm not. I'm just asking you to put the same trust in me that I have in you. I believe you have a good reason to not tell me whatever it is you're not telling. Give me that same trust. Help me get in there, just one more time."

Jake shook his head, rubbing his palms on his jeans. "But why?"

Ella's voice raised. "I can't tell you," she said. "Just trust me. Please. I'll go in and go out and Grace will never know the difference, but it will mean everything in the world to me. Everything."

Jake just stared at her.

"I need this," she said. "Please."

"I don't know what to say," Jake said.

"Say yes. Say you'll help me."

Jake shook his head, letting out a sigh. "You know that I can't say no to you."

"So you'll help me?"

He nodded, slowly, and their eyes stayed locked. And they were so close—ever so close—only a few inches, and she could lean in and finally know what it felt to have his lips on hers—she could feel, maybe, something other than pain.

But she broke their gaze before anything could happen.

"Thank you," she said. "Thank you so so much."

She'd arranged to come over the next morning. Neither of them were scheduled for the early shift, and he'd assured her that Grace would be out for a few hours. She always was.

Ella hadn't told him that today was exactly one month from *the day*. She didn't know how to say it, really; she only knew that the date was burned into her mind. It was something she couldn't forget about. No matter how many months and years and lifetimes would pass. It was one that she would always remember.

The walk to Astrid's wasn't long. Ella walked in the street because there were barely any cars around at this time of day. There were barely any cars around here ever.

It was a day awfully similar to *the day*. The sun was shining, and the sky was Monet-blue. The mountains in the distance stared back at her through open air. But in the other direction, behind her, clouds loomed.

That day, one month ago, she'd ridden, not walked. Her mom had driven her over after the phone call. Grace, her voice high-pitched and worried over the phone: Had she seen Astrid? No, she hadn't. But she said she was staying with you. But she didn't. We went to the party and she wanted to stay. So you saw her head home? No. She hadn't thought to check. She and Sydney had just bounced off to the party like nothing was the matter.

When they got to her house, Grace had asked her to take her there, to the last place she'd seen her daughter. To the cabin.

And she had.

The house came into sight, and she didn't text Jake this time. She just went right up and knocked on the door. She was tired of walking on eggshells.

He answered it quickly, almost like he was waiting for her.

"She's definitely out, right?" Ella asked, heading inside before he had time to ask her in.

"Yeah," he said. "Don't worry."

"Thanks," Ella said. She didn't want to waste any time now. Not like before, when she'd casually waited for an invitation. "Can I see her room?" she asked, as her feet headed there anyway.

"Okay," he said, but he grabbed her arm. Not roughly. Gently, but like he had something to say. "Please don't mess anything up too much, Ella."

"I know," she said. "I won't." And she felt a pang of guilt as she answered, because deep down she knew that she was lying. She'd turn the place upside-down if she had to, to find those pages. She patted the journal, tucked inside her purse. She had to finish the story.

Jake followed her into the room, and she looked up, waiting for him to excuse himself like he had before. But he didn't.

"You're going to hang out in here?" she asked.

"I just want to make sure everything's okay," he said. But she looked in his eyes, and she knew that there was more to it than that. He was saying, *Don't mess anything up, be careful,* but his eyes almost looked rebellious, hopeful, like he wanted her to win. Like he wanted her to find what she was looking for.

"Jake," she said, standing close to him. "Please. Just let me do this."

He stared at her. "What is it that you want to do?"

"I need to find something," she said.

"What?" he asked.

Ella rolled her eyes. "I thought you said you would trust me."

Jake stepped closer to her. She could almost feel his breath on her face. "I do trust you, but you have to let me in. You have to tell me what it is you're looking for. You have to at least let me help."

Ella sighed. "You promise not to judge me?"

Jake nodded, his worried eyes turning to a smile. "I haven't yet."

She looked straight at him. "And you promise not to throw me out?"

Jake shrugged. "You're here. Why would I make you leave now?"

Ella pulled out the journal and pushed it into his hands. Their fingers met for an instant, and she wished they were meeting for a different reason, not this. She pulled her hand away, leaving the journal in his.

"What's this?" he asked.

"Just open it."

He did, and his eyes widened. "Wait, is this—"

Ella nodded. "Yeah."

"But where did you—"

"I took it. Last time I came here."

Jake's jaw dropped, but she interrupted him before he could say anything.

"You told me to trust you," she said. "This is me. Trusting you."

"I know, but—"

"And you said that you weren't going to judge me."

"I know."

"I'm sorry," she said, "that I didn't tell you. But I felt like I had to, and if you just give me a second to show you, I think you'll understand."

Jake nodded slowly, but he still looked angry—hurt—he tried to put the journal back in her hands.

"No," she said. "Turn to the last page."

"Ella, I don't want to read it."

"You don't have to read anything. Just look."

"Why?" he snapped.

"Just look," she said. "Please. We're in this together, now."

Slowly, he flipped open the back cover.

She grabbed his hand in hers—it was warm, far more calloused than hers—or Ben's, for that matter—and she ran his finger down the page. "Ow," he said. "That's sharp."

Ella nodded. "The pages have been cut out," she said.

Jake's eyebrows knitted together, and even he looked shocked. "What? What do you mean?"

"She cut them out, Jake. Astrid wanted to say something, and Grace silenced her."

He just stared straight ahead. He didn't say anything more.

"Jake?" she asked. He was starting to look lost.

"Yeah," he said, looking back to her.

"Are you okay?"

He nodded. "That's fucked up," he said. "That's really fucked up."

"I know," she said. "That's why I want to find out what it says."

He handed the journal back to her, and she tucked it safely back into her purse.

"So you'll help me?" she asked. Jake nodded.

"Yes," he said. "I'll do anything you want."

They worked as fast as they could without turning the place into a total wreck. At this point, Ella didn't even care that much, but she understood why Jake did.

It was a perfect little world in here that Grace was preserving. An eerie, creepy tomb. It still looked like Astrid could walk right in any moment.

Hey lady. What's up?

Ella took the closet, while Jake checked under the bed. She pulled out shoebox after shoebox, flipping through old photos and looking for lightly lined pages. Nothing.

When she was done with the closet, she checked the nightstand. She pulled out each of the three drawers. She opened every book to make sure the pages hadn't been tucked in, while Jake fished around under the bed, uncovering old art projects of Astrid's and boxes to shoes and hairdryers—the kinds of things you keep under the bed.

"Hate to break it to you, but I'm not having any luck," Jake said, pulling out a clear Tupperware container filled with markers that probably didn't work anymore.

"I know," Ella said. "I'm not finding anything either. How long will she be gone?"

"Probably a couple of hours."

Ella looked at her watch. It had already been almost an hour. "Maybe we should check *her* room," Ella said.

"Grace's room?" Jake looked up from under the bed. "I don't know."

"Think about it," she said. "If she wanted to hide something, why would she hide it in here?"

"I don't know," Jake said. "It doesn't sound like a good idea."

Ella couldn't help it. She raised her voice. "Jake, we're way past good ideas. We either do this or we don't. Don't you want to know what she said?"

Jake sighed. "Let's just finish here first, okay?"

"We're running out of time."

"Just finish here. You still haven't checked her dresser."

Ella sighed, stomping towards the dresser—even though she knew there was nothing in there. She'd looked through it the last time she was here. But it couldn't hurt to double check. She hadn't been looking for loose pages then.

Her eyes scanned over the pots of nail polish and eye shadow. Even though Astrid didn't wear a ton of makeup, every girl still had some. Then she opened the drawers slowly, basic bras in pastel colors, the horrible diamond-studded underwear they'd bought for her as a joke, lots of socks, none of them rolled up together, all just randomly thrown in. Astrid never had matched socks.

She opened the next drawer, and as she did, she heard something behind her. She flipped back as a breeze flitted through the window, tickling the curtains. Why hadn't she noticed the open window before? She ran across the room quickly, slamming the window shut. She didn't need any distractions.

"You okay?" Jake asked.

"Don't worry about it," she said, surveying the room around her. Ella took a deep breath. There was something here, she knew, something that she needed to see. Something that Astrid was trying to tell her. Wasn't there? Or had it all been her imagination, some weird technical glitch, every cracked branch and missed call and flash of red? Had she really lost it? Was she just as lost as her friend?

Please, she thought, looking around the room.

Please, Astrid, if you're here, show me something.

Be honest with me. I'm your friend.

The floor creaked beneath her as she walked back to the dresser, and she jumped. She felt like she was on the brink of something. She felt like something was about to *happen*. She wanted something to happen and she didn't, all at the same time. She was both scared and eager.

Ella whipped the next drawer open. But she shook her head as her hands rifled through the clothes. Nothing. She slammed the drawer shut. "This is never going to work like this."

"It's okay," Jake said, putting his hand on her shoulder. "Calm down. We can look in her room, okay? We can—"

But Ella stopped listening. Her eyes locked on what stood in front of her. Astrid's jewelry tree, filled with rings and bracelets and chains, but one thing was missing. One thing was terribly, hopefully, wonderfully missing.

"The key," she said.

"What key?" Jake asked.

She whipped back around to face him.

"The necklace. She always wore it. It was here the last time. It was hanging right here. Grace must have taken it," she said. "She must have used it."

"So what does that mean?" Jake asked, but it was too hard to explain everything. She rushed out of the room and towards the living room. The desk was right there.

Shut. *Tight.*

Before Astrid left, it was never shut. That's why she could wear the key around her neck. There was no use for it. And why would it be unless Grace was hiding something? What better place to put the pages than right here?

Ella pushed at the top. But she knew it was no use. It was locked. She briefly glanced around the desk to see if the key was lying somewhere. It wasn't.

So she leaned down to inspect the lock—to see if maybe she could pick it without the key—and that's when she saw it. Three letters, carved into the wood. RNA. RNA. It was someone's name, obviously, but not Grace, not Astrid . . .

She turned to Jake. "What was Astrid's dad's name?"

"Why?" he asked.

"Just tell me. What was it?" She shook her head. "What is it?"

"Robert," Jake said carefully. "Robert Allen."

And that's when it clicked. Why Astrid had been so obsessed with that key. Why she'd never taken it off. She had always figured that Astrid had just thought it was pretty, that it was cute, that she'd found it in the desk and decided it'd make the perfect necklace. But there had been so much more to it than that.

This desk had been her dad's. It was maybe one of the only things she had to remind her of him. Ella had never seen a photo—had never heard Grace even speak his name. Hell, if she went around telling people he was dead, then she wasn't going to keep mementos of him all over the place. The topic had always been off-limits. Astrid's standard answer: "He died in a car accident when I was eight. I don't want to talk about it."

Ella stared at the desk. It had been important to Astrid. It had to be important to Grace, too. Cherished by her dead daughter, left behind by a man who'd hurt her so badly that she'd told the world he was dead. This was the place where Grace would hide something. She knew it, deep in her heart. This was it.

She just had to get inside.

"Do you have a bobby pin?" she turned back to Jake.

But she didn't wait for him to answer. She rushed down the hall and into the bathroom. She opened the drawers quickly, rifling through. She grabbed the first brassy one she saw and then ran back to the desk.

Jake moved out of the way as she knelt down, pulling the prongs of the pin apart and carefully inserting one into the lock. She twisted and turned, listening, waiting.

"Do you know what you're doing?" Jake asked.

"Shhh," she said. "I've almost got it."

She felt the pin connect with something—a ridge. She turned it, just a little bit, almost there.

And Ella let out a sigh of relief as the desk opened with a satisfying click.

CHAPTER TWENTY-NINE

Sydney had a bad feeling.

She felt like it should be raining. But it wasn't. Like the day was murkier than it actually was. Like the weather simply hadn't gotten the memo. She told herself that it was just Astrid. Just the fact that it had been a whole month. As if that weren't enough anyway.

She carried her fiddle in her hand. She felt silly, almost, walking off to the cabin to what, serenade her dead friend?

It was like something Ella would do.

She laughed to herself at how silly she was, but it didn't really work, so she walked faster down the sidewalk, trying to shake the feeling. But the bad feeling wouldn't go away.

Audie said that the women in their family had that power. A certain sixth sense, if you will. Of course, Audie, as awesome as she was, was a little kooky. *A lot kooky.*

Sydney had tried her best to ignore her aunt. People weren't psychic. The crazies who cancel their flights because they had a bad dream just ended up with some huge layover in Texas, feeling stupid when the plane that they should have been on doesn't crash.

But she couldn't ignore the fact that she got these feelings. That a tiny part of her believed them.

Sydney veered off the sidewalk, towards the empty lot that led to the woods. She didn't know why Ella still used the shortcut by Astrid's house. Sure it was faster, but it was creepy to walk right by Grace and company.

As she got closer to the woods, the feeling intensified. She could call Audie crazy, but there was no denying that this happened to her sometimes. Not often, just sometimes. It was this notion, this premonition—who knows—this sense in every bone of her body, from head to toe, that something was off.

And the sense only got stronger as she stepped inside, leaving suburbia behind, letting the woods envelop her.

Something was definitely wrong.

CHAPTER THIRTY

The first thing Ella noticed was the smell. Carnations.

Then she saw the petals, strewn across the desk. But she didn't have time to process it. Her eyes widened as she saw it all—pieces of blue chiffon, jaggedly cut on the edges. Just like Astrid's dress. Photos of Astrid, ones that they'd taken down, ones that had never been put back up. There'd been so many, Ella hadn't even realized that some of them were missing. But here they were, scattered about. Ella's heart raced brutally fast.

What is going on?

But she didn't have time to think. Because then she saw the pages. A small stack of lightly lined pages.

"Holy shit," Jake said, but she ignored him.

Slowly, she picked them up.

The first one only had a couple of sentences. May 31. A little over a week before she died:

She's only getting worse, and it drags me down, like weights in my stomach. Like if I jumped in the river I'd just sink. I know it will get bad again. I just know it. I know that it will never get better.

Ella held her breath as she turned to the next page. June 1st.

I wish there was someone to talk to, to tell EVERYTHING to. But I see their eyes when they ask if I'm okay. They don't really want to know. They want me to say yes and then we can go back to normal. It's the one thing I can't tell them. I'm not normal. I'm not okay. Maybe if they really wanted to know, I'd tell them. But they don't.

Ella felt sick, because it was so wrong—wasn't it? They would have helped her. They would have understood. They would have loved her no matter what. But Astrid didn't know it.

She died not knowing it.

Ella turned the page again. June 4. Just two days before Astrid had left.

I want her to get better, but I know that she won't. And I won't either. Sometimes I think she's going to leave me, just like he did. That if I don't go, she will first. And then it will just be me. I don't think she'd even miss me. I don't think anyone would.

Ella flipped to the next one. June 5. The night before she died.

Forgive me. I'm sorry.

"Are you okay?" Jake asked, but she didn't want to talk to him, she didn't want to see him. She only wanted to cry. *I'm sorry I'm sorry I'm sorry.* She was the one who should be sorry. She was the one who'd failed her.

I'm sorry I'm sorry I'm sorry I'm sorry I'm sorry.

But it was no use. It was too late.

Ella threw the pages down and shook her head. But then she heard something. A voice.

Help.

She heard the word, almost as if it were whispered in her ear, and it sounded, it sounded like Astrid. But Ella spun around and it was only Jake.

"Did you hear that?" she asked.

"Hear what?"

Help her.

Ella flipped back and there it was, all of it. The photos. The carnations. The blue fabric from Astrid's dress.

How many times had Grace gone there? How many times had she hung around, looking for something that wasn't coming? Just like Ella?

It's all my fault.

Who had Ella been seeing all this time?
Ella's eyes flitted across the pages, and the words rang in her head.

If I don't go, she will first.
If I don't go, she will first.
If I don't go.
She.
Will.
First.

Ella turned around and grabbed Jake by the shoulders, squeezing him so hard she could feel her fingers dig into his bare skin. "That night in the cabin," she said. "You started to tell me something. You started to tell me something about Grace." Her heart was racing now. Running fast.

"About Robert?" he asked.

"No," she said. "I mean, yes, but no. Something else. You said that she shouldn't have been surprised. Why did you say that?"

"I don't know," Jake said, stepping back. "Don't worry about it."

"No," she said, grabbing him again, squeezing tighter. "You have to tell me," she screamed, shaking him. "You have to tell me the truth. Why did you say she wasn't surprised? Why did you think she should have seen it coming? Why did you say all that? Why?"

And in moments, the words were out of his mouth. Real. Impossible to ignore.

"Because she tried the same thing herself."
Ella shook her head, stepping backwards.
"It was right after Robert left. It was awful."
"No," she said. "No."

If I don't go, she will first.

"Where is Grace?" Ella asked.
Jake shrugged. "She said she was going out."
"She didn't say where?"
"No," he said. "She never says where—"
And without thinking she ran down the hallway, ignoring Jake's cries and his confusion. She knew. Some part of her knew. She ran out the back door that led to the shortcut through the woods, not even bothering to close it behind her.

The woods were in front of her. Majestic. Eerie. Breathing with the wind.

Calling her.

She had to get to the cabin. Before it was too late.

CHAPTER THIRTY-ONE

The branches cracked beneath her feet as Sydney walked. This way had more woods, thicker woods, less trail. The feeling was deep now. Sitting in her stomach. Heavy like a rock.

And she felt a dizzying sense of déjà vu because she realized that she'd had this feeling in this same place. Not too long ago. Not too long ago at all.

One month ago, to be exact.

It was as they left her. It was the last time they ever spoke to her.

They were leaving the cabin. It was the last time they'd be in the cabin ever, all three of them. They were walking out. They were going to their party.

Sydney/Ella: Are you sure you don't want to come?
Astrid: No, I'd rather stay home.
Sydney/Ella: You sure? It's going to be awesome.
Astrid: I'm sure.
Sydney/Ella (with smiles, unaware): Okay, bye.
Astrid: Bye.

And the feeling had hit her then, as she and Ella walked one way and Astrid walked another. That familiar ache. But it had gone away. A few drinks inside her and it was gone, and she'd forgotten about it in the morning. And she hadn't remembered it until now. When she felt it so strongly. Again.

Now the wind swept around her, fluttering through the leaves of the trees as she stepped into the clearing.

She stared at the cabin. So much pain in there. And so much happiness, too. She had to go in. She knew that she did. She knew that she could. She could shake the feeling and just step inside. But before she had a chance, she heard a rustling in the trees. Cracking branches and swooshing leaves.

Someone was out there.

And that someone was coming here, too.

CHAPTER THIRTY-TWO

Ella didn't think. She ran.

Ran fast. Ran over the branches. Around the trees. Ran like she should have done that night a month ago. She should have run back. She should of run back to her friend.

By the time she reached the clearing, she was out of breath, the cabin was in sight, and—

"Sydney," she said. Syd was staring right at her, as if awaiting her arrival.

"Ella," she said. "What are you doing here?"

"What are *you* doing here?"

"I wanted to play," she started, holding up her violin. But Ella shook her head.

"Ella, is everything okay?" she asked.

"I don't know," Ella said. She had to get inside. She ran past Sydney, across the porch, and through the door—just like that day, so much like that day—and—

She screamed.

Astrid. After all this time. Astrid was here. Lying here. In that cornflower blue dress. Her red hair splashed around her. The key around her neck. Just like she'd found her that day. Ella had led Grace here, and she'd been stupid, she'd walked in first, and she'd seen her friend, dead, gone, and she'd run forward and touched her and begged her to wake. But it was too late. It was too late. It was way too late.

And she screamed and she screamed and she screamed and she screamed and then Sydney was running past her, kneeling down, saying, "Oh my God, oh my God, oh my God," and Sydney was leaning, listening for a heartbeat, feeling for breathing and yelling. Sydney was yelling something as she shook her.

Grace. Grace. Grace. Wake up, Grace. Wake up.
Wake up, Grace.
Wake up.

And then Sydney was looking to her. "Ella," she yelled. "El."
Ella closed her eyes. Shook her head.
And in a second she felt Sydney's arms around her, and she didn't hear herself screaming anymore. And the screams were replaced with sobs, sobs that shook her body. Shook her to the core. But Sydney held her still. Sydney didn't let go.
But Sydney yelled above her cries. "She's still breathing," she said. "We have to call 911."
And Ella let herself open her eyes and see that despite the blue dress and despite the red hair and despite the key that it wasn't Astrid. It wasn't Astrid at all.
It never was.

CHAPTER THIRTY-THREE

The news spread like wildfire in the town over the next few days. Sydney wasn't even that surprised. It was the story of the year. A girl had killed herself, and now her mother had tried—there was no hiding it. Everybody knew.

All over Falling Rock stories started to pop up about Grace, how she'd flipped on them once at the café, how she always looked in a daze while at the supermarket. Everyone wanted a piece of the action. Some heard about Robert, going on about how they could swear they'd seen him here and there throughout the years. Some didn't even seem to remember that Grace had ever had a husband. That's how it was in Falling Rock—once you left, you pretty much fell off of everyone's radar.

Sydney tried to avoid it all, spending her mornings with Darcy watching cartoons and her evenings at the dinner table, talking to her mom and George about the best place to find organic grapes. All the time in-between was spent with Ella, reading bad magazines and watching movies that were so stupid they were funny. The type of movies that college boys like. The ones that don't require you to think. She felt sick about every fight, every doubt she'd had about Ella. She wanted to make it up to her. In any way she could.

They didn't even talk much when they were together. They were just there for each other. Sometimes they cried and sometimes they laughed. They were what they should have been from the beginning. They were friends. Friends who could finally grieve together.

Carter called her a couple of times each day, but she didn't answer. It wasn't anything against him. She just wasn't answering for anyone but Ella.

Still, he left her messages every time.

I hope you're doing okay. I want to hear your voice. I'm here for you when you need me.

On the third day, she answered. They made plans to watch a movie. Sydney was getting awfully good at that now.

Carter gave her a big hug when she got to his house, holding her as long as he could. It felt good.

"I missed you," he said.

Sydney smiled. "I've been a little MIA, I know."

Carter shook his head. "No, it's okay. Really. I totally understand."

They walked inside, and she said hi to Carter's parents, and they made their way down to the basement. It was crazy but she didn't think that they'd ever been down in this comfy, familiar place alone. There was always Max or Ben or Ella or Astrid.

"Alright, your choice," he said. "*Killer Clowns from Outer Space* or *Wedding Crashers*." Sydney weighed her options—evil spacey clowns or crude jokes and lots of naked girls. She went with the clowns.

They sat close enough to each other but not too close. They laughed when they should laugh, and they screamed when they wanted to make fun of how horrible the movie was. At one point, she felt their legs come together, Carter's bony thigh next to hers. She didn't move away.

When the movie was over, they sat in silence for a bit while the credits rolled along the screen. They were far into the names of the grips when Carter finally broke the silence.

"How are you?" he asked.

She shrugged. "I'm fine."

"Seriously, Sydney," he said. "You don't have to pretend with me."

Sydney looked over to him. His eyes were wide open and he looked like he just wanted to take care of her. He was so good.

"I'm here," she said. "Aren't I? That's a start."

Carter nodded, even though it was obvious that he didn't really get it.

"Did you hear anything about . . . "

"Grace?"

"Yeah."

Sydney took a deep breath. "She's still in the hospital. She's fine, physically. But Jake and his mom are looking for a more long-term place, I guess."

"So you never knew?"

"That she was in a really bad place?" she asked, and Carter nodded.

Did she know, she wondered. She'd known things were bad, but not this bad. Maybe she should have. She felt guilty that she hadn't known and heartbroken that Astrid hadn't trusted her enough to really tell her. She didn't think it was the kind of feeling that would ever go away—it was a wound she'd always have, and all she had to do was poke at it to feel it again—just like Audie had said. "No, I didn't really know, I guess. I mean, I always thought something was off. She always seemed, I don't know, volatile or something. Like she could change her mood any moment."

"She probably could," Carter said.

Sydney didn't tell Carter everything that she and Ella had managed to piece together. That Grace had started dressing like Astrid, wearing her hair like hers. That it was her crazy, fucked-up way of grieving. That Ella wasn't imagining things. That Ella was just the one who'd opened her eyes enough to see. That the red hair and the blue dress had really been Grace all along.

That Astrid had a dad out there, somewhere, who probably felt more shitty about all of it than even she did.

She didn't think it was hers to tell.

So she gave the clinical version. "Apparently she stopped taking her meds after Astrid died. Which is, like, not good if you have a serious depression. I guess she did that a lot, though. According to her sister."

"Wow," Carter said.

"Yeah."

"So you think that's why . . . you know, uhh . . . Astrid . . ."

Sydney cut him off. "I don't know. Maybe it was and maybe it wasn't. I think she needed help," Sydney said. "Just like her mother.

I think she needed help and she didn't get it." There was that wound again. Aching.

Carter nodded.

She took a deep breath. "I think if I had tried harder to understand her, to ask her, then things would have been different. But I didn't."

"Syd," Carter said. "No."

But she just shook her head, and a part of her almost felt lighter—it was nice to say it out loud. "Yes," she said. "It's just the way it is. If someone had helped her, she might have been okay. I was the one who was there."

Carter started to object but she stopped him. "We saved Grace. It doesn't make up for it, but I think that somehow, somewhere maybe Astrid is proud of us for that. Like, maybe she forgives us—a little part of her."

Carter put his hand on Sydney's. "There's nothing to forgive."

"You'll never know how much there is to forgive," she said.

Carter just stared at her, the corners of his mouth turned down, his eyes trying to understand.

"So how's the band?" she asked, changing the subject.

Carter laughed, quietly, exhaustedly. "What band?"

"You mean you and Max haven't been practicing these last few days?"

Carter shook his head. "I haven't heard from Max since that night. Have you heard from him?"

"No," Sydney said. "And I don't want to."

"Well, there's your answer then. That's how the band is."

Sydney felt a pain in her heart. Not for Max so much as for what they were together. River Deep. They were just starting to get an audience. And then she got an idea.

"You and I could do it together," she said. "We could keep it going."

"Max would never go for that," Carter said.

"Screw Max," she said, and he laughed. "Seriously."

"Seriously?" he asked.

"Seriously."

Carter was quiet a moment before he opened his mouth to speak. He looked into her eyes, seemed to consider it, and then looked down at his hands, removing his from hers. "I don't think so," he said finally. "I don't think it would be a good idea."

"Why not?" Sydney asked, scooting closer to him.

"Look at what happened to you and Max. I don't want that to happen to us. You guys like hate each other now."

"That's cause Max is a dick," she snapped. "We wouldn't be like that."

"I like having you as a friend, Syd," he said, and her heart sank a little at the word "friend." They could have been so much more, and she screwed it up.

"Okay," Sydney said. "If that's what you want."

It was quiet again, and the air seemed to hang between them. All the things that hadn't been said.

Carter finally spoke up. "Sydney?"

"Yes," she said, looking right at him.

"Nothing," he said, shaking his head. "It's stupid."

"What is it?" she asked, leaning closer.

Carter took a deep breath, and his big green eyes seemed to quiver. He looked down at his hands. "You know that stuff you said that night?" he asked.

"Yes," she said, moving in still.

"The night we all fought."

"I know what night you're talking about," she said. "It feels like ages ago."

Carter smiled. "Just a few days, actually. That stuff you said about me."

"Yes."

"About your, uhh, *feelings* for me."

"Uh huh."

"Did you mean it?" And he took a risk and looked up at her, and he must have seen immediately that she was smiling.

"Yes," she said. "Yes I did. I meant it completely."

Carter smiled back. He was so goofy and cute, she wanted to just kiss him right then.

"So do you feel the same?" she asked.

He nodded. And they both laughed. Their smiles were so big they were grins.

"So does this mean we can be bandmates?" she asked.

Carter shook his head. "I still don't think it's a good idea," he said. "Plus, you're too good to play with me anyway. You were always too good to play with any of us."

Sydney's face dropped.

"We can't be bandmates," he said. "But we can be something else."

And her smile was back. Matching his.

"Alright," she said. "I guess I'll take what I can get."

CHAPTER THIRTY-FOUR

Ella was keeping busy. When her mom wasn't in the studio or teaching a class, they got to do all the things that she'd been putting off—buying a bedroom set, finding the perfect desk lamp—she'd even friended her future roommate on Facebook and made a brand-new pot—one that she hadn't thrown on the ground in a fit of anger.

She didn't see Jake. Not since *the* day, when he'd shown up shortly after they'd found Grace, ushered them out when the paramedics came, and delivered them to his mother who was waiting with a car to drive them home. Ella had taken a break from the café—it was way too much for her now—and Jake was staying busy there. He called her to give her updates on how Grace was doing. But that was it.

When she wasn't hanging out with Sydney (i.e., when Sydney wasn't with Carter), Ben would come over. They'd drive around. Do summery things. Swim in the river and play Frisbee golf. He was trying to comfort her. He was trying to be there for her. She couldn't blame him for that. She couldn't blame him for anything. And yet it wasn't the same.

One night they went to Johnny's, ordered the usual, and sat in the car, looking out at the view. Ella sipped her milkshake and munched on her fries. She looked at Ben. God, he could be gorgeous sometimes. And he was so nice and sweet. And this place was beautiful. This town, this life of hers, it was so good when it wanted to be.

They ate in silence, because she and Ben didn't have much to talk about now. She usually just updated him on her latest college purchases, and he on the news and gossip with the football guys. They didn't have much time left together anyway. In just over a month, she'd be starting down the road, and he was going an hour away on his football scholarship. Sure, they could make it work if they wanted to.

But she wondered if they did.

When they were back at her house, Ben put the car in park, turned the engine off.

She looked at him. "Did you want to come inside?"

"No," he said, shaking his head. His eyes looked sad.

She looked at him, and she wished that she felt more, that she was more scared at what he might say, what he might feel, but she wasn't. Whatever was happening between them was small compared to everything that had happened. Whatever he said, it was nothing compared to Astrid leaving, to Grace trying to, to Ella finding them both.

If she wasn't broken yet, how could she be now?

"What is it?" she asked. "Just tell me." She put her hands on his shoulders, but they didn't feel like hers anymore. They just felt like shoulders.

Ben took a deep breath. "I've been wanting to ask you this for awhile. But I didn't want to bother you with it right after, you know . . ."

Ella nodded. "It's okay, Ben. Just ask."

He stared at her a minute and then he spit it out. "Did anything ever happen between you and Jake?"

Ella took her hands from his shoulders, and she looked straight ahead. She thought of the concert, the way he'd made her feel, the night in the cabin, as she pressed him for information about Grace, the way they'd talked to each other as they'd torn Astrid's room apart, the way whenever he stood close, she was just dying for him to kiss her.

"No," she said. "Not like that."

Ben nodded. "I didn't think you had it in you."

"I don't."

"But?" he asked.

She took a deep breath. "We never even kissed," she said. "We barely even touched. It's just that, I don't know. I knew something about it was wrong."

Ben sighed then. "Just say it," he said. "Just get it out there. Say it."

Ella shook her head. "What do you want me to say?"

"That you had feelings for him. That you *have* feelings for him."

Ella breathed deep as she felt the tears start in the corners of her eyes.

"Oh Ben," she said, turning to him and cupping his face in her hands, and the numbness, the disinterest, the whatever she'd felt just a minute ago was gone, because, even though she knew he was right, even though he wouldn't be hers much longer, right now, he still was. "I'm so sorry," she said. "I didn't mean to. You've been everything I needed for the last three years. You've been *more*." She felt tears well in her eyes because even though she'd known it was coming, now that it was here, it felt different. It felt like yet another something was dying.

Ben nodded, his eyes getting wet now, too. Ella didn't think she'd ever seen him cry.

"I've loved you so much, Ben," she said. "So much."

"But not anymore," he said, his voice cracking, and his tears spilling over. She pulled him close to her, buried his face in her shoulder. "You don't love me anymore."

"No," she said. "I'm sorry."

Ben's body shook more, and hers did with him. "I wish I could say something else," she said, the words muffled in his t-shirt. "I'm sorry."

They held each other for who knows how long, holding on to the end, because they both knew that it was there. It had to be.

When they pulled away, his eyes were puffy. Her cheeks were wet.

"What a pair we are," he said, laughing if only a little.

Ella nodded, laughing a bit herself.

"You should get inside," he said.

"Yeah."

But she had to do it. Just once more. She leaned in, pressed her lips on his, and felt them so familiar, so warm and comforting, hers still, even for just one more minute.

Ben pulled away.

"Part of me will always love you," she said.

"I know."

And there wasn't anything else to say, so she gave him a half-smile, and she grabbed her purse, opening the door and climbing out of the car.

"Bye, Ben," she said. He looked at her, not smiling. But he looked okay, at least. He looked like he'd be okay.

"Bye," he said, and he put his Jeep into reverse and pulled away.

It was another week before she could bring herself to go back to the café.

She hoped Jake would be there. She wanted to see him again. She didn't know when he'd be leaving—they hadn't texted in days—and she didn't want him to go without saying goodbye.

She slowly opened the door, and she could see that he was there. Becky was, too, and there was a new face that she didn't recognize— probably her replacement—and the place smelled like it always had, and it was full of customers like it always was at this hour, and it was remarkable how little had changed.

"Ella," Jake said, as she walked inside. Without waiting for her to answer, he pulled Becky onto the register and walked around to meet her. "Ella," he said again, and he wrapped her in a hug. Right there, right in the middle of the café.

"Hi," she said.

"Hi."

"I just wanted to see you again," she said.

He smiled. "I missed you, too. Come on," he said. "Becky can cover for me. Let's sit down."

She followed him to a table in the corner, and she set her stuff down on a chair.

"Hold on," he said, and he popped behind the counter and emerged with two hot cups of coffee.

They sat down as if they were two normal customers, as if they weren't completely, tragically, wrapped up in this place. As if they were just two kids getting coffee.

"Are you okay?"

"Yes," she said, taking a bitter sip. "Are you?"

"Uh huh."

It was such a strange way to start a conversation. And yet it made perfect sense for them.

"How's it going?" he asked.

"Okay," she said. She took another sip. "Ben and I split up." And she felt stupid for saying it so quickly. Like she was purposefully letting him know or something. He'd probably expected the standard, *Fine. How are you?*

But his eyes only looked caring. Understanding.

"I'm so sorry," he said. "It must be so hard with everything else."

"It's okay," she said, trying to recover. "I mean, it was a long time coming. It needed to happen."

"Well, I'm still sorry," he said. "If there's anything I can do . . ."

There is nothing you can do, she thought. *At least nothing you should do.*

"I'm really fine," she said. "But thanks."

"Cool," Jake said, taking the cup in his hand and taking a sip. "There's something I want to tell you," he said, and for a second, her pulse quickened, like he might tell her he felt the same way, like he might confess his love to her right here in the middle of the café.

"We're selling the house," he said, and her heart sank in more ways than one. The house she'd spent so much time in. The house with Astrid's room. The shortcut to the cabin. All gone.

"Whoa," she said.

"Yeah," he replied. "I know. But there's nothing else to do. The doctors say it would be too much for Grace to come back here. And this will give her some more money for the treatment facility—it's nice," he said. "Plus, she's not going to be working again any time soon."

"Will she be okay?" Ella asked. "To stay there? Will there be enough money?"

Jake nodded. "Believe it or not, Robert's going to help her."

"Robert?"

"Astrid's dad."

"Oh."

"I know," he said. "It weirded me out when my mom told me. But he's apparently some bigshot in Manhattan or something. I guess he can afford to help."

Ella just nodded.

"I still hate him," Jake said. "But she needs the help. My parents are teachers in West Virginia. They're not exactly loaded."

Ella nodded again, processing. "And what's happening to this place?"

"My mom's going to stay awhile until it sells. She's hiring a new store manager and stuff. It will still be around, probably. Unless the new guys turn it into something lame, like a Starbucks."

"That's good, I guess."

"It is."

"I'm amazed Grace actually kept it going these last few years."

"She had a lot of help," he said. "Astrid was there a lot. My dad did all the accounting. My mom came down when she really needed a hand."

"Really?" she asked.

"Yeah, they both helped her keep it afloat many times."

"Wow," she said. "I had no idea."

"She's going to get better, Ella," Jake said, putting his hand on top of hers. "She's finally getting the help that she needs."

"I hope so."

"She is," Jake said, removing his hand.

"I've actually been meaning to call you," he said. "We're going to sell all the furniture and stuff, but we're putting all the clothes and pictures and memory things in boxes for Grace. My mom thought that you and Sydney might want to come and take a few things. For you guys to have."

"Oh," Ella said. "Yeah. Thanks."

"Anytime you want," he said. "Just swing by when you can."

"Thanks, Jake," she said.

"Thank you for doing so much for us," he said. "Thank you for saving Grace."

"Oh, it's not. I mean, it was—"

"Ella," he said. "Thank you."

She took another sip of coffee, letting it heat her up from the inside. "You're welcome," she said, and a part of her felt lighter than it had all summer. The important part.

Sydney was down with the idea. It was probably the first thing they'd straight-up agreed on all summer, besides which movies to veg out to. She picked Ella up a couple of days later, and they drove over.

When they parked, Sydney turned to her. "You definitely feel up to this, right?"

Ella nodded.

"I mean, if you don't, we can come back later. Or I could just go in. Or—"

"Sydney," Ella said, looking right at her friend. "It's okay. Trust me. I'm okay."

"Really?" Sydney asked. Her eyes lit up. "Like, really really?"

"*Really* really."

Syd pulled down the car mirror and messed around with her bangs. "What color do you think I should do next?" she asked.

"Au naturel."

Sydney kept her eyes locked on the mirror. "Yeah, I was thinking about that myself."

"Really?"

Sydney laughed, flipping the mirror back up. "I know, shocking, right? Even I still have a few tricks up my sleeve."

Ella laughed, too.

"Ella," Sydney said, turning to her. "I'm sorry."

"I'm sorry, too," Ella said.

"No, really, Ella. I'm sorry I thought you were crazy. I mean, I'm sorry I doubted you."

Ella shrugged. "I probably sounded crazy."

Sydney laughed. "Yeah, you did," she said. "But I'm sure I didn't help."

"Thanks, Sydney."

Sydney gave her a hug, and she wondered when was the last time they'd done this. A normal, friendly hug. Not a shaking sobbing hug. Just a hug. It felt nice.

"Let's go," she said.

"Okay."

The door was wide open, so they walked inside.

The house was packed with boxes. Stickers and lists of where things were to go. What was going to storage and what was being sold. You had to hand it to Claire for her resourcefulness.

"Hey girls," Jake said. He gave each of them a hug, but he held Ella the longest. He was so warm and sweet and cheerful that she wished they could just stand like this forever, holding each other.

But they couldn't.

When Ella pulled back she felt tears in her eyes, but she quickly wiped them away.

Jake pointed towards Astrid's room—the door was wide open—it looked strange. "I'll just be down the hall in the living room," he said.

Ella nodded. "Thanks, Jake."

"Sure."

Ella led the way to Astrid's room. The windows were open, and the sun was shining in. The curtains had been taken down, and Astrid's bed linens were in a box. It was the first time that Ella had been in the room and it hadn't looked like Astrid was about to walk right in. It was weird—but something about it was nice, too—a relief.

"Thanks, *Jake*," Sydney said in the most high-pitched and girlie voice possible.

"What?" Ella asked, turning around.

"Oh, nothing," Sydney said, walking over to a box half-filled with clothes. "You guys just so totally have the hots for each other."

"I don't know what you're talking about," Ella said, walking over to the mirror still covered in photos. She could see that her face was red.

"Sure you don't," Sydney said, sitting down on the naked bed.

"And shh," Ella said, turning around. "He's going to hear you."

"Aha," Sydney said. "So I'm right."

Ella crossed her arms. "You know, just because you and Carter *finally* got together doesn't mean that the whole world is as googly-eyed as you are."

Sydney blushed at that, but was immediately back to her argument. "You are such a bad liar."

"Besides," Ella said. "I just split with Ben. We were together for three years."

Sydney narrowed her eyes. "I know. And I'm sorry. I am. But you and Ben had been done awhile. As much as I love him, even I can see that now. And I can also see that you care about Jake."

Ella sighed. Obviously Ben had, too. It made her feel good and bad all at the same time. "And what if I do?"

Sydney surprised her then. She stood up and gave her a hug. When she pulled back, she looked right at her. "I'm just saying that you deserve to be happy. After everything we've been through, we deserve it. You, especially."

Ella looked down, and Sydney stepped back. There was nothing but the sound of the wind between them for a moment, and memories of Astrid, still so present in all of the things around them.

"Alright," Sydney said, breaking the silence and flopping back down on the bed. "Where should we start?"

"You hit the closet? I'll start over here?"

"Sounds like a plan."

Ella turned back to the mirror. Photos were still taped around the edges, and in a second she knew the one that she wanted the most. It was of the three of them, taken after a day of splash and sun at the rock quarry. Their hair was wet, plastered around their faces—which were red—but Astrid's was bright, different—good, really good. Maybe everything hadn't been a lie. Maybe the good times they'd had together really had been good. Maybe she and Sydney had been an escape for her. A tiny point of light in her murky world.

Astrid looked happy. She really did.

And Ella knew that Sydney was right.

She deserved it, too.

When Ella got home, she took all her stuff upstairs. She'd taken some old clothes, a hat. She and Sydney had split up Astrid's year-books, but what she'd loved the most was the photos. Visual proof that their friendship had been real. A reminder anytime she was tempted to forget.

Ella knelt down and pulled a shoebox out from under her bed. It was big—it had held a pair of high boots that she'd never quite been able to pull off. She put the yearbooks inside. And the photos. And one of Astrid's favorite dresses. But there was still space left.

She went to her purse and pulled out what she'd been carrying with her all week. The journal. The beat-up, leather-bound journal. The story of Astrid's life.

She set it inside—carefully—and as she did her body rocked and the tears started, harder than ever. Here was all that she'd missed. All her friend had wanted to tell them. All that she hadn't. All that they'd never thought to ask.

And Ella closed the box and shoved it back under the bed, and lay down on the floor and just let the tears come.

Ella spent the next week helping Jake and Claire when she could. Scrubbing. Packing. Getting everything in tip-top shape. She'd thought the house would be too much for her, but once she'd gone the first time, she knew it was okay. It wasn't Astrid's house anymore. It was just a house.

In their downtime, she and Jake hung out—they listened to music, walked around town; she tried to teach him the potter's wheel, and he failed miserably. She and Jake and Sydney and Carter went miniature golfing and out to dinner together. Or they all went to Carter's basement and watched bad movies.

They didn't touch, and they didn't kiss. It was all so beautifully undefined.

That Saturday, August 4, was Sydney's birthday. Carter's parents were—oddly enough—on a weekend trip with Max's—so a party was in order. A good party. One without a fight and without any secrets. One where they could just have fun.

Ella and Jake arrived together, and Sydney's face lit up as soon as she saw them.

"Yay," she said. "My favorite people!"

"Hey," Carter said, and Sydney gave him a sideways glance. But one of those cute, we're-a-couple-now ones.

"Happy birthday," Ella said. And she hugged her friend.

"Thanks," Syd said, pulling back. "Now first thing's first. You guys need a drink. We have beer or Mike's Hard Lemonade."

Ella saw Jake make a face at the latter. "Beer," she said.

"Fab." Sydney hopped over to the cooler and grabbed two.

"Salut," Jake said, holding up his drink. She and Sydney raised their beers with him. "Cheers," Ella said. And she tipped it back, and it tasted good.

It was the perfect night for a party. The air was cool, but not too cool. The night was clear and star-speckled. The lightning bugs glowed and the smell of honeysuckle reminded them of where they were.

Carter had a porch that opened onto a wide yard, which met a flowing creek, and people were scattered across the lawn, drinking and dancing, while Sydney and Carter serenaded them between drinks.

Everyone was there. Becky and the other guys from the café. Ben and his football buddies. Half-friends and acquaintances that Ella had forgotten to think about since Astrid died.

After a couple beers and a few hugs and the unavoidable, *How are yous* and the, *Oh my God, I heards*, she and Jake made their way down to the creek where there weren't so many people. Ella pointed out the constellations she knew, which weren't very many.

"You having a good time?" she asked, when she'd run out of stars.

"Yeah," he nodded, smiling, his shaggy dark hair catching a bit of the moonlight. "I am. Is it crazy to say I love this place?"

"What?" she asked. "Carter's house?"

Jake laughed. "Yeah, Carter's house. And Aunt Grace's house. And everything. The whole place. The way you guys get together and drink and dance and play good music. The way the mountains and the rivers and the houses are all just mixed in together. It's like twenty-four-seven camping."

Ella laughed, but she knew it was bittersweet. Once the house sold, Jake would be gone. There'd be no more reason for him to be here.

"I guess it's not this way in Chicago," she finally said.

"No," he said. "Not even in my part of West Virginia—it's just strip malls, there. This place definitely has its charms."

She smiled.

"And you do, too," he added.

And at that she didn't know what to say. *Thank you? My stomach just did a somersault? Do you really think that?*

So she stayed quiet, but Jake kept on. He was so cool like that. He never let anything get the best of him.

"Is it weird that it's been like the worst and best summer of my life?" he asked.

In the distance she could hear Sydney's fiddle, going a mile a minute, and screams from people probably chugging beers or taking shots. But right here she heard the coo of the creek, and the sound of Jake, so close to her, breathing in and out.

"No," she said. "No, it's not."

His eyes locked on hers, and she couldn't look away. She wouldn't look away. She didn't want to.

"I'm going to miss you," she said, but he didn't answer, he just leaned forward, and before she knew it, his lips were on hers, and his arms were wrapped around her, and he was holding her, supporting her, *kissing her* like she'd wanted him to all this time. But it was even better than even imagined. It was real.

He pulled back, and she caught her breath, and he smiled. "I've wanted to do that all summer," he said.

She smiled back. "Me, too."

He leaned in again, and she felt light and weightless, like the gravity tethering them to this world was nothing, and they could float out, up into the sky and be their own constellation.

And in that moment, everything felt right.

They found Sydney back up on the porch.

"And where have *you two* been?" she asked, flitting her eyes from Ella to Jake. Jake just laughed, but Ella felt herself blush.

"Let's get a drink," she said, pulling Sydney aside and pushing her towards the cooler. Ella grabbed two beers and handed one to Syd, who was practically jumping for joy.

"You guys totally did it, didn't you, like right in the grass."

Ella looked at her friend. "You're disgusting."

"Okay, okay," Sydney said, pulling Ella to the railing where there were fewer people. She leaned up against it and took a sip of her beer. "So really, tell me what happened."

Ella smiled, taking a sip herself. "Okay, so we kissed."

"Yay!" Sydney said, jumping up and down. Her honey-brown roots were really starting to show.

"Get ahold of yourself," Ella said.

"Okay, okay," she said. "I'm good. But seriously, *finally*. Cheers to that."

"Cheers." And they clinked bottles.

"So was it good?" Sydney asked.

Ella nodded. "Yes, very."

"Awesome," she said. "Now who says I don't throw an amazing party? Apparently that was all you guys needed to, like, confess your love to each other."

Ella rolled her eyes, but she leaned on the railing, looking out at the people scattered across the yard. "It is a good party."

"I know," Sydney said, looking out at everyone herself. "It certainly is."

They were quiet for a moment, silently sipping their beers, and Ella knew that they were both thinking the same thing. That it was good. That it was very good. But that Astrid wasn't here.

Because even though the night was beautiful and Sydney was happy, and Ella could close her eyes and think about how good it was to kiss Jake, and Ben—even Ben—was here, there was someone who should have been here, too. Either standing with them on the porch, sipping on a beer, and jumping up and down at the latest Jake news, or out there on the lawn, with her hair falling across her back and her long hippie skirt spinning and her favorite key dangling around her neck. But she wasn't. And she never would be.

And even when they went to college and they made new friends and graduated and went into the real world and found husbands and started families and gained weight and clipped coupons and made time to watch the news every night and yelled at their own teenagers for drinking and throwing parties, there would be a hole, a missing piece, bigger some days than others, but always there nonetheless.

Ella took a sip of beer, and stared at the stars, and moved closer to Sydney, so their arms just barely touched.

No matter what happened, it would always be *after*.

But for tonight, at least, that was okay.

ACKNOWLEDGMENTS

Many thanks to my agent, Danielle Chiotti, for ingenious ideas and moral support; to my editor, Jacquelyn Mitchard, who helped bring this story to life; to Micol Ostow and the Mediabistro crew, for spot-on notes and advice; to all the NC and NY friends who encouraged me and generously read my stories and drafts; to my mom and dad, for teaching me to do what I love and never doubting that I could; to my sister Kimberly, teen-fiction expert, stand-in editor, grassroots publicist, and best friend all in one; and to Thomas, for adventure, positivity, and much-needed laughter along the way.